Born and raised in the Philippines, **Paulia Belgado** has worn many hats over the years, from office assistant, flyer distributor, singer and nanny to farm worker. Now she's proud to add romance author to that list! After decades of dreaming of seeing her name on the shelves next to her favourite authors' books, she finally found the courage—and the time… thanks, 2020!—to write her first story. Paulia lives in Malaysia with her husband Jason, Jessie the poodle, and an embarrassing amount of pens and stationery art supplies. Follow her on X @pauliabelgado or on Facebook.com/pauliabelgado.

GW00504247

Also by Paulia Belgado

May the Best Duke Win
Game of Courtship with the Earl
The Lady's Scandalous Proposition
The Marquess's Year to Wed

Look out for more books from Paulia Belgado
coming soon.

Discover more at millsandboon.co.uk.

THE LADY'S SNOWBOUND SCANDAL

Paulia Belgado

MILLS & BOON

First published in Great Britain 2024
by Mills & Boon, an imprint of HarperCollins*Publishers* Ltd,
1 London Bridge Street, London, SE1 9GF

www.harpercollins.co.uk

HarperCollins*Publishers*, Macken House, 39/40 Mayor Street Upper, Dublin 1, D01 C9W8, Ireland

The Lady's Snowbound Scandal © 2024 Paulia Belgado

ISBN: 978-0-263-32100-5

11/24

MIX
Paper | Supporting
responsible forestry
FSC
www.fsc.org   FSC™ C007454

This book contains FSC™ certified paper
and other controlled sources to ensure responsible forest management.

For more information visit www.harpercollins.co.uk/green.

Printed and Bound in the UK using 100% Renewable Electricity
at CPI Group (UK) Ltd, Croydon, CR0 4YY

For Dr. Ana Maria Belgado Naluz,
or simply Ate Ana,
who left us much too soon.
Thank you for giving me the gift of
loving romance novels.
I will forever be grateful for this.
And to Gelo, her son and the person she loved
wholeheartedly.
Your mom's love will never fade or disappear,
and we will never forget her generosity
and selflessness.

Chapter One

London, England,
1st December 1853

No seven words could strike more terror into Lady Georgina Abernathy's heart than those her new companion Miss Sophia Warren was about to utter.

'Shall we go for a walk outside?'

Lost in her embroidery, Georgina was distracted by the dreadful suggestion, causing her to poke her finger with her needle. 'Ouch!'

Drat.

She quickly drew her finger into her mouth, thankful the blood hadn't stained the expensive white silk handkerchief. She scowled at Miss Warren.

'You cannot spend another day cooped up inside.' Miss Warren gestured to the window. 'It's an unusually warm winter morning. Why would you object to going for a stroll outdoors?'

Truly, Georgina had no objections to most of the seven words in that sentence. 'Shall we' implied that

Miss Warren would be with her, to which she did not take issue. Even the 'go for a walk' part sounded like a good idea, if her sore bottom, which had been seated for hours, had any say in the matter.

No, Georgina could only protest to one of those words.

Outside.

She shuddered.

That earned her a stern look from the companion. 'Lady Georgina.'

Georgina placed her embroidery into her basket and splayed out on the settee in a most unladylike manner. 'Going outside requires that I put on my coat and my hat, as well as my gloves and boots.'

'Yes, and…?'

'But that also means I must leave this lovely warm sitting room and my tea.' She nodded to the tray next to her on the table. 'And step out through the door.'

'Yes, that is the general idea of outside.'

'And why would I want to do that?'

'Lady Georgina, since I arrived here at Harwicke House, all we've done is embroider, read, paint watercolours, drink tea, and occasionally sit in the gardens.' A wry smile played on Miss Warren's lips. 'You don't mean to stay indoors for the remainder of the year, do you?'

'I do.'

'Truly?'

'Yes.' Rising to her feet, she brushed her hands over her skirts. 'Miss Warren, when you assumed the role of my companion from Great-Aunt Leticia a few weeks ago, you probably expected a young debutante, not an unmarried lady of seven and twenty.'

'To be quite honest, I did not know what to expect, Lady Georgina.'

'In any case, as you will learn, I do not participate in society. At least, I haven't for three Seasons now.'

In her first Seasons she had attended every ball, gathering, and social event Leticia had deemed necessary. Under the watchful eye of her chaperone, she'd had no choice after all. But then Leticia's health had declined and while she did not rejoice in her chaperone's failing health, it had been an excellent excuse not to attend any social gatherings in the last three years. Besides, six failed Seasons seemed quite pathetic and she wasn't about to humiliate herself for a seventh.

'Here I am, in my tenth year since I came out. I think it is quite apparent that I will never find a husband.'

'That is simply not—'

'Oh, it's all right, Miss Warren, I have accepted this fact and rejoice in it.' She paused. 'My brother, the Duke of Harwicke, has pledged to take care of me for as long as I need.'

It had been after her last Season, when no gentleman had offered for her, that he had made the remark. Trevor was not being unkind, only pragmatic. Georgina was painfully shy, and too plain, and despite years of being on the so-called marriage mart, no man had come close to buying what she had to offer.

'Did you not wonder why my brother did not find me a chaperone? And why you were hired to be my companion instead?'

Miss Warren's mouth pressed tight. 'I did not think it my place to ask.'

'I am no longer a fresh young debutante with a reputation to protect—meaning I'm much too old for a chaperone. I have no other close relatives, and with my brother unmarried, there is no other lady of the house.'

'And propriety requires that another woman, such as a chaperone, be present when he is not around?'

'Exactly. I didn't want him to find another distant relative who would drag me to balls and society functions, so we compromised by hiring a companion for me.' Trevor had been against it, but she'd told him that eventually, once she was old and feeble, she would need one anyway, so why waste time when she could just have a companion now and be done with it.

'Surely you could still find a husband, if you searched hard enough.'

She snorted. 'The Ton, if they remember me at all, has already placed me on the shelf.'

'The shelf?'

'Oh, you know, *the* shelf.' She gesticulated with her hands, raising her arms high up. 'The spinster shelf, where all the other old, unmarried ladies of the ton gather dust. Frankly, I am relieved that I no longer have to go into society.'

'Ah, so it is not the outside you object to, but the people.'

'Precisely. I would find the outside quite tolerable, except for the pervasive presence of people.'

She shuddered again at the thought of bumping into acquaintances and having to exchange pleasantries with them, never mind actually making conversation. No one could ever speak their mind or be honest or even just excuse themselves when they grew tired of the interaction because it was impolite.

How everyone simply agreed that this was how society worked was beyond her. People were always such a drain on her mind and body—whenever she came back from any sort of event she often found herself exhausted for hours afterwards.

And when she thought of those events where crowds of people gathered…

No, she did not even want to think of that.

With her great-aunt indisposed, she no longer had to worry about *that*.

She also didn't have to be around *people* any more. And while she said a silent prayer to the heavens to keep Leticia in good health, she also added one of thanks—because now she stayed at home all she wanted and never had to see any member of the Ton for as long as she lived.

'So you do not plan to attend any balls, accept invitations to teas, musicals, or even take morning calls?'

'No, no, no and no,' she said decisively. 'I have packed up my ball gowns, left my dancing slippers to gather dust, and tossed out all my dance cards.'

'I see.' Slipping her hand into her pocket, Miss Warren retrieved an envelope from her reticule. 'I suppose that means you do not want to attend the planning meeting for this year's Christmas fundraiser for St Agnes's Orphanage for Girls?'

'I—' Georgina stopped short. 'When?'

'The day after tomorrow.' Her companion waved the envelope around. 'This was addressed to Miss Leticia Abernathy but, seeing as she is no longer your chaperone, Dawson thought to give it to me. The people at the orphanage probably hadn't been informed about Miss Abernathy's retirement. It's a wasted effort, though, seeing as you don't—'

'Of course we will attend—we always do,' Georgina exclaimed, snatching the envelope from Miss Warren's fingers.

'Is that so?' Miss Warren asked wryly. 'I thought you said you didn't venture into society?'

'This is not society,' said Georgina, holding the envelope to her chest.

Aside from her brother, there were only two other things she loved most in the world—St Agnes's Orphanage and Christmas, and this yearly fundraiser was a convergence of the two, which was why she made an exception to her no-socialisation rule for this particular event. Besides, many of the ladies who participated in the efforts preferred to plan the event and not necessarily do any of the work, or even mingle with the children. Why on earth they would do that, she never would understand, but it didn't matter to Georgina.

'And the people?'

'These are not just people, either. These are *children*.'

And how she adored the girls at St Agnes's. Children were such a joy to her—so refreshing and so honest. They spoke whatever was on their mind about anything that interested them, and with such varied conversation Georgina never found herself bored or impatient to leave. If there was one regret she had with regard to her spinsterhood, it was that she would never have her own children. But that was why she enjoyed visiting St Agnes's and did so regularly throughout the year.

'We must prepare for our visit,' Georgina declared as she crossed the room towards the door.

'Now? But the committee doesn't meet for another two days.'

Looking over her shoulder, Georgina said, 'Which means we have very little time.'

And so, two days later, Georgina and Miss Warren, with the help of the Harwicke House staff, loaded up the carriage with baskets of goodies for the children and the staff at St Agnes's.

Miss Warren peeped out of the window when the carriage stopped. 'That didn't take too long at all. Have we passed Hanover Square?'

'Yes. We're just at the end of Boyle Street.'

'Right in the middle of the busy commerce district?' the companion asked, astonished. 'I know there are a few orphanages around London, but most of those are in the East End or far in the outskirts of the city. How ever did St Agnes's manage to acquire a building in this neighbourhood?'

'It's quite unusual, I know,' Georgina began. The door opened, and as she took the footman's offered hand she continued. 'But according to Mrs Jameson— she's the matron here at St Agnes's—one of the orphanage's first benefactors was a wealthy merchant who offered to let the entire building to them for a very reasonable price.'

'Interesting…' When she alighted, Miss Warren glanced up. 'This is not what I expected.'

The carriage had stopped outside the doorstep of a four-storey building made of red brick and stone. On one side was a milliner's shop and on the other was a solicitor's office, while a bank occupied the building across from it. There was no sign outside proclaiming what it was, and it certainly did not look out of place on the busy commercial street.

'It was not what I expected either, when I first came to visit,' Georgina said. 'And I assure you, the children here are treated well. It's not very old—established only three years ago. There are twenty-seven girls living here and the oldest is about ten years old. They have tutors who help them learn to read and write, and one day, when the children are old enough, we hope to help them find a trade or learn skills to help them into adulthood.'

Georgina walked up to the door and knocked. Seconds ticked by, but no one answered.

'Do you think perhaps they are out?' Miss Warren asked.

'There's always someone here, and the children don't usually all leave at the same time.' She looked around them. 'Hmmm...there doesn't seem to be anyone else here yet.' Usually by this time carriages would be waiting in line to drop off the other ladies in the planning committee. 'Are we sure it's today?' She had glanced at the letter last night, but wondered if she'd read it wrongly.

'Yes, I'm quite certain, and the letter said ten o'clock in the morning,' Miss Warren said.

'Then why—?'

The door flew open, cutting Georgina off.

'I'm sorry, we— Lady Georgina!' The harried-looking woman on the other side curtseyed. 'What are you doing here, milady?'

'Mrs Jameson,' she greeted here. 'Miss Warren, this is Mrs Jameson, the matron of St Agnes's. Mrs Jameson, this is Miss Sophia Warren, my new companion, who has replaced Great-Aunt Leticia.'

Mrs Jameson wrung her hands together. 'Oh, dear, is your aunt...?'

'Great-Aunt Leticia has simply retired,' she said.

'I see. That must be why you did not receive the letters.'

Georgina frowned. 'We received one letter. I thought the planning committee was to meet today for the Christmas fundraiser?'

'Oh, milady, I sent out the *second* set of letters yesterday, but yours was addressed to Miss Abernathy. We have had to cancel the fundraiser.'

'Cancel?' Georgina exclaimed. 'Why ever would you cancel the fundraiser? It's the biggest event for St Agnes's, and raises enough money to cover the rent for the year.'

'I... Please come in and I'll explain.'

The matron ushered them inside into the foyer. Georgina could not help but notice how the house seemed unusually quiet. Usually as soon as she entered, children were running up and down the stairs or rushing about, not to mention laughing or shouting down the corridors.

'Would you like some tea, milady?'

Georgina searched Mrs Jameson's face. The usually pleasant woman had dark circles under her eyes and the lines on her forehead were etched deeper than the last time she had seen them. 'Please just tell us what happened, Mrs Jameson.'

The older woman sighed. 'I'm afraid there's no nice way to say it. We are losing our home.'

'What?' Georgina exclaimed. 'How? When? Why?'

Mrs Jameson's lower lip trembled. 'We received notice to vacate the premises the day the invitations for the planning meeting were sent out.'

'Vacate? But what about your patron?'

'Unfortunately, Mr Atkinson passed away a few weeks ago.' Mrs Jameson sniffed. 'I didn't even know he had died. His heirs have sold the building and now we are being evicted.'

'When?'

'On December the twenty-fifth.'

Miss Warren gasped. 'What cruel man would make orphans homeless on Christmas Day?'

Georgina had the same thought, though the words she would use to describe such a man were much more severe than 'cruel'—not to mention something she would never say in polite company. 'Who is the new owner? Do you have the eviction letter?'

'Yes, it's in my office. Come, I'll show you.'

They followed Mrs Jameson to her office, where she produced the letter. 'Here.'

Georgina took the letter and began to read it, her blood simmering with rage as she read its contents. '"Notice seeking possession…vacate premises… December the twenty-fifth…"' The edges of the letter crumpled under her fingers. '"Face legal action…"' Her gaze scanned up to the letterhead on top of the document. '"ES Smith Consolidated Trust"?' She chewed at her bottom lip. 'What is the "ES Smith Consolidated Trust"?'

'The name of the business who bought the building from Mr Atkinson's heirs,' Mrs Jameson supplied.

'Have you tried to speak with the heirs?' Georgina asked. 'Or with the owner of this company?'

'The solicitor who brought the letter said that Mr Smith—that's the new owner—was not interested in any counter offer unless it was for more than the amount he paid.'

'And how much is that?'

'Much more than we can afford.'

'And that is?' Miss Warren enquired.

When Mrs Jameson said the amount, Georgina gasped. 'He paid *that* much?'

The matron nodded. 'And see…there's not much we can do except pack our things and prepare—' The creaking of the door hinges interrupted her. 'Charlotte! Eliza! What are you doing here?'

Two children rushed inside, both of them running to Georgina. 'Lady Georgina! Lady Georgina,' the smaller of the two cried as she wrapped her arms around her legs. 'You're finally back in London.'

'Yes, Eliza, I'm so sorry I took so long. Great-Aunt Leticia needed more time to settle into her new home in Hampshire, then I had to wait for Miss Warren to join me—' She nodded up at the companion '—before I could come for a visit.'

'Lady Georgina, we have to leave St Agnes's,' said the taller one, Charlotte, her blue eyes sombre.

'Yes, Mrs Jameson told me.'

'Where will we go?' Eliza's eyes filled with tears. 'I don't want to leave at Christmas.'

As Georgina knelt down to their level to wrap her arms around both girls, her temper beginning to rise once more. 'Do not fret, girls. I shall take care of this. Mrs Jameson, Eliza, Charlotte—if you'll excuse us…' Rising, she straightened her shoulders. 'We must be on our way.'

'And where are we going, Lady Georgina?' Miss Warren asked, puzzled.

Georgina waved the eviction letter in the air. 'To the offices of the ES Smith Consolidated Trust.'

'I'm happy to report profits are up.'

No seven words made Elliot Smith happier than those just said by his recently hired man of business in London, Andrew Morgan.

Well, usually they did.

However, he'd heard it so many times that the effect on him had lessened over the years. Indeed, he had more money now than he knew what to do with, and would not be able to spend it all in ten lifetimes. His reputation for making spectacular returns on his investments had earned him the nickname 'The Midas of San Francisco'. Others said he had the luck of the devil.

Elliot scoffed silently. Only fools and dreamers sat around, hoping and waiting for their luck to turn. Everything he had now, he had earned with his own sweat and blood.

Having grown up dirt-poor, Elliot only had two assets: himself and time. He'd seen how his own wastrel of a father had squandered both, barely eking out a living, throwing away his hard-earned money on drink and women while Elliot and his mother nearly starved at home. When Ma died, when he was ten, he'd vowed to never waste a single second of his life. Sitting in that grubby hovel alone, next to his mother's lifeless body, his father nowhere to be found, he'd vowed that he would make something of himself.

Still, he did not discount the fact that he had a knack of being in the right place and time. If one could call such a thing 'luck', then he supposed his first stroke of luck had been his mother passing and his being forced to work, finding odd jobs in New York City's harbours, doing everything from selling papers to shining shoes just so he could eat. But it was at this time that Elliot had observed the ferries crossing the river, carrying dozens and dozens of passengers to and from their destinations. This had given him the idea to run his own service. And he'd begun to form a plan in his mind—specifically, a ten-year plan with one goal: get himself out of poverty.

So, he'd worked even harder, saved every penny he could, borrowed some, and purchased his first periauger when he was fifteen. He'd ferried people from Staten Island to Manhattan, and in a few short years had a fleet of ships plying New York's rivers.

Having seen success with his first ten-year plan, he'd created another one with a different goal: expand his business interests. It was then that his second stroke of luck had come, when gold was discovered in California. Elliot, however, had not rushed west to mine for the precious metal. No, he'd moved to San Francisco and invested in steamships to transport the gold back to the east coast. By focusing on transport, and monopolising the routes southward through Nicaragua, he had expanded his business empire and grown his fortune.

Perhaps some might say that his third turn of luck

had been selling his steamship business for a king's ransom and moving to New York just before all the gold had dried up. However, it hadn't quite been *good* luck that had made him move back east, and then even further east across the Atlantic to London.

'Mr Smith?' Morgan repeated.

His voice was firm, but polite, in the way that only these posh English people could sound.

'Apologies, Morgan.' Elliot sat up straight behind his desk and drummed his fingers on the surface. 'You were saying the owner of that textile factory in Manchester is ready to sign the contract for the purchase?'

While he might have been lost in his thoughts, Elliot never missed any business-related chatter.

'Yes, Mr Smith.' Morgan slid a piece of paper across the table. 'Here are the final figures. Mr Davis is quite eager for the sale to proceed as soon as possible.'

Elliot quickly scanned the document, checking the final number at the bottom. From his calculations, after investing in newer looms, he'd be able to turn a profit in two years—three years at the most.

'All right.' He quickly signed on the line at the bottom. 'See that the payment is released.'

'Of course, Mr Smith.'

Though Morgan did not say it aloud, Elliot could tell from the man's tone and countenance that he did not believe the factory was a wise investment. Indeed, if one were merely looking at profits for the last five years, Davis Mills' numbers were abhorrent. They were bleeding money faster than a dinghy with holes.

Elliot, however, had seen the potential in the business, as well as in the textiles industry in England. And with Davis eager to sell, he was getting it at a bargain.

Morgan's scepticism was rather refreshing at this point.

Back in San Francisco, everyone waited for Elliot to make his move before making theirs. After his success in the steamship trade, he'd invested in various businesses and real estate around the city, and everything he'd touched had indeed turned to gold, earning him the 'Midas' moniker. Word had spread around town and soon every businessman and investor watched his every move. Stocks would rise and fall based on his decisions, and the value of companies would skyrocket if he even expressed an interest in them.

Elliot had made more money than God, and continued to expand his empire in San Francisco. And, seeing as his previous ten-year plans had brought him great success, he'd created another one—only this one would cement his legacy. At that time he'd been a man thirty years of age, and there were things expected of him. He was not immortal, but there was one way he could live for ever and be remembered after he passed.

And so he'd set the goal for his next ten-year plan: marry a refined woman of quality who would elevate his status and give him a passel of bright young children to pass his legacy on to.

But, as he had learned, one could plan for any eventuality, but life could always drop an unexpected situation at his doorstep.

'If that is all, Mr Smith…'

Elliot rose, signalling an end to their meeting. 'Yes, that's all. If you could—'

'Mr Smith!' The door flew open and a flustered-looking young man of about twenty rushed inside. It was his assistant, Michael Grant. 'Apologies for the intrusion—'

'We were just finishing up.' Still, he crossed his arms over his chest and scowled, as Grant knew better than to interrupt his meetings. 'What is it?'

Grant swallowed. 'S-Sir, one of your house staff just arrived and asked to see you.' As he stepped out of the way John, one of his footmen, hurried inside. He looked even more harried than Grant.

'M-Mr S-Smith, I… I…' he stammered.

Elliot tapped his foot impatiently. 'Why are you here?'

'Er…' He took a deep breath. 'I came to tell you that the governess is quitting. Again.'

Ah, yes.

The unexpected situation.

Quite literally dropped at his doorstep five years ago on a foggy night, in the form of two little girls, aged four and eleven.

'And that is all?' he said, irritated. 'Why rush here like the sky is about to fall on our heads? Surely my sisters are not alone, fending for themselves in a ten-bedroom house in Mayfair?'

He employed a staff of nearly two dozen people at

his newly purchased London home, all hand-picked by him, from the butler to the scullery maid.

'Er...no, sir. B-But there is the matter of the fire.'

He sprang from his chair, slamming his palms on the table. 'Fire?' Terror struck him straight in the chest. 'Where are Anne-Marie and Lily? Are they safe? Was the fire brigade called? Well, John? Speak!'

The footman turned even paler. 'I—I—I...'

'Breathe, man,' Morgan urged. 'Then speak.'

John took a great heaving breath before words spilled out of his mouth. 'Everything is under control. Your sisters are safe and the fire was limited to the drawing room. The staff was able to put it out. But Miss Jones is quitting—and not *quietly*, she says, unless you come and pay her this month's wages, plus severance.'

So the shrew wants money.

While Elliot had lots of money—he could certainly meet her demands without even blinking—that wasn't the point. When he'd hired Miss Jones as a governess, he'd had the most peculiar inkling about her. Her references were impeccable, and she was in demand, having just left the employ of a baronet whose children were now full-grown. However, something about her just hadn't felt quite right. But he'd been desperate because he'd already had three governesses quit, and they'd only been in England for six months. He'd hired Miss Jones anyway, because he was far too busy, but he should have trusted his instincts.

It was obvious Miss Jones was much too nosy and

shrewd for her own good. It was likely she'd figured out why Elliot had left New York and was now in England, and was using that to her advantage.

She was blackmailing him, plain and simple, and threatening to ruin his and his sisters' reputations if she was not paid out.

Damn, if he didn't hate her right now, he would admire her audacity.

'Grant, grab my coat, my hat…' He let out a huff. 'And my cheque book. John, go back to the carriage and wait for me.'

The footman nodded and his assistant scurried off. 'Morgan?'

'I'll be on my way, Mr Smith,' the older man said. 'I'll see you in the morning.' Tipping his hat, he turned and left.

Elliot drummed his fingers on his arm as he waited for Grant to retrieve his things. Too anxious to sit, he faced the large window behind his chair, the grey London winter sky greeting him. There was something soothing about the scene outside, in some ways reminding him of foggy days in San Francisco. Ironically, it had been on a day like today that two little girls had appeared on his doorstep all those years ago.

Well, not so little any more.

Lily was now nine years old and Anne-Marie sixteen, practically a woman.

Still, he would never forget the sight of the two of them in threadbare clothing, shivering and clinging to each other at his doorstep. There'd also been a woman with them, who claimed to have known his father—in the most biblical sense—and said these two waifs were his half-sisters.

He hadn't seen nor heard from his father, Harold Smith, since he'd left New York for California. When his ferry business had begun to prosper, he'd spent a good deal of money trying to reform his father—employing him on his ferries, paying off his debts, and even setting him up in a modest apartment in Queens. Yet his father had always turned to drinking and gambling, never showing up to work and running up more debts. Before he'd moved to San Francisco, he had given Harold a generous bank draft and told him that after this he would never receive a single cent from Elliot ever again.

Seeing as his father had conveniently died a year prior, and could not be there to prove her claims, Elliot hadn't been about to take this stranger's word for it. But then the two girls had looked up at him with the same green eyes he had inherited from Harold. He could not deny that they were related to him, so he'd had no choice but to welcome them into his home. The woman—their mother—had not been interested in staying, but she'd been very aware of Elliot's recent good fortune. She'd happily left with a fat roll of bills, leaving behind her daughters.

The sound of the door opening jolted him out of his thoughts. Running his fingers through his hair, he spun around. 'Damn it, Grant, what took you so—?' He sucked in a breath. 'You're not Grant.'

No definitely not.

For one thing, the figure standing in the doorway was a woman.

'No, sir, I am not.'

Elliot fixed his gaze on this woman who had dared to enter his office without an appointment. She looked like any of the dozens of fashionable English women he'd seen shopping or having tea on Bond Street. The fabric of her white and red walking dress was fine silk, and the wool cloak around her shoulders was trimmed with mink. He couldn't tell what colour her hair was, because most of it was hidden under a large bonnet, though he spied a bit of blonde. Her face was nothing out of the ordinary, with round cheeks and the tip of her nose all pink from the chilly air. As he locked his gaze on hers, he found himself staring into large eyes the colour of bright copper pennies.

He cleared his throat. 'Can I help you, Miss…?'

'Lady Georgina Abernathy,' she said.

A lady.

Now he was intrigued. 'Lady Abernathy.'

'It's Lady Georgina,' she corrected. 'There is no Lady Abernathy.'

His interest was piqued further, and his mind began to form possibilities.

'So it is a courtesy title? From your father?' As part of his preparation for his move to England, he had read *Debrett's Peerage*.

'Yes. He was a duke.'

Now *that* caught his attention. Dukes were the highest ranking of all titles in England, save for royalty.

Her pink nose twitched. 'Are you Mr ES Smith?'

'Yes, I am.'

'The owner of ES Smith Consolidated Trust?'

'Yes, I am Elliot Smith and I own this company, as well as a few others.'

Her brows snapped together. 'You're American?'

'Yes. May I ask a question as well?'

'And what is that?'

'What are you doing here, Lady Georgina?'

'I…' She hesitated, then straightened her shoulders. 'I've come to ask you not to evict the residents at number fifty-five Boyle Street.'

'Boyle Street?' He rubbed at his chin. 'Ah, yes. I purchased that building from a Mr Andrews…no, Atkinson.'

And it had been a fine deal as well, as Atkinson had been eager to sell to stave off his creditors. Desperate sellers always offered the best bargains.

'But why would I need to evict the residents? Isn't it some shop or factory?'

Lady Georgina's mouth pursed. 'I'm afraid it is not, Mr Smith. Number fifty-five Boyle Street happens to be St Agnes's Orphanage for Girls.'

'An orphanage? In the middle of a busy commercial district?'

She let out an exasperated sigh. 'You bought it, didn't you? You didn't know it was an orphanage?'

'I did not.' He frowned. While he had instructed

Morgan to clear the building, Atkinson definitely hadn't mentioned there were any occupants, nor that they were orphans.

Damn.

'Oh, now I see!' She clapped her hands together. 'There was a mix-up then? And you really aren't evicting the girls?'

'I didn't say that.'

She blinked. 'You mean to throw over two dozen orphaned girls onto the street?'

Elliot ignored the knot forming in his gut and erased the vision of shivering waifs out in the cold her words had conjured in his mind. He'd made many cutthroat decisions in business before, and this one would be no different.

But his next move would no doubt be the most ruthless one he would ever make.

'I could change my mind. I mean, *you* could change my mind.'

'Me?' Her delicate brows slashed downwards. 'And what is it I can do to change your mind?'

'Marry me.'

Her bright coppery eyes grew to the size of saucers. 'I—I b-beg your pardon?'

'You heard me. Marry me and I will rescind the eviction notice.'

'You can't be serious.'

He was deadly serious. After all, this was the very reason he'd come to England: to marry a refined, blue-blooded English lady.

To say that the two little girls had thrown his entire life into chaos would have been an understatement. The children had been practically feral, for one thing. They hadn't known how to behave in polite company and both had run wild, sending his household into disarray. From what little bits and pieces they'd told her, their mother was likely a whore and they'd lived in a bawdy house before they'd left for San Francisco. He'd immediately hired a nanny for them, but had known a paid staff member would not be enough to turn the girls into proper and civilised young women. It had been evident that the girls needed a strong feminine influence.

Then there was his ten-year plan to marry and have children he could pass his legacy on to. If news came out that he had two illegitimate sisters—and it would, because San Francisco was still a small town—no woman would want to marry him. Unless he sent his sisters away, which he would never do.

And so he'd decided to move back to New York, setting them up in a grand house on Fifth Avenue where he could simply pass the girls off as his legitimate sisters. He had determined to find a suitable wife with all the graces and refinement necessary to raise his sisters and ensure that they, too, would make good matches when they were of age.

Flush with cash from the sale of his steamship business, he'd bought and sold a few properties in and around the city, invested in some businesses, and after a few years had once again been reaping the benefits of his golden touch.

But Elliot had miscalculated this move.

He had mistakenly thought his newfound wealth would allow him to mingle with the Knickerbocker set, so he could find a suitable wife—preferably with the pedigree that could open the right doors for him and his sisters. New York's high society salons, however, had remained closed to those who were not one of them. Though the society matrons of New York had not known about the girls' illegitimacy, they also had not known about *him*—and that had been the problem. Except for business acquaintances, Elliot had no social connections in the city—at least none that mattered. To the elite of the Fifth Avenue, no matter how much money he made, how many properties he owned, or stocks he traded, he would never be good enough to marry one of their daughters.

After three years of attempting to infiltrate New York's upper crust, with no victory in sight, he'd been about to give up when he'd seen a story in the newspaper about a duke and duchess from England visiting New York. There was to be a grand celebration that would take place at the home of the Commodore and Mrs Baldwin, *the* foremost socialites in the city. Apparently the Duchess was a born-and-bred American—the former Miss Grace Hathaway from Rockaway, New York, daughter of Richard Hathaway, who owned hotels along the beaches in Queens. Elliot didn't know the girl, but he remembered Hathaway—a jovial old fellow who swore like a sailor and drank like one too, with the manners of a goat. Elliot couldn't believe that Hathaway would be invited to this celebration and not him, just because his daughter had married some fancy duke from England.

This news, however, had given him an idea for a new ten-year plan. If Miss Grace Hathaway of Rockaway could marry into English society and come back as a celebrated success, why couldn't he?

However, he'd been in London for more than six months now, and he had yet to meet any eligible ladies. It seemed the English elite were even more prejudiced than New York's. In fact, Lady Georgina was perhaps the closest he'd come even to speaking with anyone who had a potential to be his bride.

'Well, Lady Georgina? What is your answer?'

The entirety of her face had turned red. 'I am not a chattel to be exchanged or bargained for,' she blurted out. 'I will not sell myself to you. How dare you suggest something so utterly offensive?'

'When you say it that way, it does sound offensive…' He paused. 'But what is marriage anyway? When you take it down to its barest bones, it's nothing but a contract between two parties from which both benefit. Not much different than let's say…a deed of sale. There's even property and money exchanged. In this case, if you become my wife, I will simply void the contract.'

And he would have his refined English bride, who would not only elevate his status, but that of his sisters.

Once they came of age they, too, would marry well and provide him with nieces and nephews who could continue his legacy. Why, Lady Georgina wouldn't even have to bear him an heir. After the wedding they could live separately, like most married couples of the Ton.

'Y-You are insane, Mr Smith,' she spluttered.

'Why not? I'm very wealthy, you know, and would be generous to my wife. I could buy you jewels, gowns, houses, a yacht. I have several houses in America and I am negotiating to purchase a lovely estate in Surrey. Anything you want that I don't have, I can provide.'

It was just money after all.

Her face turned even redder and her hands curled into fists at her sides. 'I will not marry you. I will *never* marry you.'

Elliot ignored the small pang in his chest at her words. 'All right, then. I guess your orphans will have to find another home.'

'You're a fiendish, miserly...' She seemed to struggle to find the words to describe him. 'Scrooge!'

'A what?'

'Scrooge,' she repeated. Her eyes turned bright with fury. 'As in Ebenezer Scrooge! Ha! You even have the same initials—ES. I can't believe you would be so cruel as to toss orphans out of the only home they've ever known! And on Christmas Day too.'

'Christmas?' He looked at the calendar on the wall. 'Is it Christmas already?'

'It's December the first,' she informed him.

'Ah, so it's not Christmas yet.'

'But it is the season of Christmas,' she said. 'Does that not mean anything to you?'

If she had thought that would help her in pleading her case, she was, unfortunately, deeply mistaken.

Because, for him, Christmas wasn't a special day. It wasn't even an ordinary day—at least not since he'd woken up that one Christmas morning and found his mother coughing, her body weak as a baby bird's. She'd been hiding her illness for some time and the cold weather had made it worse. They'd had no money for a doctor, so she'd died in their makeshift shack on the Lower East Side.

'Elliot, come here,' she had rasped. *'There is something I need you to do for me...'*

His mind blocked off that memory instantly.

As the years had gone on, Christmas had become just another day to him. He never celebrated, or decorated, and he certainly never gave or received presents. The closest he'd come to celebrating it had been in the last five years, if only to indulge Lily and Anne-Marie, watching them open presents on Christmas Eve. However, he let his staff deal with the festivities, and on Christmas Day itself he preferred to spend the day at the office, where he could actually get some work done as no one was around to disturb him.

Lady Georgina turned those pleading copper eyes on him. 'Can't you find it in your heart to allow the children to stay, Mr Smith? Their rent was paid to Mr Atkinson every month without delay.'

He'd seen the figures, of course, and had to bite his tongue to stop himself from laughing at the dismal amount they'd been paying. It had been barely enough to pay the taxes.

'You know my terms, Lady Georgina.'

Her eyes blazed once again. 'I told you, I will not—'

'Then we have no deal.' He crossed his arms over his chest in a firm, final motion.

She let out a small high-pitched sound as her lips pressed together. 'Good day to you, then, Mr Smith.'

'Good day, Lady Georgina.'

He didn't even wince when she slammed the door behind him. Instead, he turned back to the window and glanced out. Moments later, Lady Georgina marched out of his offices and into the magnificent carriage waiting on the street. He continued to watch the carriage as it rolled away, disappearing into the distance.

'Mr Smith?' Grant poked his head in. 'I heard voices and didn't want to interrupt.' He held up the coat and hat in his hands. 'The cheque book is in the front pocket, sir. Shall I cancel the rest of your meetings for the day?'

'No need.' Elliot blew out a breath and forced Lady Georgina out of his thoughts. 'This shan't take very long. I expect we'll be back within the hour.'

Chapter Two

4th December

'And there is truly nothing you can do about it, Trev?'

Trevor Abernathy, Duke of Harwicke, who also happened to be Georgina's brother, shook his head. 'I'm sorry, Georgie. As much as I want to help you save the orphanage, we simply cannot afford it.'

'You've looked into it? There's nothing we can sell to purchase the building? What if I go without new dresses for a year? Two years?'

'All of our lands are entailed, and therefore I cannot sell any of them.' Trevor smiled fondly at her. 'And I'm afraid it would cost more than two years' worth of dresses to purchase a building like that.'

Drat.

'How about your friends? Couldn't you pool your resources together and make an investment?'

'Yes, but that would take time. And, Georgie…' He took her hands into his. 'It's not really an investment—you do understand that?'

'*Pfft.*' The breath she blew out made a stray lock of wispy hair fly off her forehead. 'I know.' She stared up at her brother's kind face. 'I appreciate you trying.'

And she also appreciated the fact that he was not condescending to her—never had over the years. Perhaps because since they had lost both their parents in a terrible carriage accident twelve years ago they'd understood that they only had each other from then on, and their relationship had grown stronger over the years. Truly, there was no one else in the world she adored more than Trevor.

'I shall continue to search for alternative lodgings for them,' he said. 'And you should perhaps reach out to the other patrons and patronesses to start a new fundraising effort? Even if I can find a new place for them, the landlord will still expect rent.'

'Of course.'

Unless the Good Lord dropped another generous donor into their laps, any location they secured for the children would have to be paid for. Raising funds would be a good start, but December the twenty-fifth was fast approaching and the orphanage could be shut down before Trevor secured anything for them.

'I've also enquired about this Mr Smith fellow, to see if I can find anything he would want in return for giving up the property. From what little I've heard, he's supposedly a very rich and shrewd businessman. He's called the Midas of something—everything he touches turns to gold. We would have to find something truly valuable to make him want to change his mind about the eviction.'

Georgina avoided Trevor's gaze and bit the inside of her cheek. After all, she already knew *one* thing Mr Smith wanted.

No. Never.

She crossed her arms over her chest and pouted.

And how dared that boorish man even suggest such a thing?

'Are you all right, Georgie?' Trevor cocked his head to the side. 'You seem rather piqued all of a sudden.'

Georgina managed to smooth out her frown. 'I… yes, I was just thinking about that…er…the last bit of the banister in the main hall. It's still missing evergreen and holly. Mrs Harris didn't order enough, and now it's all lopsided.'

Trevor chuckled. 'You're still not finished? You've been decorating for three days now. Why, we must have more baubles, bits and bobs than Windsor Castle.'

After her encounter with Mr Smith, Georgina had been so fraught that she'd thrown herself into decorating Harwicke House for the festive season. Since she loved Christmas, she always dressed the house in yuletide finery, but this year she'd added more decorations, leaving not a single inch of space uncovered by fir branches, holly, ivy leaves and sparkly ornaments.

'I doubt that,' she said. 'But you know how much I love Christmas. Which makes it even more awful for the orphaned children.'

'I know, Georgie.' Standing up, he walked from behind his desk and placed a hand on her shoulder. 'We will do our best. If anything… I suppose we could place the girls in different orphanages.'

Her heart sank. That was what Mrs Jameson had said they would have to do if they didn't find a new home. It was something she dreaded, as she'd heard about the conditions in other orphanages around London. Many of them were not well kept and the children were squeezed into small spaces. And those were the better ones.

'Thank you, Trev.' Rising to her feet, she covered his hand and squeezed it. 'I should go and find Miss Warren.'

She left her brother's office and found her companion in the library, having a cup of tea.

'What did your brother say?' Miss Warren asked as soon as she entered.

Georgina sighed. 'What do you think?' She sank down on the settee next to Miss Warren. 'It's hopeless.' She relayed the conversation with her brother to her companion. 'Trevor tried his best to soften the blow, of course, but I do not think we will find a new home for the children by the twenty-fifth. We might not have any choice except to place them in different orphanages around the city and beyond.'

'I am so sorry.' Miss Warren placed a sympathetic hand on her shoulder. 'You tried your best.'

'I know, but it's not good enough!' She rose to her

feet and paced across the Persian rug. 'There is still time…surely there must be something else I can do.'

'It seems to me you've run out of options. Was Mr Smith truly stone-hearted? Did he not even budge or offer to delay the eviction? At least until after the New Year?'

'Yes, he truly was an uncharitable, greedy scoundrel.'

Her temper flared once more, thinking of that lout. Did he think everything could be bought and sold, like goods at a market? And to think the moment she'd laid eyes on him she had thought him quite handsome, in a rugged sort of way. He was quite tall, and his shoulders were unfashionably bulky, even under his tailored shirt, and he seemingly spent too much time in the sun, judging from his swarthy complexion. His dark hair had stuck up at angles, as he'd raked his fingers through it, and those eyes…bright green, like jade… had been so stark against his tanned skin. She'd never seen anything quite like them before.

'And very rich too, from what I heard.'

Georgina stopped pacing and planted her hands on her waist. So, he had not been exaggerating when he'd said he was wealthy and could provide all those things for her when he proposed. But she wanted to know more.

'What *have* you heard, Miss Warren?'

'He's only been in London for a few months or so, but has already bought property and businesses all over England,' Miss Warren relayed. 'A man like that has to be sitting on a very large fortune indeed.'

'Well, Trevor did say they called him a...what did he say? Oh, a Midas of something. But why come to England, then, if he's already wealthy in America?'

'London seems to be teeming with these moneyed foreigners lately.'

'Lately?' Since Georgina hadn't participated much in society these last few years, she hadn't noticed.

'Yes. And many of them are obscenely wealthy, having made their money from industry and commerce back in America.'

'And what are they doing here? Are many of them doing business in England?'

Miss Warren's eyes narrowed. 'Actually, I've only encountered the wives of these rich businessmen. And their daughters. They travel all the way here, hoping to catch husbands.'

'These girls travel across the Atlantic for marriage?' Georgina chuckled. 'Is America bereft of eligible men?'

'Yes. At least, titled ones,' Miss Warren clarified. 'America has no royalty and aristocracy, after all. Apparently these young women arrive at our shores to marry titled lords.'

'Not much different from any woman in England,' Georgina said dryly.

'Yes, except for their very, *very* generous dowries. And many of them do succeed in attracting those lords who have been left in dire straits, due to their failing estates. These young women then return to America with their shiny new titles and elevated social status.'

To her irritation, Mr Smith's words about marriage being a contract surfaced in her mind.

'What's wrong?' Miss Warren asked. 'Is the idea of the exchange of a dowry so disagreeable to you? You yourself have one, do you not?'

'I do, but...' She sat down next to her companion. 'I just wonder why Mr Smith would ask me to—' She covered her mouth with her hands, muffling the audible gasp that had escaped her lips.

'Ask you to *what*?' Miss Warren's face was scrunched up. 'Lady Georgina...did something happen in that office that I should know about?'

'Well...' Georgina shifted in her seat uncomfortably.

The companion let out an outraged sound. 'I knew I should not have allowed you to go up there alone. Did he say or do something improper?'

'He wasn't improper! Or not in the way you think.'

'I can think of a great many things that could be interpreted as "improper". Tell me now or I shall be forced to tell your brother—'

'No! Please...' It wasn't that she was afraid of her brother, but it was difficult to describe how she felt about the whole fiasco. Embarrassed, perhaps?

'Lady Georgina...'

'All right.' She folded her hands in her lap. 'Mr Smith asked me to marry him in exchange for not evicting the children.'

'What?' Miss Warren's eyes widened. 'I… How…? I cannot even comprehend.' Her nose twitched. 'No one heard him, I hope?'

She shook her head.

Miss Warren's mouth puckered. 'I will never allow you to be alone anywhere from now on. I was foolish, staying in the carriage and allowing you to go in there by yourself.'

'You'd think you'd be happy that I have finally received an offer of marriage,' she said dryly.

'I thought you said he was a scoundrel?'

'He is, but…' Georgina could not explain it, but she attempted to. 'Despite the ridiculousness of his request, he sounded…well, sincere.'

And perhaps that was why she could not forget Mr Smith's proposal. She was insulted and shocked by his forwardness, but knew he'd been deadly serious about it. He'd acted and sounded as if he really, truly wanted to marry her.

'Sincere?' Miss Warren echoed.

'Yes.'

'Do you know why he would ask such a thing of you?'

'I don't—' She gasped. 'That's *it*!'

Miss Warren's eyebrows snapped together. 'What's it?'

'Why he wants—and how we can save the—' The ideas bounced around in her mind so fast she could barely form a coherent sentence.

'Lady Georgina? You look ready to faint. Are you all right?'

'Yes, I'm all right.' She inhaled a deep breath. 'And I know how I will save the orphanage.'

'How?'

Smirking, she crossed her arms over her chest. 'I will find Mr Smith a wife.'

'You will? Why?'

'It's quite apparent to me now—thanks to what you've told me about these American women—why he asked me in the first place. He wants a titled wife to elevate his own status. That's why he asked me to marry him.'

'I was speaking of the American *women*, and Mr Smith would not gain a title if he were to marry you.'

'Yes, but a titled wife would open so many doors for him,' she pointed out. Being a shrewd businessman, as Trevor had said he was earlier, such an association would be priceless for Mr Smith. 'He was very much interested in the fact that I was a duke's daughter. He knows that by marrying me he would be able to raise his position in society, both here and in America.'

'I suppose that makes sense...'

'Then you agree that I must go to Mr Smith and tell him that I will find him a bride, in exchange for his allowing the orphanage to remain.'

'Now, *that* I did not agree to,' Miss Warren retorted sharply. 'As I mentioned, I will never allow you to be in the company of a man by yourself—and certainly not Mr Smith.'

'Then you shall accompany me,' she said, rising to her feet. Sensing Miss Warren's protest, she pre-empted it with a plea. 'Won't you do this with me, Miss Warren? This is for a good cause. And your job is to be my companion, after all, so…accompany me. Think of those poor children.'

Miss Warren's stern expression softened. 'I suppose…'

'Excellent! Let us leave now, so we may catch Mr Smith in his office.'

To her surprise, Mr Smith's assistant ushered them into his office even without an appointment. Once again, those jade-green eyes pierced right through her the moment she stepped in.

'My lady,' he greeted her. 'I'm surprised to see you return.'

From his tone, Georgina didn't think he sounded surprised at all. 'My companion, Miss Warren,' she introduced with a quick nod. 'Thank you for seeing me today.'

'Of course.' He gestured towards the chairs in front of his desk. 'Please, have a seat.'

As soon as they'd both sat down, she spoke. 'Mr Smith, I've rethought your…er…proposal.'

'I see.' He threaded his fingers together and rested his chin on top of them. 'And you are accepting it?'

'No.' When his eyebrows lifted, she quickly added, 'I mean, yes. Or no. Er…' She glanced at Miss War-

ren helplessly, who only shrugged, as if it say, *What
do you expect me to do?*

'No and yes? You do realise those words are the
opposite of each other?'

'Yes.' Georgina straightened her shoulders. 'What
I am trying to say, Mr Smith, is that while I still decline your first proposal, I have a different one to
make to you.'

'You do, do you?'

'Yes.' Trying to appear confident, she placed her
hands on the table as she leaned forward. 'I know why
you asked me to marry you. You want a proper English bride with the right background, preferably the
daughter of a titled lord. Correct?'

Mr Smith's expression remained impassive, but she
didn't miss the glint in his eyes. 'Go on.'

'And I suppose the reason you asked me, despite
the fact that we had only just met, is that you've had
no luck on your own?'

'Your powers of deduction are astounding,' he said
dryly.

'So I have a counter proposal.' She folded her hands
together in a similar manner to his. 'Or rather, a *business* proposal for you: I will help you find a bride, and
in return you will rescind the eviction notice.'

'You believe your assistance has equal value to a
prime piece of property?'

'You certainly believed *I* was when you made your
first offer,' she pointed out. 'Surely one lady is no different from another? And wasn't it you who said mar-

riage is nothing but a contract? In this case, I will act as your…er…'

'Agent?' he supplied. 'Middle man?'

'Matchmaker,' she said.

Mr Smith lifted an eyebrow at her sceptically. 'Tell me, Lady Georgina, what exactly do you bring to the bargaining table? London is full of eligible debutantes and unmarried misses searching for a match. If I, a wealthy man of considerable means, have yet to find a bride amongst the stable of eligible ladies, what makes you think you could?'

'Ah, but I have something you do not.'

'And that is?'

Scrounging up every bit of confidence, she said, 'The right pedigree and connections. My brother is a duke, after all. Our family is invited to all the best balls and events in town, and we know everyone in London.'

'Everyone?'

'Why, yes. Everyone who is anyone.' She thought she had sounded quite convincing, so she continued, 'I can make the necessary introductions for you.'

'Introductions are one thing, but delivering an actual bride is quite different,' he said. 'I would need something solid if I am even to consider your proposal.'

Desperation crept into her chest. 'How about…an engagement by Christmas? To a lady from one of England's finest families?'

Miss Warren's eyes enlarged, as if sending her a

warning. But the words were already out of her mouth, and Georgina could not take them back.

The corner of his mouth curled up into what appeared to be a smile. 'An engagement? In...' he looked at the calendar '...less than twenty days.'

'That's plenty of time. A quick courtship is not unheard of, after all, and once a woman begins accepting calls from you, that means she is already considering a proposal.'

'You said "an engagement by Christmas".'

'Not in the literal sense. I will do my best to lead the right lady to you, but it is up to you to propose, now, isn't it? It won't be my fault if you fail to ask the question. Surely you don't think I will be asking on your behalf?'

The look on his face told her that, yes, he did expect that.

She stifled the urge to roll her eyes. 'Allow me to explain to you how things work here in England, Mr Smith. A lady's father or guardian will not allow you even to begin courting her unless the lady already has an inkling to accept. Otherwise, if she continues to toy with numerous men, she will be branded a flirt. The best I can do—the best anyone can do—is advise you which ladies would be most...er...suited to your needs and open to accepting your proposal. Besides, you will need at least a full year's engagement before you can marry.'

She paused, trying to gauge his thoughts, but found

his face was unreadable. She would have to do her best to persuade him to give her a chance.

'Of course, you could keep on with your current method of finding a wife, as that certainly seems to have brought you success.' She tapped a finger on her chin. 'Oh, wait—it hasn't, has it? Because otherwise you wouldn't have made that offer to me two days ago.'

He remained silent, though his nostrils flared. Finally, after what seemed like an eternity, he spoke. 'All right.' He huffed. 'I will propose to the most suitable woman you introduce to me by Christmas, and if she accepts I will rescind the eviction.'

She clapped her hands together. 'Excellent. I accept the terms.'

'Of course, you do know this means that your choice must be guaranteed to accept my proposal?'

Well, she hadn't quite thought of *that*.

'Of course.' She ignored the growing lump of stone in her stomach. It would be a Herculean task, but it wasn't as if she had any other way to save the orphanage. 'Should we have a contract drawn up?'

'No need.' Rising from his chair, he leaned over the desk and extended his hand. 'We shall seal our deal with a handshake. A fiancée by Christmas for me, and in exchange your orphans can stay in their home.'

Elation shot through her, and before she could even think she took his hand. 'We have a deal.'

As his ungloved fingers closed around hers, she couldn't help but notice how much larger his hand was compared to hers, nor how warm they felt even through her gloves. She wondered how they would feel if her fingers were bare too. The very thought sent a strange flutter behind her ribs. Lifting her head, she met his jade-green gaze, and warmth spread up her neck.

Miss Warren cleared her throat, and both of them released each other's hands.

'So,' Mr Smith began, sinking down into his seat. 'What is your exact plan, then?'

'Plan?' She gawked at him. 'Do I need a plan?'

'Yes. Every goal requires some sort of plan of action in order to achieve it. What are the steps in your plan and how will you execute them?'

Georgina swallowed a gulp. She honestly had not thought she would get this far—at least not far enough to require an entire plan from beginning to end.

'Well?' Mr Smith asked. 'You *do* have a plan, don't you?'

'Of course I do,' she said quickly. 'I just…left it at home.'

'You left it at home?'

'Yes.' Quickly, she stood up. 'Silly me—how could I do that? Miss Warren, we should head back to Harwicke House immediately, before…er…one of the maids throws it away whilst tidying up.'

Mr Smith rose as well. 'And when will I be made a party to this plan of yours, my lady?'

'I shall send you a note,' she said. 'As soon as possible.'

'I hope so.' He glanced at the calendar. 'After all, you only have nineteen days left.'

She let out a nervous laugh. 'Of course. Come now, Miss Warren. Good day, Mr Smith.'

Before he could even bid her goodbye, she rushed them out of the office and into the street, where they hurried into her carriage.

'What in the world were you thinking?' Miss Warren admonished.

Georgina wilted into the plush velvet seat. 'I'm afraid I was not.' But then again, she would do any-thing—almost anything—to save the orphanage.

'You do realise fulfilling your end of the bargain and finding him a bride requires the one thing you swore you would never do?'

Her head snapped towards the companion's. 'And what is that?'

'Venturing into society.'

'I— Oh…'

Drat.

'So, am I to assume we should unpack your ball-gowns, dust off your dancing slippers, and perhaps acquire some new dance cards?'

Double drat.

While she hated to admit it, Miss Warren was right. To find Mr Smith a bride and save St Agnes's, she must re-join society. After all, how was she to make introductions and find these potential brides while sipping tea and doing embroidery at home? No, she would have to leave the comfort of her home and attend those dreadful balls and parties.

The very thought of it made dread pool in her stomach.

But she reminded herself this was for a good cause. *Think of the children.*

'And what of this plan Mr Smith expects?'

'I haven't got to that yet,' she confessed. 'But I have an idea of where to begin.'

Chapter Three

5th December

Elliot had expected never to hear from Lady Georgina again. After all, her 'proposition' was absurd. Surely, if she had any sense, she would have stayed away. She was far too young and naive, now that he thought of it, and he never should have offered to marry her in the first place.

So he was very much astonished to receive a note the next day, unsigned, and written in a loopy, feminine handwriting.

> *Please come to Harwicke House for tea today at two o'clock.*

And so that very afternoon he found himself on the steps of an elegant mansion at Mayfair's most fashionable address, Grosvenor Square. The two-storey villa itself—red brick, with white window frames and a gabled roof—was well-kept, and obviously belonged to someone very important.

Not that Elliot didn't already know that the Duke of Harwicke was a leading member of society. After all, he always did his due diligence when it came to both his business and personal life. One of the first things he'd done when he'd arrived in London had been to hire a private investigator to ferret out information on anyone he was to have dealings with. In the last twenty-four hours, he'd had his man gather every bit of available information on Trevor Abernathy.

Trevor Charles William Abernathy, aged twenty-nine, had received his title upon the untimely death of his parents twelve years ago, when he was only seventeen. His estates were well-maintained and profitable, he had made a number of wise investments over the last few years. While his assets paled in comparison to Elliot's, the Abernathys were still rich. No wonder Lady Georgina was not at all tempted by his wealth.

'May I help you, sir?' The stodgy-looking butler on the other side of the door asked as soon as it was opened.

'I'm Mr Elliot Smith. I'm here for—'

'Yes, come in.' The butler glanced around, as if he were checking for robbers outside—or perhaps for any prying eyes watching the house. 'She is waiting for you.'

Before he'd arrived here he had pictured in his mind what Lady Georgina's home would be like. He'd imagined elegant decor, antique furniture, plush carpeting and portraits on the wall sneering down at him, telling him he didn't belong here.

As he followed the butler inside, however, he was unprepared for the sight that assaulted him.

It seemed every square inch of the entrance hall had been covered in evergreen and ivy. Boughs of holly hung from the doorways, and red and green ribbons were wrapped around the fir-covered banister. Glass balls and bulbs sparkled from where they hung from the ceiling, tinkling as they clinked against each other. The smell of pine and sugar wafted into his nostrils. He suspected it came from the large tree he spied in the drawing room, just to his left—were those actual sweets and biscuits hanging from its branches?

'Dear God, man, what happened here?' he exclaimed. 'Did they bring in an entire forest?'

The butler merely sniffed. 'This way, if you please.'

He followed the butler through the richly decorated corridors of Harwicke House. He did not think it were possible, but the deeper he was drawn in, the more bits and baubles he saw, hung from the walls and springing forth from the ceiling and floors.

When they reached a door at the end of the corridor, the butler stepped inside first. 'Mr Smith is here,' he announced, then stepped aside to allow Elliot inside what appeared to be a sitting room.

Like the rest of the house, this room was decorated with all kinds of Christmas trinkets and knick-knacks. However, this time the garish display faded from his vision as something else caught his eye—Lady Georgina herself, who sat by the window.

Now that she was not wearing a hat, he could finally see what colour her hair was—light blonde, the colour of wheat. It was swept up in wispy waves around her head and threaded through with a blue ribbon that matched her day dress. He wondered how long it was and what it would look like undone.

'Thank you, Dawson. You may leave,' she said. 'Mr Elliot, welcome to Harwicke House.'

'Thank you for your invitation.'

'You remember my companion, Miss Warren?' she said, gesturing to the woman who sat in an armchair to her left.

'Miss Warren,' he greeted her.

Of course he had not expected to be alone with her, though he did think her much too young to have a companion. He'd thought companions usually accompanied doddering old women. Perhaps in England a chaperone and a companion were the same thing.

Miss Warren murmured a greeting in return, her suspicious gaze remaining on him for a few seconds before she bowed her head curtly.

'Would you like tea to be served now or later, after we speak?' Lady Georgina asked.

'If you don't mind, perhaps we could proceed with our business,' he replied.

'As you wish.' She motioned for him to sit on the chair across from her.

He spoke first. 'So, Lady Georgina, are you ready to tell me about your plan?'

'Ah, yes.' She cleared her throat and placed her

hands on her lap. 'My plan. The one I have thought up to help you find a suitable bride.'

'Exactly.'

He tried not to sound impatient, but he'd had a distinct feeling yesterday that she had no plan at all. Why, if he were to trust his instinct, he would guess she'd simply thought up her proposal just before she rushed over to his office, hoping to entice him not to evict the tenants at number fifty-five Boyle Street.

'So, my plan consists of you and myself—but not together, of course—g-going to several balls so that you can meet the right people.'

He paused, waiting for the next part. When a few awkward seconds passed without another peep from her, he said, 'That's it?'

'Er...yes.'

'But surely there must be more? You need several steps, at least, and a timeline...milestones you must achieve.' He curled his hands on the arms of the chair, stifling the urge to stand up and walk away. 'And you must also put in some contingencies in case of failure.'

She stared at him as if he had declared himself the King of England. 'Failure?'

'Yes.' He clicked his tongue. 'You don't actually have a plan, do you?'

'Of course I do,' she spluttered. 'I have just told you.'

'But not a real plan,' he countered.

She crossed her arms over her chest. 'Love cannot be planned.'

'I do not need love, Lady Georgina,' he stated firmly. 'I need a wife. If you cannot help me find one, then I will bid you goodbye.'

He stood up.

'No, please.' She sprang up from her seat, her hands grasping at his forearm. 'I do have a plan…it's just that…he's late.'

He froze at her touch. Much like it had yesterday, when they'd shaken hands, his body seized at the contact, and a curl of lust coiled inside him. He had brushed it off as a fluke—after all, it had been months since he'd been with a woman…not since New York. He'd been much too busy with the move to London, and dealing with his sisters, not to mention establishing his company here. Too busy to have time for dalliances. That had to be it. Because by most standards Lady Georgina was no stunning temptress.

Yet now, this close, he couldn't help but notice how velvety her skin seemed, and how the sun shining through the window highlighted the streaks of gold in her hair. He took in a deep breath, and he swore he could smell the light, powdery scent of her perfume.

'Apologies for my lateness.'

The new and very male voice caused them to jump apart. Lady Georgina's face turned crimson as she turned away. 'I…ah… Trev, you're finally home.'

'There was an accident outside my solicitor's office. Overturned cart. Took bloody for ever to clear the street so my carriage could get through.'

The man—whom Elliot guessed was His Grace the Duke of Harwicke himself—walked over to him.

Lady Georgina cleared her throat. 'Trev…er… Your Grace, may I present Mr Elliot Smith? Mr Smith, this is His Grace the Duke of Harwicke.'

'A pleasure to meet you, Mr Smith,' the Duke said.

He was fair-haired, like his sister, but that was the end of the resemblance between the siblings. Harwicke was nearly as tall as him, with broad shoulders, and he had a handsome face with strong, masculine features and sharp blue eyes. Blue eyes that, much to Elliot's frustration, were unreadable. While the Duke was putting on an affable demeanour, as if they were being introduced at a dinner party, Elliot could not help but feel that Harwicke was hiding his true feelings behind that facade.

He bowed his head. 'Likewise, Your Grace.'

'I'm not usually late to meetings,' he said. 'I see you've started without me.'

'You're to be part of this meeting?' Elliot asked, incredulous. 'Lady Georgina has told you everything?'

Did Harwicke know he'd proposed? From the nervous look he saw on the lady's face—because she, on the other hand, was very easy to read—he guessed not.

'Of course.' Harwicke walked over to his sister, ruffling her hair affectionately before sitting down next to her. 'She has told me she needs my assistance, so what is a brother to do but offer it?'

'This is the first part of my plan, Mr Smith,' she

said. 'My brother will make you the necessary introductions to the right people in London. Fathers, brothers, guardians of potential brides...that sort of thing. I didn't mean to make it seem I was unprepared, but I was hoping to stall you before Trevor arrived and I could explain.'

'And you have agreed to this?' he asked the Duke.

'Well, my sister certainly can't make you introductions to these men. She is unmarried and still under my protection.'

'I see.' Elliot sat back down. 'And then what, Lady Georgina?'

'Once you become associated with us—with Trevor—then you'll be invited to various society events around town.'

'And you'll be there too?'

'Of course,' she said.

Elliot observed that the smile forming on her face did not reach her eyes, but he did not mention it. After all, her plan was solid for now. Having the Duke as an acquaintance would definitely get him into the right places.

'All right, that sounds like a logical plan.' He wouldn't say it was good but, as Lady Georgina had said yesterday, what did he have to lose?

'Excellent.' Harwicke patted his sister's arm, then stood up. 'Now, Mr Smith, would you mind joining me in my study for a moment?'

'But, Trev, Mrs Harris is preparing tea.'

'You and Miss Warren will enjoy it, then.' His blue

eyes speared right through Elliot. 'Mr Smith and I need to speak alone.'

Not missing the Duke's serious tone, Elliot rose and followed him out of the sitting room to his study, just across the corridor.

Harwicke walked over to the liquor cabinet. 'Drink? I have whisky, sherry, port—'

'No, thank you, I don't drink.' He occasionally had a glass of wine with dinner, but nothing stronger—not after he'd seen how it affected his father.

The Duke's eyebrows shot up, but he said nothing as he poured some brown liquid from a decanter into a glass. 'Let me get straight to the point.'

'That's how I like it myself,' said Elliot.

'As I mentioned, Georgina is unmarried and under my protection.' The edge in his tone could have cut through a rock. 'Ever since our parents died, it's just been her and I. She is my sister and my only remaining flesh and blood. You may not understand why, but I will do anything for her.' He took a sip of his drink. 'But I will also do anything to protect her. I am only agreeing to this because of her—I don't care about your reasons. And while I know Georgie may never marry, that does not mean that I will risk her reputation.'

Never marry? What in God's name was Harwicke talking about? Any man would be lucky to marry Lady Georgina.

Except him, which she had made abundantly clear that first day she'd barged into his office.

'Do we understand each other?' asked the Duke.

'Of course,' he said.

'Good.' Harwicke downed the rest of his drink. 'Meet me tonight at Brooks' for dinner. Eight o'clock sharp. You do know where that is?'

'Yes.'

Brooks' was one of the most exclusive gentlemen's clubs in London—of course Elliot knew where it was. If Harwicke could get him in there, even for just a meal, then the Duke truly was influential.

'I'll see you there,' he said in a dismissive tone, then turned his back on him.

Elliot guessed that was the signal for him to show himself out, and so he did. Thankfully, he managed to follow the trail of fir branches and crystal baubles and found his way out of that festooned madhouse.

As he climbed into his carriage, Harwicke's words rang in his head.

'You may not understand why, but I will do anything for her.'

He scoffed to himself. If only Harwicke knew.

'Home,' he said to his footman.

The trip back to his house took only a few minutes, as it was only a small number of streets away, on Upper Brook Street. As soon as he entered, the lingering traces of smoke invaded his nostrils. Elliot glanced left at the door to the drawing room.

'We're doing our best to air it, Mr Smith,' said his butler, Fletcher. 'Mrs Jenkins, the housekeeper from next door, has recommended we place bowls of vinegar all over the room to absorb the smell.'

'Then the entire house will smell of vinegar and not smoke.' His eyes slid heavenwards. 'All right... do what you must.'

He was just glad no one had been hurt in the fire. When he'd arrived home two days ago, to deal with the situation, Miss Jones had been in a fiery mood. Lily had clung to him the moment he'd stepped through the door, but Anne-Marie had stood there, defiant, as Miss Jones had lashed out.

'Your sisters are the worst charges I've ever had!' Miss Jones had screamed at him. 'And if you do not give me what I demand, everyone will know what devil spawn they are.'

Elliot had done his best to control his temper. 'What happened here?'

'They tried to set me on fire!' the governess had raged.

'Is that true, Anne-Marie?' he had asked. 'You could have hurt Miss Jones and razed the entire house to the ground.'

'She's a liar!' His sister had shot back. 'She knocked that candle over by accident.'

'Because you attempted to assault me.'

Anne-Marie had bared her teeth. 'You had grabbed my sister and twisted her arm until she screamed in pain!'

Cold fury had risen in him. 'Lily?' The child had

not answered, but instead had tightened her grip on him. 'Girls, please go up to your rooms.'

'But she—'

'Now.'

Once both girls had left, Elliot had focused that splintering rage on the governess. 'Listen to me, you insignificant flea. I will pay you your wages until the end of the month and nothing more. And if you dare say anything about my sisters to anyone, or attempt to ruin them, I will make it my life's mission to thwart your every move and prospect. I will find every family, every position you apply to, and make it worth their while not to hire you. You will never find a job in this city higher than scrubbing floors or washing dishes in a public house. Am I making myself clear?'

The way the blood had drained from the old hag's face had been almost satisfying enough to make him forget his problems.

Sighing now, he looked up towards the stairs, making his way to the schoolroom, where Lily sat at one of the tables, writing something down as the new tutor, Mrs Howard, kept a keen eye on her.

'Very good, Lilian,' Mrs Howard said. 'Your penmanship has vastly improved.'

'Hello,' he called to Lily.

The little girl looked up from her writing, her face lighting up. 'Elliot!' she screamed as she pushed away from the desk and jumped off her chair.

'Oomph!' he exclaimed as a tiny bundle of red curls and lace jumped into his arms.

'You're home early!' she said.

'I am.'

'Are you home so we can go somewhere? Maybe you can take Anne-Marie and I skating on the Serpentine.'

'Anne-Marie and *me*,' Miss Howard corrected.

'That's what I said,' Lily said with a small huff. 'So, are you taking us?'

'Perhaps—but not today. It is already dark out, and the skating is finished.'

'Oh…' Her tiny lips pursed. 'Another time, then?'

'We'll see.' He kissed her forehead. 'In the meantime, please do pay attention to Mrs Howard's lessons. She's making sure you grow up to be a proper lady.'

Her little nose wrinkled. 'All right.' She beamed up at him and then bounded back to her chair to resume her lesson.

Elliot watched for a few more seconds, then left the room, closing the door behind him and leaning against it with a heavy sigh.

Now the easy part was done. Glancing down the corridor, he stared towards his other sister's rooms.

Perhaps it was unfair to compare Lily and Anne-Marie. Lily had been so young, after all, when she'd come to live with Elliot. Still, he recalled Anne-Marie as a quiet, sweet young thing, and it seemed only recently that she'd grown a rebellious streak.

Trudging down the corridor, he stopped outside her room and knocked. 'Anne-Marie? Anne-Marie, are you in there?'

No answer.

'Young lady,' he said in a sterner voice, 'I would like to speak with you.'

He hadn't seen her in three days—not since he had sent them up to their rooms so he could deal with Miss Jones.

'Anne-Marie, open this door now!'

He heard some rustling from inside before the door opened. Anne-Marie's pretty face was drawn into a scowl. With the same curly red hair and green eyes, she was an older, ganglier version of her younger sister.

'What do you want?' She crossed her arms over her chest.

So much for that sweet young thing.

'Mrs Murphy has told me you haven't eaten since yesterday.'

'I'm not hungry.'

'Surely that's not true,' he said. 'You must eat. And you must leave your room for lessons.'

Her pretty face scrunched up. 'Which ones? Those futile dancing lessons or the pointless lectures on social graces?'

'They are not pointless,' he said through gritted teeth. 'Those lessons will help you later in life. And I've paid for the best tutors in London to come here and teach you girls so that you may become elegant young ladies when you enter society.'

'That's all you care about, isn't it? Your money? Why don't you just stop wasting it on me?'

'Young lady, how—?'

Blam! The door slammed shut.

'I hate this damned place,' came the muffled sob from the other side.

Elliot blew out a breath and knocked his head against the wooden door. Could he really blame Anne-Marie for being angry with him? For the past five years he'd dragged them from one coast of the United States to another, and then all the way across the Atlantic to a strange place. Anne-Marie in particular had been furious when he'd announced the move to London, as she was finally making friends in New York.

He straightened his shoulders. 'I'll send a tray up and you won't leave this room until you've eaten every last bit of food,' he said in a determined tone before he walked away.

Elliot raked his fingers through his hair. How could one slip of a girl thwart his plans? He was halfway through this ten-year plan and he was nowhere near achieving his goals, nor had he even met any of the milestones he had set.

But perhaps his luck had turned—not that he believed in such a thing. He'd been in the right place at the right time, after all, when he'd decided to purchase number fifty-five Boyle Street and a certain flaxen-haired lady had barged into his office. If Lady Georgina's plan worked, then before the year ended he would have a blue-blooded bride who would solve all his problems.

A knot of anticipation formed in his chest at the

thought of Lady Georgina. He wasn't quite sure why. Perhaps he'd seen something different in her this time. How he had thought her ordinary that first time she'd burst into his office, he didn't know.

In any case, he had to set his sights elsewhere. Since Lady Georgina would never marry him, she would have to be the key to the success of his ten-year plan.

7th December

Just as Harwicke had promised, he dined with Elliot that evening at Brooks'. The Duke made the introductions to other members they encountered as they made their way to the dining room, though they dined alone. The other members watched him curiously, but said nothing out of politeness. After dinner they had port and cigars, while watching some members play cards, and then they left.

The next two evenings were spent at Brooks' too, though they were joined by more of Harwicke's acquaintances for dinner and they lingered on much longer each time. Elliot allowed Harwicke to lead the conversation, and he was quite surprised when some of the men asked him questions. In fact, when he started speaking about investments and such, they listened with rapt attention.

'Is it true you are called the Midas of San Francisco?' asked Lord Kensington, whom Harwicke had said was a schoolmate from Eton, during the third evening they were at the club.

'Midas?' echoed Mr James Galwick, another of their schoolmates.

'Yes. I heard Smith here made more money than God in the gold mines,' Kensington added. 'Did you strike a particularly rich vein?'

Elliot grinned. 'No, I'm afraid I've never entered the gold mining business.'

'And why not?' Galwick asked. 'I heard of one claim that resulted in nearly twenty thousand dollars' worth of gold in one week.'

'Ah, yes, the Weber's Creek claim.' That had happened the year before he'd arrived, but it remained the talk of the town for years. 'Unfortunately, for every Weber's Creek claim dozens of others turned out to be worthless. The risk was much too high for me, and I didn't know the first thing about mining. I did, however, spend ten years building my ferry company.'

And he told them about how he'd invested in building the shipping lines from west to east.

'What great luck. And very perceptive of you,' Kensington remarked. 'Perhaps I should have gone to California and sold… I don't know…perhaps picks and shovels.'

All the men laughed—even Harwicke.

While Elliot was certainly having a grand time—it had been much too long since he had done anything except read reports in the evenings before going to bed—his patience was running thin. He'd been running around with Harwicke for three evenings, but he'd only met gentlemen.

Still, he didn't say anything to the Duke, and they continued with their merriment. By the time they made their way out of Brooks' the sky was streaked with the pinks and purples of dawn. Elliot cursed himself as he hadn't noticed the time. It was also a reminder that another day had passed.

'I'll see you tonight,' Harwicke said as they awaited their carriages. 'We'll be—'

'When will you introduce me to some potential brides?' Elliot asked, frustrated. 'We've been wasting time here, while the deadline grows closer.'

Harwicke lifted an elegant blond eyebrow. 'I was beginning to like you, and then you had to bring up that damned agreement with my sister.' He sighed. 'This is but a first step, as Georgina explained to you.'

Elliot ignored the way his heart jumped at the sound of her name.

'Normally, these connections take weeks to foster. But because of this deadline of yours I've had to make these introductions quickly.'

'And these gentlemen…do they have daughters? Perhaps sisters I can marry?'

The corner of Harwicke's mouth twitched at the mention of sisters. 'No, but they have wives.'

'And?'

'As you will quickly learn, when it comes to matters of society it is the wives who matter. With your wealth, some impoverished gentleman with a languishing estate will definitely want you for a son-in-law, but ultimately it's the mamas you must win over.

I've learned over the past few nights that I do not need to choose my words with you, so I shall be blunt: any lady you marry will be stepping down from her station, so you must convince the mothers that you will be a worthy enough match that they can overcome your background.'

'I see.'

The Duke's words made sense. Men, after all, were in charge of the money, while the women were in charge of the home and the children.

'If you had allowed me to finish my earlier sentence,' said the Duke, 'I was about to tell you that tonight we will be at the opera.'

'Opera? I hate the opera,' he said. 'A waste of a perfectly good evening.'

'But that's where you'll be seen by the wives of the Ton,' Harwicke explained. 'You'll sit in my box, with myself and Georgina.'

His heart quickened again at the mention of her name. It seemed so long since he had seen her. Last night, he'd come to Harwicke House to pick up the Duke, as his carriage was being repaired. He hadn't even seen a glimpse of her, though he had spied her companion walking across the hall, which had meant Lady Georgina was home.

'She'll be there? At the opera?' he asked.

'Naturally,' said Harwicke. 'You'll have a grand time with her, I'll bet. She hates the opera, too—hasn't joined me in years. But she'll go because she needs to. Being acquainted with me will help you, but Georgina, being a duke's sister, will open doors for you, and with her approval, you will be allowed access.'

'But she isn't a society matron. She's not married, I mean.'

'True, but she is still one of them. As the daughter of a duke, she still outranks many of the women of the Ton—even the married ones. And, though she's approaching spinsterhood, her reputation has remained un-besmirched all this time.'

That last sentence certainly sounded like a warning to Elliot's ears. 'Why is it that you think your sister a spinster? She cannot be that old. Surely she's had many proposals over the years? Why has she not chosen anyone?'

'My sister is seven and twenty, which I personally do not believe makes her a spinster, but unfortunately that's what society believes. And as for your last question—that's her business. My sister is sheltered, but she knows her own mind. I will do whatever it takes to make her happy, and I have promised I will support her whether she marries or not. Now, I'll see you tonight—seven o'clock,' the Duke said as he got into his carriage.

As Elliot waited for his own carriage, Harwicke's words about Lady Georgina rang in his head. How could she have remained unmarried all this time? Perhaps she was a shrew—she's certainly acted like one when she called him a... What was it? A Scrooge or whatever the hell it was?

But still he couldn't help but admire her bravado,

entering his office all by herself like some avenging angel, though she'd looked more like a cherub with her cheeks and nose all pink from the chilly air. He wondered what it would be like to warm those cold cheeks and those lips. She had looked so damn lovely in the sitting room, her hair and her lush curves on display in her casual morning gown, instead of bundled up in her coat and outdoor finery. He wondered how soft those wisps of blonde hair would feel in his hands, or how they would look splayed on the pillow—

He huffed, pushing down the surge of lust that had made his cock twitch and his heart race once more.

He shook his head. He could not let his thoughts go astray, and certainly not in her direction. Lady Georgina had struck a bargain with him and she was there to help him as a means to an end. He'd best remember that, no matter what certain parts of his body might think.

Chapter Four

8th December

'Do you like the opera, Lady Georgina?' Miss Warren asked.

'Not particularly,' Georgina replied, whipping her fan faster to circulate the air around her. They had arrived minutes ago in the Abernathys' private box and sat down in the two front seats. 'The air in here is stifling. Why are there so many people here tonight? I don't recall it ever being this crowded.'

Ever since she could remember, large groups of people in one place had frayed her nerves. She had got used to it in her earlier Seasons, since her come-out, but it seemed that ever since she'd withdrawn from society it had become worse.

Miss Warren placed a calming hand on her shoulder. 'Breathe, Lady Georgina. That's it…open your mouth…inhale…'

Georgina took two big gulps of air. 'Th-thank you.'

'See? It's not so bad, being out and about, is it?'

'I suppose not. At least I'm not expected to speak to anyone, like at Lady Chisholm's tea party.'

'It wasn't that terrible, was it?' Miss Warren asked.

'I nearly passed out in the necessary,' she reminded her.

Her companion rolled her eyes. 'You ran there because the Countess of Allenvale asked what you thought of the weather.'

'Exactly.' She snatched Miss Warren's fan, opened it, and fanned herself with it as well as her own.

Ah, much better.

Perhaps it was just the stale air inside that set her nerves on edge.

'You've been doing splendidly, dear,' Miss Warren said. 'I'm so proud of you.'

To be honest, Georgina was rather proud of herself too. She had managed not one, but two social events in the last three days, after all. Aside from the nearly disastrous tea, she'd called upon an old friend, Cordelia Wentworth, now Viscountess Gilliam, who'd used to live near their estate in Northamptonshire.

Actually, Georgina wasn't quite sure if the woman she'd met *had* been her friend, as she could only vaguely recall playing with her a few times when they were little. However, during their short call, the Viscountess had regaled her with stories from their childhood, to which Georgina had nodded and smiled, though she couldn't remember any of them. The call had ended with Cordelia promising to return her call, which of course had sent her into a state of dread, because etiquette deemed that after *that* call Georgina would have to pay her a call and so on, with the cycle never ending until one of them died.

Georgina seriously hoped she would be the first to go, because the thought of attending Cordelia's funeral with all those mourners around them made her want to hide in a closet.

'While I still do not approve of this bargain you have struck with Mr Smith,' Miss Warren began, 'I am glad it is compelling you to come out. And you do look lovely tonight, dear.'

Georgina scratched at the lacy edges of her cream-coloured satin opera gown. 'I'd forgotten I had this dress made three years ago. I should have asked the modiste to remove the lace. And perhaps raise the décolletage another inch or two.'

She felt rather exposed, and now she wished she'd worn a larger necklace to cover her chest, which threatened to spill over the edge. Sadly, she had filled out these last years, and the dress now hugged her more generous body. When they'd arrived at the opera house she had stared enviously at all the beautiful, slim ladies walking about, not worried about having to limit their breathing to keep their modesty.

Miss Warren cleared her throat. 'Lady Georgina...' She nodded behind them.

'What is—? Oh.'

Her brother had entered the box, but he was not alone. Mr Smith came in after Trevor, his bulky frame seemingly filling the confined space. Georgina's dress seemed to lace itself tighter, and she wished she had a third hand to fan herself with. She'd seen him twice now—thrice, really, if she counted that time she'd peeped through the window when he'd come the other night to fetch Trevor—but never in formal attire. His swarthy complexion against the white of his cravat and shirt was a startling contrast, and the near-perfect fit of his coat on his large shoulders made him appear even more imposing.

'Georgie… Miss Warren.' Trevor's voice, thankfully, interrupted her thoughts.

'Good evening, Your Grace.' Miss Warren stood up and curtseyed.

'Apologies. I couldn't escort you here. But it was probably fortunate as I found Mr Smith wandering outside and was able to guide him here.'

'My lady… Miss Warren.' Mr Smith greeted them, his jade-green eyes lingering on her.

For the past few days she'd been wondering what it was about them that she found so unique. Now she realised that it wasn't just the colour—no, there was a keen sense of alertness in them, perhaps even a hunger that she'd never seen in anyone before. He had the look of a predator, ready to consume anything he deemed prey.

Trevor indicated for him to take the seat behind her companion—which was unfortunate, because from where Georgina sat she could catch him from the corner of her eye.

'What's playing tonight?' Mr Smith asked.

'*The Marriage of Figaro*,' Miss Warren replied.

Georgina stifled a laugh as she spied Mr Smith wince. Mercifully, the lights were turned down, indicating that the performance was about to start, and everyone settled into their seats.

While she was no fan of going to the opera, Georgina actually adored opera music. It had been years since she'd come here to watch a performance. How she loved the elaborate scenes, the dramatic singers and the sound of the orchestra blaring into the audience! If there was a way for her to enjoy music without leaving her home, she would truly be in heaven.

Tonight, however, she couldn't help but be distracted by the presence of the person sitting just at the edge of her vision. The temptation to turn her head and watch Mr Smith was strong, but she managed to resist it until the lights were turned on again for the interval.

'That was lovely,' Miss Warren said. 'Mozart is truly a genius.'

'Yes, he is. But now the real work begins,' Trevor said. 'I spoke briefly with the Earl of Rutherford when I saw him in the lobby earlier this evening. He's invited us all to their box for champagne during the interval.'

Ugh. Georgina winced inwardly. This was why she didn't come to the opera. All that socialising just ruined the experience.

'Must we?'

'Lord and Lady Rutherford are hosting their annual

ball tomorrow,' Trevor reminded her. 'We've already accepted their invitation.'

She blinked. 'We have?'

'Yes. And once we have become reacquainted with Lady Rutherford, I will ask her to extend the invitation to Mr Smith, as there will be many eligible ladies there.'

'Oh. Of course.' Good Lord, was she truly about to subject herself to the torture of conversing with near strangers?

Think of the girls at St Agnes's.

This would be a small price to pay to keep them in their home.

'Shall we head over to them, then?'

Seeing as she had no choice, she followed Trevor out of their box and down the crowded corridors to a box a few doors down.

'Your Grace,' the Earl of Rutherford greeted Trevor. 'Welcome.'

'Your Grace.' Lady Rutherford curtseyed. 'How wonderful to see you. I was so delighted when my husband told me he had invited you and your party to join us.'

She nodded to a footman in the corner, standing next to a table with champagne flutes and an ice bucket. The footman quickly filled several glasses.

'And Lady Georgina, is that you? You look lovely tonight. That lace on your gown is so elegant. French, I think?'

'Lady Rutherford,' Georgina said with an acknowledging nod.

Trevor sent her a meaningful look, likely meant to remind her that she had to respond to the Countess's compliments. However, she had a difficult time finding something nice to say because she was nearly blinded by the obscene amount of diamond jewellery around Lady Rutherford's neck and wrists, not to mention the heavy tiara on her head that looked as if it might snap her neck.

She attempted to compliment her gown, which was actually the colour of what could only be approximated to a baby's vomit.

'Your gown…it's an interesting shade of green.'

'Thank you. The brocade is Italian.'

It reminded Georgina of the wallpaper in one of the guest rooms at Harwicke House.

The Countess snapped her fan open and flapped it against her chest. 'Why, it's been a while since I've seen you last. And where is your Great-Aunt Leticia?' She lowered her tone. 'She's not…passed on, has she?'

'No, but she's been ill for a few years. She recently decided to return to Hampshire and enjoy the peace and quiet.' She gestured to Miss Warren. 'Miss Warren has replaced her.'

'Ah…' The Countess closed her fan and slapped it on her palm. 'That is why we have not seen much of you these days, is it? Such a devoted niece you are… caring for her all this time.'

'Er…yes.'

Thank you, Lady Rutherford.

The Countess had now given her a plausible excuse for her absence in society.

'Lord Rutherford… Lady Rutherford,' Trevor interrupted. 'May I introduce you to my guest for this evening? Mr Elliot Smith of New York City.'

The Earl and Countess turned to acknowledge Mr Smith. 'Welcome to London,' the Earl said.

'Thank you, my lord…my lady.' He bowed his head.

'We also have a guest,' the Earl said, gesturing to the young man behind him. 'Your Grace, this is Viscount Bellamy. Bellamy, this is His Grace the Duke of Harwicke, his sister Lady Georgina Abernathy, Mr Elliot Smith and Miss Sophia Warren.'

'Lovely to meet you,' Bellamy said.

Taller than herself, the Viscount was slim and fairhaired, with light blue eyes. As his gaze passed over her, Georgina could not help but feel it linger slightly, and the corner of his mouth curled up with the tiniest smile. She guessed him to be perhaps her age, maybe a year or two younger, and like many of his peers, he was dressed and groomed fashionably.

The Earl tutted impatiently at the footman, who had just finished filling the glasses and was now scrambling to bring the tray. 'And what brings you to London, Mr Smith?' he asked.

'Business,' Mr Smith replied.

'Now, now, Smith,' Trevor said with a short laugh as he took a glass of champagne from the tray the footman offered. 'We are here to enjoy ourselves. Don't get him started on business—he won't stop. There are other more enjoyable things we can speak of. Such as your ball tomorrow, Rutherford. Georgina and I are looking forward to it.'

'We are? Er… I mean, yes, we are,' Georgina said, taking a glass from the footman. Glancing over at Mr Smith, she managed not to down the entire flute by thinking of the girls at St Agnes's once more.

'How go the preparations?' Miss Warren asked smoothly. 'You must be very busy.'

'Very,' the Countess said in a dramatic tone. 'But I'm quite proud of how it's turning out. This year, we are doing a yuletide-themed ball.'

'Yuletide-themed ball?'

Georgina and—much to her consternation—Mr Smith spoke at the same time.

'Why, yes.' The Countess clapped her hands together. 'The Duchess of Haverston threw such a ball last year. It was the most lavish and splendid event I'd ever seen, and ever since then I've wanted to do one of my own. This year, the entire ballroom at Rutherford Hall will be decorated with Christmas trees—'

'And a lot of them,' the Earl interrupted with a laugh. 'What a strange tradition, isn't it? We didn't have that when I was young… In fact it didn't become all the rage until ten years ago, when the Queen herself started putting up these trees inside the palace and decorating them. I was told it was a tradition from the Prince Regent's side of the family.'

'If it's good enough for the Queen, then it's good

enough for us. There will still be the usual merriment and dancing, of course,' the Countess added.

'Sounds splendid,' Trevor said. 'Lady Rutherford, I believe my friend from America has never been to a proper English ball. Wouldn't it be a privilege to be the first to show him how we throw a ball on this side of the pond?'

'I…' Lady Rutherford hesitated, but when her husband sent her a warning look, she smiled and said, 'Of course, we would love to have you, Mr Smith. If you are not too occupied with business.'

It was evident that Lady Rutherford was hoping he would decline, but Mr Smith raised his flute to her and said, 'Thank you, my lady, I accept.'

'And I will see you all there,' said Bellamy, raising his near-empty champagne glass. 'And perhaps you can save space on your dance card for me, Lady Georgina.'

She was tempted to tell him that, sadly, there would be no competition for the very empty spaces on her card, but instead said, 'Of course. Er…if you'll excuse me? I must refresh myself.'

Handing her half-empty flute to the footman, she exited the box and made her way to the necessary, holding her breath as she waded through the throng of people. If it wasn't for her urgent need, she would just leave, but she braved the crush.

After finishing her business, she quickly left—but had forgotten where the Rutherford box was located. Had she turned left or right when she'd left it?

Drat.

The crowds in the corridor seemed to grow, enclosing her, making her vision swim.

Sometimes the strain of being surrounded by too many people, or barraged by the presence of others, gave her these spells. It made it hard to breathe, as if a heavy weight was pressed on her, and all her energy would drain away.

Breathe, Georgina.

Somehow, she managed to remember the way back to their own box, and she reached the door just before her nerves completely unravelled. Hurrying inside, she let out a loud, cleansing sigh.

'I thought you'd head back to the Rutherford box.'

Her heart leapt into her throat at the sound of the familiar voice. 'I thought you'd still be there, Mr Smith.'

'The conversation turned boring,' he said. 'I— Are you all right?'

'Yes, I'm perfectly fine, Mr Smith.'

'You look pale, and you're sweating like you've run a race.'

'Isn't it impolite to remark on a woman's appearance?'

'Not if she looks ready to fall down.'

Clicking his tongue, he strode over to her, placing a hand on her gloved elbow to guide her to her seat. To her surprise, he planted himself on the seat next to hers, instead of retreating to his own.

'Here.' He offered her his handkerchief.

'Th-thank you.' She patted it on her brow. 'The crowds…'

'Yes, it seems all of the Ton is here tonight,' he remarked. 'But you look like you've gone through a harrowing experience. Would you like me to fetch you some water?'

'Do not bother yourself,' she said. 'I am fine.'

'Did anything happen?'

'No, but…' How was she to explain to him? 'There's just not enough air in places like this. It's suffocating. They should have built more windows.'

'True…but then again I don't think that would be very good for the acoustics. But still, you seem—'

'I'm looking forward to tomorrow's ball,' she interrupted, hoping to steer him away from further questions about her current state. 'I don't think I've ever attended a Christmas-themed event. I love Christmas.'

He stared at her as if a second head had grown out from her shoulders. 'Why?'

'Why not? I love how everything looks festive, and it feels as if people are nicer to each other. Giving gifts, sharing meals, contributing to charity and whatnot.'

He harrumphed. 'I truly do not see what is so special about it. It used to be just another day in the calendar and now there are celebrations and expectations around it. And think of all these decorations and baubles that must be tossed into the rubbish after the season is done—it seems incredibly wasteful to me.'

That, she couldn't argue with, and guilt crept into

her as she thought of what she'd spent on decorations for Harwicke House and what the staff did with them every year once Christmas was done.

'But what about sharing with the less fortunate? And giving to charity?'

'I happen to contribute to several charities all year round.'

His tone did not sound arrogant, or boastful, just matter-of-fact.

'And not just once a year when "the spirit of the season" expects it.'

'Ah, so it is not giving you are against.' She smiled wryly at him. 'And I thought you were as miserly as Scrooge.'

His lips pressed together. 'Who exactly is this Scrooge character you keep comparing me to?'

'He's from a book. *A Christmas Carol* by Charles Dickens. The lead character is Ebenezer Scrooge.'

'Ah, ES.'

Embarrassment warmed her cheeks at this reminder of their first encounter at his office. 'You should read it sometime, Mr Smith,' she told him. 'It might be enlightening.'

He leaned closer. 'Do you think that, since we will likely be in each other's company more in the next few days, that perhaps you may call me Elliot?'

That bold question so took her by surprise that she did not respond right away. Then: 'I beg your pardon?'

'I would still call you Lady Georgina, of course.

But I give you permission to use my first name. Is that not done here?'

'I d-do not think so.' At that moment she couldn't recall what was deemed appropriate as she was much too distracted by the luminous jade-green eyes and the handsome face that was now mere inches from hers.

'You don't? Well, in any case, do feel free to use it at any time.'

'I—'

He pulled back before she could say anything further, then stood up—which was fortunate because Trevor and Miss Warren entered the box at that very moment.

'Georgie, there you are,' Trevor said. 'You had me worried. We were waiting for you in the Rutherfords' box.'

'I got lost,' she said. 'So I just made my way back here.'

'And so did Mr Smith,' Miss Warren said. 'How—' The lights began to dim, interrupting her. Sending Georgina a knowing look, she sat down beside her.

As the orchestra began to play Georgina allowed herself to sneak one very quick look at Mr Smith.

Elliot, she corrected herself. The name had sounded strange to her own ears, but she supposed it didn't hurt to refer to him by his first name in her mind. After all, he did spend an inordinate amount of time there.

Not that she could help that. After all, she needed to think about him—or rather, think about finding him a bride to save her orphanage. And, despite what he'd said about giving to charity, she reminded herself that he would still evict the children if she did not succeed.

And he hated Christmas.

That still made him a Scrooge, in her opinion.

9th December,
Lady Rutherford's ball

'My, my, it seems Lady Rutherford has truly been imbued with the Christmas spirit,' Miss Warren remarked as they entered the ballroom at Rutherford Hall. 'I wonder if there are any trees left in the forests?'

Georgina laughed. 'You're jesting, of course. I only count thirteen—no, fourteen Christmas trees in here.'

'You must be in heaven,' the companion remarked.

'Oh, yes.'

The Rutherford ballroom showcased a true Christmas scene. Aside from the scattered trees, fir garlands had been strung across the ceiling and sparkly crystal ornaments that mimicked icicles hung from them. The magnificent chandelier was decorated with baubles and trinkets, while swathes of white fabric were strewn across the floor to mimic snow. Meanwhile, roaming footmen offered guests Christmas treats—sweetmeats, merengues, candies, mini-plum puddings and chocolate creams.

Georgina had to stop herself from taking more than one of each. Thankfully, her maid had found her something to wear that didn't need to be let out. The green satin gown wasn't new, but it was good enough for tonight. And as she'd been coming downstairs earlier tonight, one of the holly berry twigs had fallen from its perch on the balustrade. Instead of replacing it, she'd instead stuck it in her hair, to add a more festive look to her outfit.

'Is Mr Smith here?' Miss Warren enquired.

'I don't know.'

Georgina craned her neck, trying to find him, but didn't see him. She wasn't sure if he would be coming with her brother, though Trevor had said that he would travel in his own carriage, as he was going to Brooks' for dinner first.

'He will probably hate this ballroom,' she said with a chuckle. She could already imagine him scowling at all the 'waste' and 'frippery'.

'And why is that?'

'Because he hates Christmas, apparently. Thinks it's much too wasteful and unnecessary.'

'And how do you happen to know that?'

Georgina avoided her companion's suspicious gaze. 'Perhaps it's time I begin fulfilling my end of the bargain with him by finding him a potential wife. I will start tonight.'

'How exactly do you plan to do that?'

'I may be out of practice, but my social graces have not completely left me.' After all, she'd had six Seasons under the watchful eye of her Great-Aunt Leticia, who had taught her all the proper manners and conversation topics when meeting acquaintances. 'And so—' she swallowed audibly '—I will mingle and socialise.'

'I see…'

'And as I go I will make a list of potential brides.' She opened her reticule and retrieved a small card. 'I will write them down here, then present them to him.'

Miss Warren peered at the card in her hand. 'Is that your dance card?'

'Yes. I won't be using it for dancing anyway.' Straightening her shoulders, Georgina inhaled a large gust of air. 'Come, Miss Warren, we must begin at once.'

If only so she could finish sooner.

'You look as if you're about to go into battle,' her companion remarked. 'It's just conversation.'

Georgina sighed. 'Exactly…' But she would do it, if only to save the orphanage.

And so she roamed the ballroom, reacquainting herself with the women of the Ton, though she approached her subjects thoughtfully. She avoided most of the women her age, because after all, they would be of no use to her as they were already married and only had children who were a few years old. She sought out the older matrons whom she spied protectively shielding young women of marriageable age like mother hens. Thankfully, many of them remembered her, though a few raised their eyebrows at her unmarried state.

'Good heavens, I am exhausted,' Georgina declared eventually.

They had been speaking with Lady Mary Hammersmith about the latest trends in hats when Georgina had decided she'd had enough and excused herself.

'It's only been an hour,' Miss Warren pointed out.

'Feels like it's been days…' Her body felt sapped of all strength. 'But our efforts weren't for naught. I have collected a few names of possible brides.' She waved the card triumphantly at Miss Warren. 'And I—'

'Lady Georgina, here you are.'

'Lord Bellamy,' she greeted as the Viscount approached them. 'What a surprise.'

'I told you I would be here.' His gaze went to the card in her hand. 'Ah—I see your dance card is filled.'

'What—? Oh.' She quickly hid it behind her. 'N-Not at all. I mean, I'm all finished.'

Bellamy's face lit up. 'Ah, then perhaps I might have the next dance?'

Georgina glanced at Miss Warren helplessly. 'Er…'

'I'm afraid she's already promised me this next one,' came a voice from behind.

She didn't need to turn around, as she immediately recognised the low drawl, but she did anyway. Mr Smith—*Elliot*, she reminded herself—once again looked impressive in formal wear, and that curious flutter in her chest returned.

'Ah, Mr Smith,' Lord Bellamy said. 'How are you enjoying your first English ball? Is it just as you imagined?'

Elliot glanced around the room. 'Yes…exactly as I imagined.'

Georgina had to bite the inside of her cheek to stop herself from giggling as he looked less than enthused.

'As I mentioned, I would like to claim my dance now, Lady Georgina?'

'I will wait for the next one, then,' Lord Bellamy said. 'I shall be ready whenever you are, my lady.'

Elliot offered his arm, which she took, and led her to the dance floor, where the waltz was announced. Georgina thanked the heavens as it was one of the dances she remembered, and would require very little from her except to follow her partner's lead.

'*Is* it exactly as you imagined?' she asked in a teasing tone as she placed her hand on his shoulder.

For a moment she could have sworn the muscles under her palm jumped, but the movement had been so fleeting she wasn't sure if she'd imagined it.

'Why, yes. It's just as extravagant and excessive as I pictured it. Maybe even more.'

She chuckled. 'Why am I not surprised to hear you say that?'

'What did Bellamy want?' His hand landed on her waist.

'He—' The unfamiliar grip of his fingers on hers made all the air in her lungs disappear. It had been a long time since her last waltz—were partners really supposed to stand this close? 'Just a dance—as he said. Oh, that reminds me… I have made a list of potential wives for you.'

'You have?' The music began and he led them around the dance floor. 'Who are they?'

'Well…' The card was tucked between her fingers on his shoulder, so she shifted her hand to read it. 'To preface: you gave me no other requirement for your bride except that she has to be the daughter of a peer.'

'Correct.'

'All right, then. There are eight women on my list…'

'I'll take any one of them—whoever you think wants to marry as soon as possible.'

'I b-beg your pardon?' She would have stumbled had he not pulled her closer to him. 'I haven't even asked on your behalf—they do not even know you are interested. You can't just pick a name from a list and be married on the morrow.' She clicked her tongue at him impatiently. 'That's not how things work, Elliot.'

Those muscles jumped again at her use of his name, and the strangest look passed over his face, though it was gone in a moment and that serious mask slipped back on.

'Then tell me, how *does* it work?'

'First you will be introduced to them—which I can do tonight. Then you must meet them once more, and then you can call on them. After that, you may ask permission from her parents to court her.'

'That seems a rather drawn-out process.'

'If you want a quality bride, then you must go through it.' She blew out a breath.

He let out a resigned sigh. 'All right. Which of the eight women do you think would be the most amenable to marrying me? Your top three choices.'

She squinted at the card. 'My first choice would be

Lady Amanda Garret, daughter of the Earl of Hastings. This is her third Season, and I hear her father is eager to curtail her spending on the new gowns and jewellery she and her mother buy each year. Lady Hastings has lamented that her husband is complaining of the last bill from their modiste.'

'Excellent. Who else?'

'Lady Lavinia Wright, the Marquess of Arundel's daughter,' she said. 'Her sister, Lady Genevieve, is said to be the most beautiful debutante of this year, so she's overshadowed poor Lady Lavinia.'

Which was a crime, in her opinion, as she thought Lady Lavinia was lovely.

'The Duke of Waldemere wants to court Genevieve, but her father refuses to allow the younger sister to marry before the older. Thus, the mother wants Lady Lavinia married off.'

'Acceptable. And the third?'

'The Honourable Miss Penelope Philipps. Her father is a viscount, the only son of the Earl of Halifax. Supposedly, he is awaiting the Earl's death, so he can take over the estate and open up the coffers. He's always been put on a very limited allowance.'

'Sounds like Miss Penelope would be the best candidate.' He paused. 'But your frown tells me you do not approve.'

'I just find it distasteful…waiting for a parent to die,' she said. Though distasteful was perhaps too mild a word.

'Because you lost your own parents at a young age and so suddenly?'

Her head snapped up to meet his jade-green gaze. 'How did you know that?'

'I have my ways. Now, perhaps it's time for you to make those introductions.'

'What—? Oh!' She hadn't noticed that the dance had ended. 'Of course.'

They bowed to each other, and he led her away from the dance floor. Lady Amanda had been dancing with Lord Dorset, so Georgina steered Mr Smith towards her mother, Lady Hastings, and they reached the Countess at the same time.

'Lady Hastings,' she greeted the Countess. 'And Lady Amanda—did you enjoy the dance?'

'Oh, yes. Lord Dorset is an excellent dancer.' She nodded to the older man, whose arm she clung to.

'We were also dancing—oh, allow me to introduce you to my brother the Duke's very good friend from America.' She quickly introduced Elliot.

'An American,' Lady Hastings said, the sneer in her tone evident. 'How many more of you are coming over to our shores?'

Georgina winced, but before she could say anything Elliot spoke. 'With the advancements in steamship mechanics, a great many more, I imagine. Good evening to you, ladies…my lord.'

Placing a hand on her elbow, he guided her away from the trio.

'Wait…wait!' She stopped, forcing him to halt. 'We

weren't finished. You did not even get a chance to speak with Amanda.'

'Oh, I think we were very much finished,' he said. 'From the look of disdain on Lady Hastings' face, it's clear she will never accept me for a son-in-law, and Lady Amanda seems to be already enamoured of Lord Dorset, and he of her.'

She hadn't even noticed that.

'Who's next? Where is Lady Lavinia?'

'I last saw her there, by the lemonade table. The one in the blue dress. The two women beside her are her mother and her sister.'

Crossing the crowded room, they made their way to the Marchioness and her two daughters. After a pretence of fetching some lemonade, she quickly introduced Elliot to them.

'How is New York these days?' Lady Arundel enquired. 'I travelled there a few years ago with one of my very good friends—Jane, the Countess of Landsdowne. She grew up in New York, and moved here when she married the Earl. I found New York to be delightfully exciting.'

'New York is still exciting—perhaps even more so, my lady,' Elliot answered smoothly. 'Lady Lavinia, have you ever been?'

'No,' she said. 'I'm afraid not. I never go anywhere,' she added with a sigh.

'She was still but a child then, and I had to leave her here,' Lady Arundel said.

'But perhaps one day I might,' Lady Lavinia added. 'I mean, perhaps my mother will take me.'

'Mayhap, if the Countess visits her childhood home again,' the Marchioness said.

'I think you will enjoy it.' Elliot flashed her a charming smile—something Georgina had never seen before—which made the young lady blush.

'I think I might,' she replied.

A short stab of unknown emotion pierced Georgina's chest. Ignoring it, she turned to Lady Genevieve. 'How about you, Lady Genevieve? Would you like to visit America?'

Her brows snapped together. 'I do not think so. I am rather fond of England. If I ever do travel, it will perhaps be for my honeymoon, and I should like to go to Paris or the north of Italy.'

As Elliot and the ladies continued their conversation, Georgina felt as if she were fading into the background. Which was, she told herself, exactly what she wanted, so she didn't have to make further conversation. But the problem was that she couldn't leave either. No, she was trapped there, watching as Elliot and Lady Lavinia chatted amiably. Frankly, she was surprised that he could be so charming when he wanted to. And that unknown emotion seemed to bury itself deeper as she continued to watch them.

'I nearly forgot.' Lady Arundel slapped her fan on her palm. 'We will be attending the Earl and Countess of Landsdowne's musicale tomorrow, at their home. I'm sure I could persuade Jane to extend you an invitation, seeing as you're her countryman.' She turned to Georgina. 'Of course you and your brother the Duke have probably already received an invitation. So, what do you think, Mr Smith?'

'If you think it won't be an imposition…'

'Not at all. It is already a large gathering, and there is always room for more.'

'I should like to come, then.' Elliot glanced at Lady Lavinia. 'And you will be there as well, my lady?'

'I never miss it,' she replied with an expectant smile. 'And now there's more reason for me to attend.'

The stab in Georgina's chest turned into a flickering hot sensation.

'Oh, dear, I've been away from my chaperone for far too long,' she exclaimed. 'She must be worried. If you'll excuse me, I must go and find her.'

The other ladies nodded, and she turned on her heel. Despite being faced with the crowd of people, she managed to push herself through the throng.

Georgina rubbed her fist on her chest. Good Lord, what was happening? Her heart raced, her breath came in coarse pants, and the burning sensation in her chest would not go away. And when she thought of Elliot's smile directed at Lady Lavinia it worsened. It was like one of her 'spells', but it manifested a physical pain within.

'Lady Georgina!'

Surprise at hearing Elliot's voice—as if she'd conjured him up just by merely thinking of him—made her halt.

He quickly caught up to her and obstructed her path.

'What's the matter?' He searched her face. 'Why did you leave all of a sudden?'

'I… I told you… Miss Warren is probably looking for me.'

'You're acting strange again,' he said. 'Though this time your face is red instead of pale. Are you ill?'

'No!' Heavens, she wished she could escape this crowd. And him. 'It's so stuffy in here…with all the people around.'

'I see.' Gently, he took her by the arm and led her away. 'Come.'

'Where are you taking me?'

'To your brother.' He nodded ahead, to where Trevor and Miss Warren stood, just off to the side of the dance floor. 'Your Grace,' he said when they reached them. 'I think your sister is ill.'

'I'm fine,' she insisted, now annoyed with Elliot. 'Mr Smith is exaggerating.'

Trevor frowned. 'Perhaps all this pine is making her sick.'

'Never,' she insisted. 'I am not sick.'

'I will have the carriage brought round,' Trevor said, concern on his face. 'And you can go home.'

Home?

Oh, the thought of leaving this place and going back to her own rooms, where she could be alone, made her nearly weep with relief. She pressed a hand over her forehead.

'Perhaps I am feeling faint…'

'I should retire for the evening as well,' Elliot said.

'Of course. Miss Warren, would you mind watching over Georgina while Mr Smith and I bid goodbye to our hosts?'

Miss Warren hooked her arm through Georgina's. 'I shall take care of her, Your Grace.'

As Trevor and Elliot hurried off in search of the Earl and Countess, Miss Warren led her out of the ballroom and towards the front door. Georgina took a quick glance at Elliot's retreating back as he quickly disappeared into the crowd.

While she was thankful that she was finally going home, she couldn't help but feel disappointed that her time with him had been cut short. That dance between them had actually been pleasant. More than pleasant. She'd never felt so at ease in a man's arms.

'Hurry along, Lady Georgina,' Miss Warren urged as their carriage arrived.

Putting Elliot out of her mind, she climbed into the coach and closed her eyes, feeling the silence and darkness like a soothing blanket around her.

Chapter Five

10th December

It was just Elliot's luck that, as well as Lady Lavinia, the Honourable Miss Penelope Philipps was also in attendance at the Landsdownes' musicale the very next day. He was introduced to her by their hostess Jane, the Countess of Landsdowne, who had taken an immediate liking to Elliot because she too was a New Yorker. Her father had founded one of the largest banks in New York City and, much like him, she'd been shut out of society there because of her humble beginnings.

'Are you finding London to your liking, Mr Smith?' Miss Philipps asked as she accepted the lemonade offered to her by a passing footman.

'Indeed, I find myself settling in quite nicely,' Elliot replied, waving the footman away. 'Have you lived here all your life?'

'I have,' she said. 'But while I mostly spent my childhood here, summers were spent at Colworth

Hill—that's my grandfather the Earl's seat in Devonshire—where we would...'

Elliot's mind drifted off as he pretended to listen to Miss Philipps wax lyrical about idyllic summer days at her grandfather's estate. All he could think about was Lady Georgina and the fact that he hadn't yet seen her tonight. Harwicke had said last night that both he and his sister would be in attendance, but perhaps she had been taken ill.

Guilt turned his stomach to stone. Had he been asking too much of her these past days? First it was the opera, then last night's ball... She was likely exhausted from attending two evening events in a row. The fact that he did not know her current condition was driving him to distraction.

But there was nothing out of the ordinary about his concern for her. After all, they had a bargain, and if she were unwell then she would not be able to fulfil her end. He needed her for the doors that she would open for him. Of course, he did not require her tonight, as he had already met Miss Philipps on his own.

Where the devil was she?

Harwicke was nowhere to be found either, so perhaps they'd had some trouble on the way here. It wasn't unusual for carriages to break down... Or perhaps they'd had to attend to a family matter.

'Mr Smith?' Miss Philipps' voice broke into his thoughts.

'Yes?'

'I was asking if you've been anywhere outside London.'

'No, I haven't.'

'You should take a trip to the countryside, then.' She batted her eyes at him. 'There's nothing like it… especially in the spring.'

'I will have to take your word for it. Perhaps—'

He stopped short as he saw a flash of blonde hair at the edge of his vision. Sure enough, it was Lady Georgina. And, once again, he found himself unable to tear his gaze from her.

That gown she'd worn at the opera had been indecently snug, pushing her full breasts up for anyone's perusal. He had shifted in his seat several times during the performance lest anyone—Harwicke especially—catch him embarrassing himself, like a young man seeing a woman for the first time. Last night's gown had been much more modest. But holding her close and feeling her hands on him had been torture of the sweetest kind for that entire three-and-a-half-minute dance.

Tonight was no different as she was once again a vision of loveliness in a violet gown that showed off her shoulders and creamy skin, as well as a modest amount of décolletage. Her blonde hair was swept up in a simple hairstyle, away from her face and pink cheeks, the chandelier above lighting the gold strands in them like a halo. She didn't seem ill, thank goodness, though her face was full of apprehension as she quickly perused the room.

'Miss Philipps,' he began, 'if you would excuse me, I think I see my friend, the Duke of Harwicke. I must give him my thanks, for if it wasn't for his intervention I would not have received an invitation to this soiree.'

'Of course, Mr Smith. The programme should begin soon. Perhaps I could save a seat for you?'

'Yes, I would very much like that.'

Nodding at her, he turned and walked in the direction of Lady Georgina, who was, as usual, accompanied by her companion, though Harwicke was nowhere in sight.

'Lady Georgina… Miss Warren,' he greeted them.

Her head snapped up to meet him, her copper-brown eyes widening. 'Mr Smith,' she replied. 'How lovely to see you here. I'm glad the Countess extended an invitation to you tonight. Trevor sends his apologies. He's taken to his bed with an illness.'

'Nothing too serious, I hope?'

She shook her head. 'Just a run-of-the-mill cold. His constitution has never agreed with the cold weather.'

'And you? I hope you are all right after last night?'

'Yes, I'm fine.' She let out what sounded like a forced laugh. 'Nothing a good night's sleep couldn't cure. Unlike my brother, I adore the winter weather.'

'Excellent. When I didn't see you here, I was beginning to think you were reneging on our deal.'

'Never!' Her tone was light-hearted. 'In fact, I have it on good authority that not only is Lady Lavinia here tonight, but Miss Penelope Philipps as well. I could introduce you to her, if you like.'

'There is no need as our hostess has already made the introductions.'

'Is that so?'

'Yes.'

'And how do you find her?'

'She is as you described her.'

Eager, that was for sure. He had not missed Miss Penelope Philipps' interest in him either, from the way her eyes roamed all over him—including his three-carat diamond tie pin and matching cufflinks.

'Excellent, then. There are many more unmarried young ladies here, and I can enquire about them. Or perhaps I could invite Miss Philipps and Lady Lavinia, plus a few more ladies and some gentlemen, for tea at Harwicke House tomorrow? After you meet them for a second time you may call upon them at home.'

'Do you know any gentlemen who would come?' he asked. 'Since your brother is currently indisposed?'

'Hmm...' She tapped her finger on her chin. 'You're right... Oh, wait! I know at least one gentleman I could invite. Lord Bellamy.'

That name left a sour taste in his mouth. He had not missed the young fop eyeing Lady Georgina's *assets* that night at the opera. His eyes had lingered on her chest much too long, and Elliot had had to stop himself from pulling them out from their sockets. When he'd seen him approach her last night, during the ball, he'd sprung into action to obstruct him, lest he molest her with his eyes again. He would be damned if he would let that lech near her again any time soon.

'What do you think, Mr Smith? Shall I approach them tonight?'

'Perhaps it would be a more efficient use of your time to find at least two more candidates before you invite anyone to your home.'

'True. I will have to find more candidates—'

'Excuse me…forgive me for the intrusion…but are you Mr Elliot Smith?' An older man in a black and white uniform asked the question as he approached them.

'Yes, I am. Mr…?'

'Bourne, sir. The butler.'

'And what can I do for you, Bourne?'

'Your footman, John, is waiting outside and wishes to speak to you. He claims it's urgent.'

'John?'

For a moment, a sense of foreboding washed over Elliot, as he thought of the last time John had come to him for an urgent matter. But surely it couldn't be bad news from the household again, because the footman had accompanied his carriage here and now waited with it outside. Perhaps there was a problem with the carriage or his coachman. 'Bourne, I believe the programme is about to start. Do you think you could ask John to come in and explain?'

'Of course, Mr Smith. Why don't you wait in the hall and I shall bring him in? All the guests we expected have arrived, so I shall be closing the doors shortly.'

'Thank you, Bourne.'

'What do you think is the matter?' Lady Georgina asked.

He shrugged. 'Something with the carriage, I presume.'

But then again how urgent could it be that John would interrupt his evening? He could always take a hansom cab if the carriage had broken down.

'Lady Georgina, Miss Warren, why don't you take your seats and I shall deal with this?'

'Let us stay here and wait for you,' she said.

'I—'

She placed a hand on his arm. 'Please. Then we can all sit together, even if it's at the back.'

It was difficult to say no to those sweet brown eyes. 'If you wish.'

They followed Bourne out to the hall, where he left them to go outside. When Bourne returned, however, he was alone.

'Mr Smith, he insists that you come outside to see to your carriage.'

'My carriage?'

Why the devil would he need to see the carriage? If it was broken, it wasn't as if he could fix it.

Irritated, he stormed out through the door. 'John, what is the matter?'

The footman paled as soon as he saw Elliot. 'Mr Smith, sir, we have…er…a delicate situation.'

'What is it? And why are you whispering?'

John swallowed, making his Adam's apple bob up and down. 'Please, Mr Smith. You must see for yourself.' He nodded to his carriage. 'I-In there, sir.'

He grabbed the handle and yanked the door open—and a bundle of black fabric tumbled into his arms.

'Whee!'

Though the voice coming from the bundle was muffled, he immediately recognised it.

'Anne-Marie!' he whispered as he righted the bundle and pulled off the dark cloak covering his sister's face. 'What in the name of all things holy are you doing here?' His nose picked up a suspiciously familiar scent, so he leaned closer and sniffed. 'Have you been drinking?'

Anne-Marie smiled dreamily up at him. She opened her mouth to speak, but only a belch came out. 'Whoops! 'Scuse me!'

'How the—? What the—? Why—?' The fury building in his chest tied his tongue in knots. 'John—explain.'

'She—she says she followed us here, Mr Smith,' the footman began. 'I saw her walking in the street and put her up inside the carriage.'

'Why didn't you take her home?'

Anne-Marie let out the most godawful wail. Elliot was pretty sure it would leave his ears ringing for days. He covered her mouth in an attempt to muffle her.

'That's why, sir,' John said. 'She wouldn't stop

screaming when we tried to drive away. The coach-man—'

'Elliot, let go of her. The poor thing can't breathe.'

He froze—not just because of the feminine voice that had spoken his name, but because of who had said it. He immediately withdrew his hand. Anne-Marie, thankfully, stopped screaming.

'What are you doing here?' In his haste, he had for-gotten about Lady Georgina, but here she was, along with her companion, standing right behind him. Had she been there the entire time?

'You left us in the hall.' She sounded rather miffed, or perhaps like a mother scolding a child. 'What is happening here? Are you all right, dear girl?'

Anne-Marie, for the first time in her life, looked stunned as she stared at Lady Georgina, her mouth hanging open.

'She's fine…just a little…er…sick.'

'Smells as if she's drunk,' Miss Warren said, her tone laced with acidity. 'Do you often keep intoxicated young girls in your carriage, Mr Smith?'

'She's my sister,' he snapped at the companion.

'Half-sister,' Anne-Marie slurred. 'My father was also his father, but my mother was a dock—'

'Enough, Anne-Marie!'

Shame pooled in his gut. This was not how he'd wanted Lady Georgina to meet his sister. Damn it, he hadn't wanted them to meet *at all*. Surely now Lady Georgina would be utterly scandalised and would never want to associate with him again, even if it meant losing the orphanage.

'Are you feeling ill, dear girl?' Lady Georgina said as she pushed past him and placed a hand on Anne-Marie's forehead. 'You're pale and chilled.'

'I don't feel so good...' she murmured. 'The floor won't stop spinning.'

When she swayed to one side, Lady Georgina caught her and propped her against her shoulder.

'There, there...' She patted Anne-Marie on the shoulder. 'What happened?'

'I got into Cook's special cabinet and saw the bottle...drank most of it...felt good.'

'And then what?'

'I hate it here,' she sniffed. 'I wanted to tell him how much.' She sent Elliot a seething look. 'I saw the invitation on his desk and so I walked here.' She moaned as her eyes rolled. 'I don't think that was a good plan.'

'No, I'm afraid not, dear girl. You're shivering, and now you're turning an alarming shade of green. Why don't we take you back home? Wouldn't it be nice to have a hot cup of tea and a thick, soft blanket?'

'Uh-huh...'

Lady Georgina nodded at the carriage. 'Mr Smith—the door, if you please.'

Unsure what else to do, Elliot opened the carriage door for them.

'There you go.' She assisted Anne-Marie up the step. 'Now—'

'No!' Anne-Marie moaned when Lady Georgina

released her. She grabbed her arm. 'Don't leave me, please!'

'You must go home,' she said. 'And I must stay here.'

'Don't leave me alone,' she cried. 'In that big old house. With no one but my silly little sister.'

'Anne-Marie,' Elliot began, 'Lady Georgina cannot go home with us.'

'Please! Please come home with me.'

'I...' Lady Georgina looked at him helplessly, and then to Miss Warren. 'Perhaps—'

'Do not even think about it,' Miss Warren warned, her voice steely. 'You cannot go with an unmarried man to his home in the middle of the night!'

'It's not the middle of the night,' she said. 'It's barely eight o'clock.'

'And what if someone sees you? Or notices that both of you are missing?'

'Everyone is seated inside at the musicale,' she reasoned. 'No one will see us. And no one knows Mr Smith so they will not note his absence. Lady Landsdowne didn't even see us arrive—she will just assume we are ill, like Trevor. We will ride in the carriage, deliver the girl to her home, and be back here in no time. Or we could just go home. Please, Miss Warren, if you come along no one will think anything of it.'

Miss Warren pursed her lips, as if contemplating her request. 'Do not make me regret this, Lady Georgina.'

'I won't. Now, Mr Smith, does that sound like a good plan? May we ride with you?'

Elliot could only stare at her, a million thoughts in his head. Once again Lady Georgina had robbed him of his ability to think straight. But he had to consider Anne-Marie's reputation. If anyone were to find her out here, three sheets to the wind, she would be ruined even before she came out.

'Yes, please. Go right ahead.'

They all settled in the carriage, Elliot on one side and the ladies across from him, Anne-Marie in between them, clinging to Lady Georgina like a vine on a trellis. The absurdity of this whole situation slowly dawned on him, and he couldn't blame the companion for the glares she shot him every chance she could. Lady Georgina was risking a lot, being here. If anyone saw them she would take the brunt of any scandal.

But should all go well, and no one would ever know she was with him. Once they arrived at his home he would take Anne-Marie inside and then have his coachman deliver them back to Harwicke House.

His plan, however, was thwarted by Anne-Marie, who began to wail drunkenly once more as soon as Elliot tried to take her into the house when they arrived.

'I want Lady Georgina to take me in and tuck me under some soft blankets with tea,' she said, and pouted.

'For God's sake, Anne-Marie.' He raked his fingers through his hair. 'She's a lady, not a maid. She can't undress you and put you to bed.'

'You promised!' Anne-Marie cried to Lady Georgina. 'You promised tea…and blankets.' She hiccupped.

'I… I suppose…' Lady Georgina's voice drifted off as she stroked Anne-Marie's hair. 'A few minutes…'

Miss Warren sent Elliot a murderous look. 'Do not even think it! The Duke will sack me if he finds out.'

'Well, maybe he doesn't have to find out?' Lady Georgina said. 'Five minutes. We will be in and out. Won't we, Anne-Marie?'

'Five minutes…' she echoed. 'Please, Miss Warren? I want you to come too. You're so nice and pretty… I wish I had a friend like you.'

Miss Warren let out a strangled sound. 'I— Fine. Five minutes.'

They quickly bundled up Anne-Marie and hurried into the house, rushing past a startled Fletcher.

'Do not let anyone upstairs,' Elliot barked.

The butler could only nod.

Once the three of them had led Anne-Marie up the stairs, Elliot thought his troubles were over. However, the sound of small feet running across the carpeted floor made him groan inwardly.

'Elliot! What—? Anne-Marie!' Lily stood barefoot at the top of the stairs, red curly hair all wild, green eyes wide as she watched them. 'Who are you?'

'I'm…er…a friend,' Lady Georgina said as she prised Anne-Marie's hands from the banister. 'We're friends. Ah… Come now, dear girl, just allow me to help you. That's it…one step at a time.'

'I like your gown,' Lily called.

'Lily, go back to bed,' Elliot ordered.

Lily, however, did not budge. 'Are you a lady? Elliot keeps talking about bringing a lady home to live with us.'

The most delicate blush appeared on Lady Georgina's cheeks. 'I'm afraid not, poppet.'

Lily's mouth pursed. 'What's a poppet?'

By this time they had reached the top of the stairs, so with her free hand Lady Georgina brushed back a lock of wild red hair from Lily's face and tucked it behind her ear. 'Why, you are a poppet.'

'I'm not a poppet. I'm a Lily,' she said. 'But... I suppose you could call me poppet.'

Elliot sighed. 'Go to bed, please, Lily.'

'But why?'

'Because it's bedtime and I said so—that's why.'

'You're being mean.' Lily crossed her arms over her chest. 'Why can't I come with you?'

'We're just putting your sister to bed,' Lady Georgina said. 'We aren't going anywhere fun.'

'We never do anyway,' Lily retorted. 'Elliot, you said we could go skating on the Serpentine.'

'It's not cold enough yet, poppet,' Lady Georgina said. 'Winter has only just begun. And the ice isn't quite hard enough to go skating on.'

'Oh. Then why didn't you say so, Elliot?'

He could not stop himself from grinning at the exasperated expression on Lily's face. 'I'm sorry, Lily.'

'*Ahem...*' Miss Warren cocked her head to one side.

Lady Georgina clicked her tongue. 'Er… Lily, is it? Why don't you help us get Anne-Marie ready for bed.'

'What happened to her, anyway?' She sniffed. 'And why does she smell odd?'

'Your brother will explain later.' She offered her hand to the little girl. 'Well? Are you coming?'

'Yes!' she replied, taking Lady Georgina's hand.

Elliot led them to Anne-Marie's door. 'This is her room.'

Lily opened the door and let Lady Georgina and Anne-Marie inside. When he attempted to enter, Miss Warren blocked him.

'I think we can take it from here.'

'But—'

'Please.' She raised a palm. 'I'm already risking a lot, allowing Lady Georgina to be here. Your sister is safe with us. Just allow us to help her into bed so that we may leave as soon as possible.'

'All right…' He relented, then stepped back.

As soon as the door closed he leaned against the wall and closed his eyes. What a mess this whole situation was. And what kind of brother was he? Allowing Anne-Marie not only to become intoxicated but to escape the house and wander the streets of London?

A terrible one.

He scrubbed his hand down his face. What was he to do? He'd come here so that he could do what was best for the girls, but no matter how hard he tried he couldn't do anything right.

I just want what's best for them.

'Mr Smith?' Miss Warren called.

His eyes opened and he stood up straight. 'Miss Warren? Is she all right?'

'We have changed her into her nightrail and put her to bed. She has brought up her dinner, but aside from that your sister is fine. Nothing that some water, rest and food won't cure.'

And didn't he know it? He'd often come home to see his father in a drunken state. 'I assure you, Miss Warren, this is not a common occurrence in the house. I'm going to have everyone responsible for this sacked.'

She raised a dark brow. 'If you are seeking the source of this misbehaviour, perhaps you should look a little closer.'

'I beg your pardon? Are you implying—?'

Lady Georgina's sudden appearance in the doorway made him close his mouth.

'She's asleep,' she whispered as she quietly closed the door behind her. 'They both are. Lily's curled up beside her.'

'Thank you…both of you,' he said.

'You are very welcome,' Lady Georgina said. 'I'm sorry your evening was spoiled and you were unable to spend more time with Lady Lavinia and Miss Philipps.'

'Who?' He shook his head. 'Oh, yes. But your evening was spoiled as well, thanks to my sister's impetuousness. I should be the one to apologise.'

'I didn't know you had sisters,' she said quietly. 'I—'

'I believe it is time we leave,' Miss Warren declared.

'Of course.' He bowed his head. 'I shall not impose on you any longer.'

'Do not worry. I will find more eligible ladies of the Ton,' Lady Georgina said. 'With Trevor sick, we won't be able to attend any functions tomorrow, but I will shortly arrange that tea we spoke of. I will send you the details.'

Miss Warren took her elbow. 'Come along, Lady Georgina. Mr Smith, we will see ourselves out.'

He didn't bother to protest, but he continued to watch Lady Georgina as she walked away. It was such a strange sensation, seeing her inside his home. It was like the merging of two different worlds.

Once he heard their footsteps fading, he cracked open the door to Anne-Marie's room open and poked his head inside.

His heart lurched at the image that greeted him. Anne-Marie and Lily were facing each other under the covers, their arms over the sheets as they held hands.

The first few years after the girls had come to him, they'd refused to be separated, even while sleeping. He would often come home after a long day at work to see both girls curled up in the same bed, clinging to each other.

The lump in his throat grew, and he quietly backed away and closed the door.

This plan had to work.

For them.

Chapter Six

11th December

Georgina loved nothing more than a quiet afternoon of reading by the fire on chilly days. Today was especially nippy as she settled down on one of the well-worn wingback chairs in the library with a brand-new novel. This truly was heaven for her.

Except that she'd re-read the same page for the last half-hour and hadn't understood a single word of it.

'Oh, bother!' She placed the book on her lap and rested her forehead on her palm.

'What is the matter, Lady Georgina?' Miss Warren paused from her mending to glance up at her. 'Is the novel not to your liking?'

'It's not that.'

'Do you have a headache?'

'No, I'm fine.'

She picked up the book once more. Unfortunately, the words refused to make sense.

It was all Elliot's fault.

The events of last night repeated in her head, making it difficult to focus on anything else. Recalling parts of it made her laugh—like the absurdity of the three of them trying to abscond with one young lady without being discovered. Other parts of it made her sad—like Anne-Marie saying how much she hated London or how Lily had seemed such a lonely child, from the bits and pieces Georgina had picked up from their conversation while she'd helped them dress Anne-Marie for bed. And as for the rest of it… She could not quite describe the emotions elicited in her when Elliot had shown such obvious love and concern for his sisters.

I didn't even know he had sisters.

He hadn't said a word about them this entire time. Granted, they had only known each other a few days, and he did not owe her anything. Still, it would have been nice to know about them. Questions fired in her mind: where were their parents? Why were they in his care? Why had he dragged them all the way to London if Anne-Marie hated it here?

'You are still thinking about them, aren't you?' Miss Warren said.

'And you are still angry about last night,' said Georgina.

'Yes.'

'But nothing happened.'

Miss Warren sighed and put her mending down. 'Yes. But still, it could have been a disaster—someone could have seen us, and then we would be having a very different conversation at this moment—if we would even *be* conversing, as I'm quite sure your brother would have sent me away by now.'

'But nothing *did* happen,' Georgina said. 'So we should not worry about what *could* have happened.'

'I assume you are still determined to help Mr Smith find a bride by Christmas?'

'Yes.'

The reminder of their bargain sparked a different thought in her. When she had first hatched this scheme to find him a bride, she'd thought he had a very selfish motive, which was to elevate his own status and gain a foothold in society. But now that she'd met his sisters… Perhaps she was not entirely correct.

'Miss Warren, do you suppose that El— Mr Smith wants a wife because—?'

A knock interrupted her, and Dawson appeared in the doorway. 'I beg your pardon, Lady Georgina, but you have callers.'

'Callers?'

Miss Warren's nose twitched. 'Tell them to return tomorrow, during Lady Georgina's calling hours.'

'I do not have calling hours.' At least, she couldn't remember the hours Great-Aunt Leticia had set when she had still been receiving. 'Who are they, Dawson?'

'Mr Elliot Smith, with Miss Anne-Marie Smith and Miss Lilian Smith,' he said.

Elliot and the girls were here?

'Send them in, Dawson, without delay.' She shot

to her feet. 'No, wait... Bring them to the parlour instead, and have Cook prepare afternoon tea.'

'Yes, my lady.'

'Are you truly going to entertain them?' Miss Warren asked as the butler disappeared through the doorway.

'Why not? Is it not proper that we welcome guests?'

'Your brother is still abed with a cold, and Mr Smith has not left his card or even asked the Duke for permission to call on you. This is all very improper.'

The idea of Elliot calling on her as if he were courting her sounded absurd—yet it sent a zing of excitement all the way to bottoms of her feet.

'Nonsense. He is my brother's friend and has been here before, and therefore he is welcome in this house. It is also past the middle of the day, my brother is present in the house—as are you, and Mr Smith's sisters, not to mention a house full of servants. There is nothing improper about this.'

'You sent no invitation to them,' her companion reminded her.

'Who would know that? And I did promise Anne-Marie a hot cup of tea—which, in my opinion, is a good enough invitation. Now, let us see to our guests, shall we?'

If Miss Warren protested further Georgina didn't hear it, because she hurried out of the library, practically skipping all the way to the parlour. Before she entered, she paused and took a deep breath, trying to control her excitement.

'Good afternoon,' she greeted them.

'Good afternoon, my lady.' Elliot nodded to the girls. 'Allow me to introduce you to my sisters, Anne-Marie and Lily.'

She found it odd that he would introduce them so formally, but then again, they had never been properly introduced, and her presence in their home last night was to remain a secret.

'Hello, Anne-Marie... Lily.' She smiled at them. 'Welcome to Harwicke House.'

Anne-Marie acknowledged her with a bow of her head but said nothing, her expression taut with tension. Lily, on the other hand, flashed her a bright grin.

Elliot bowed his head. 'Thank you for agreeing to see us, my lady.'

'Of course. Now— But wait...why are you still wearing your coats? Dawson should have taken them.'

He shook his head. 'There is no need. We aren't staying long.'

'Not staying long? But Cook is preparing afternoon tea. We have cucumber sandwiches, petits-fours, scones, trifle and teacakes. Doesn't that sound lovely?'

The two girls looked at each other, excitement brimming on their faces, but they remained silent as Elliot spoke again.

'Thank you, but we must decline. We are here because Anne-Marie would like to apologise for her behaviour last night.'

'Is that so?' No wonder the poor thing looked as if

she was off to the gallows. She turned to Lily. 'And why are *you* here, poppet?'

Lily's smile grew wider. 'I'm here because Elliot said if I promised to forget what I saw last night, I could come.'

Georgina could barely stop the laugh bubbling in her chest. 'Ah, I see you've stooped to the bribery of children, Mr Smith.'

The corner of his mouth pulled up. 'Only when necessary, my lady. Now, Anne-Marie, is there something you would like to say?'

The girl stepped forward. 'Lady Georgina, Miss Warren, please accept my apology for my behaviour last night. It was unladylike and I will never do it again.'

Georgina strode over to her and took her hand. 'I will accept your apology—'

'Good,' Elliot interjected.

'But only if you stay for tea.'

Jade-green eyes so much like Elliot's widened. 'Really?'

'Yes. Well, Mr Smith?'

He crossed his arms over his chest. 'She's supposed to go straight back home after this, because she is being punished for her actions, not rewarded for them.'

Unable to help herself, she repeated his words back to him. 'You know my terms, Mr Smith.'

He snorted—although it sounded as if he was trying to stop himself from chuckling. 'All right. But we are staying for half an hour, not a second more.'

The two girls exchanged delighted looks.

'Come, let's sit down,' she said. 'Tea will be served at any moment now.'

'Just so you know,' Elliot began as they made themselves comfortable in the parlour, 'I didn't force Anne-Marie to come here to apologise.'

'You didn't?'

Anne-Marie smiled weakly at her. 'I felt terrible about what happened, and I asked Elliot if I could write an apology letter.' She took a spot on the empty settee and patted the space next to her, indicating to her sister to sit there. 'But he said I should do it in person.'

'She's scared of you,' Lily said.

'Lily!' Anne-Marie whispered, her face turning red.

'I don't know why she would be scared of you,' the youngest Smith said as she fiddled with the lace hem of her dress. 'Elliot said she was sick and you helped her. Why would that scare her?'

Ah, so that was his explanation. 'She…er…ripped my favourite dress while I helped her,' Georgina offered.

Lily cocked her head to the side. 'Elliot said it was your glove.'

'That too,' she said smoothly. 'Anyhow, Anne-Marie, I'm glad to see you are feeling better this morning.'

'Thank you, Lady Georgina, I am,' she replied sombrely. 'I had a headache, but the housekeeper gave me some powder that helped ease the throbbing.'

'Are you a real lady?' Lily interjected.

'Lily, you can't ask questions like that,' Elliot said with an apologetic look. 'I'm sorry—you don't have to answer that.'

'No, not at all,' Georgina said with a chuckle. She found children's questions so honest and refreshing—they were asked with curiosity and not malice. 'To answer your question, poppet, yes. My father was a duke and so I am, indeed, a lady.'

'Can I be a lady too?'

'If you marry a lord. Would you like to be one?'

She cocked her head to one side and wrinkled her nose. 'Maybe… I don't know if I want to get married. I don't like boys. All they want to do is play with sticks and throw mud at my dress.' She stuck out her tongue. 'Except Elliot. I like him very much. Do you like him?'

It took all of Georgina's willpower not to glance over at him as heat crept up her cheeks. Mercifully, Dawson entered at the precise moment, a silver tea service in his hands while a maid carried a tiered tea stand heaped with food.

Lily's eyes lit up. 'Is that all for us?'

'Yes!' Georgina chuckled. 'And there's more, so please help yourselves.'

'Tea in the Abernathy household tends to be an elaborate affair,' Miss Warren said as Dawson and the maid began to serve them. 'I'm surprised we have any appetite for dinner at all.'

'It's a tradition,' Georgina said. 'My mother loved

afternoon tea, and she and I would have all these treats until we…' Her voice faded as a lump formed in her throat at this reminder that her mother was no longer here. 'I…' Though she attempted to dislodge it, it remained there, and an awkward silence crept into the air.

'Lady Georgina, your Christmas decorations are quite…er…interesting,' Elliot said, though he seemed to struggle with finding the right adjective. 'They look to be made of the highest quality materials.'

Her head swivelled towards him. She was surprised he would even notice the decor, or say anything nice about it, given how much he hated Christmas.

'Everything looks beautiful,' Anne-Marie remarked. 'Is the entire house decorated?'

'From the roof to the cellar—and I did most of it myself.'

Elliot took a sip of his tea. 'You did an excellent job.'

Now that, at least, sounded like a true compliment.

'Thank you.'

'Do you decorate your home for Christmas?' Miss Warren asked.

'Only for Christmas Eve and Christmas Day. Then it all gets packed away as soon as we go to bed,' Anne-Marie said, taking a sip of her tea. 'But we have gifts, and a feast, with roast goose and all the trimmings.'

'And cake!' Lily added, her eyes growing large as saucers as the maid placed a generous portion of trifle on her plate. 'But none as nice as this.'

Georgina sneaked a glance at Elliot. 'And I thought you were a Scrooge.'

'Oh, Elliot doesn't celebrate with us.' Anne-Marie sniffed at a scone before taking a bite. 'He's at the office all day, and we don't see him until the next morning.'

'But why not?' Georgina asked.

'I'm always working.' He waved away the plate the maid was about to put in front of him. 'It's the only time I can get anything done.'

She tsked. 'I take back what I said, then.'

Anne-Marie snorted. 'Oh, I see.' Her eyes darted to Elliot. 'Yes, definitely a Scrooge.'

Georgina, Lily and even Miss Warren all looked at each other with knowing smiles.

'Am I the only person to have never read this novel?' He grumbled as he fiddled with his teacup.

'Oh, hello, there…good afternoon,' came a booming voice from the doorway. It was Trevor, up and about, and though he was fully dressed, his hair remained dishevelled and the stubble on his chin indicated he hadn't shaved. 'No, don't get up,' he said. 'And please don't let me interrupt.'

'Trev, you're supposed to be in bed.' Georgina rose to her feet and strode over to him. 'Are you still feverish?'

He waved her hand away as she attempted to touch his forehead. 'No, no, I am fine, Georgina.'

'That wasn't what you said last night,' she said wryly. 'You said you were on your deathbed.'

'I did not.'

'And you promised me I could have Odin when you passed.'

'I know you are definitely lying, because not even on my deathbed would I give you my best stallion.' He turned to the other occupants of the parlout. 'Pardon me for my rudeness, ladies,' he said to Anne-Marie and Lily. 'Trevor Abernathy, Duke of Harwicke, at your service.' He waved his hand with a flourish as he bowed. 'And who might you lovely ladies be?'

Anne-Marie blushed and Lily giggled.

'These are my sisters, Miss Anne-Marie Smith and Miss Lilian Smith.' Elliot gestured for them to stand. 'Girls…?'

'Delighted to make your acquaintance,' Anne-Marie said as she executed a clumsy, though serviceable curtsey. 'Your Grace.'

'I thought his name was Trevor?' Lily said in a loud whisper.

'It is…but you're supposed to say "Your Grace" to a duke, you ninny,' Anne-Marie admonished. 'Don't you remember anything from those lessons?'

'I'm sorry.' Lily hung her head low.

'It's quite all right. Since I am the first duke you've met, you are hereby granted a pardon,' Trevor said. 'I didn't know you had sisters, Elliot. Why have you never mentioned them?' He scratched his chin. 'And, by the way, what brings you here this afternoon?'

Panic rose in Georgina as she met Miss Warren's gaze. 'Er… Mr Smith told me about his sisters last night, during the musicale, and so of course I had to invite them to tea. Can you believe they've never had a proper English afternoon tea?'

'Ah, yes…' Striding over to the table, he plucked a cucumber sandwich from the tray and popped it in his mouth. 'And you've never had afternoon tea until you've had it in the Abernathy household.'

'Do you want to join us?' Georgina asked. 'I can have Dawson bring a chair from the library.'

'No need. I think I shall head back upstairs for a nap and eat at dinner.' Still, he leaned down to contemplate the tiered tray of goodies. 'But I heard voices, and my valet said we had guests, so I had to investigate for myself. Oh—' Standing up straight, he whirled to face Elliot. 'I'm glad you're here, actually.'

'Why?'

'I meant to tell you last night. Georgina and I will be heading up to Foxbury Hill, my estate in Northamptonshire, in a few days. We mean to stay until the eighteenth.'

'Oh, dear, is it that soon?' She hadn't even noticed. Usually she'd be brimming with excitement in the days leading up to their stay at Foxbury Hill.

'Northamptonshire? What for?' Elliot asked.

'It's where we celebrate our First Christmas.'

'First Christmas…?' he echoed.

'Another Abernathy tradition,' Georgina explained. 'And perhaps my favourite one.'

'Papa abhorred town during Christmas, while Mama hated being away from the social whirl during the festivities. So they compromised—First Christmas mid-December in Northamptonshire and Second Christmas on the twenty-fifth in London.'

'Ah, I see.' Elliot folded his hands on his lap. 'I suppose I'll be on my own, then.'

Georgina's stomach dropped. With her away in Northamptonshire, how was she to continue with her work on finding him a bride. 'Trev, perhaps we can...' she swallowed '...postpone First Christmas?'

'Nonsense.' He waved a hand at her. 'I was going to invite you, Elliot.'

'You were?' Georgina and Elliot said at the same time.

'Yes. And, Georgie, you should invite your potential candidates as well.'

'Candidates for what?' Anne-Marie eyed them suspiciously.

Georgina sent her brother a warning look, then said, 'Er...best friends. Yes, I'm looking to find some very good, very best friends.'

Lily's jaw dropped open. 'You must be very popular if people are vying to be your best friends. Can I help you find some friends?'

'Er...yes, poppet. Whatever you want.'

'And we can celebrate your First Christmas with you?'

'Of course you can.'

Anne-Marie let out a small squeal. 'We are leaving London!' She grasped the edge of the table. 'I can't believe it.'

Lily let out a whoop. 'Hooray!'

'Girls, girls!' Elliot exclaimed as he raked his fingers through his hair. 'The Duke has not invited you—he has invited me.'

'Well, of course they are invited,' Trevor said. 'You can't leave them alone in London while you go gallivanting off to Northamptonshire. Elliot, bring as many of your staff as you need—including nannies, tutors and governesses...'

'We don't have a governess any more,' Lily said. 'Anne-Marie set her on fire.'

'I beg your pardon?' Trevor said, looking taken aback.

Elliot let out a strangled cry. 'No, you girls will be staying in London.'

'But Lady Georgina said we could,' Lily whined.

'You *always* do this,' Anne-Marie seethed at Elliot.

'I am your brother and what I say goes,' he retorted. 'Now, girls, please compose yourselves.'

Georgina deftly manoeuvred herself between them. 'Anne-Marie, Lily, have you ever seen a winter garden before? No?' She glanced at her companion. 'Perhaps Miss Warren can show you. If you don't mind, Miss Warren?'

'Of course, my lady.' Rising to her feet, Miss Warren urged both girls to do the same, then deftly shepherded them out of the parlour.

'We have the room to host all of you,' Trevor assured him. 'I—ah—' He inhaled a breath, then covered his mouth. *'Achoo!'*

'I knew you were still sick,' Georgina admonished. Taking his arm, she hauled him towards the door. 'Go back to your room and rest.'

'But—'

'Go.' She pushed him out and then shut the door behind him. Brushing her hands together, she turned back to Elliot. 'It truly is no trouble to have your sisters come with us.'

'That is very kind of you, but—'

'They don't know, do they? That you are looking for a wife?'

His expression darkened, like the sudden arrival of dark clouds on a sunny day. 'I would rather they not know my personal business. They are children.'

'Anne-Marie is what—? Sixteen? Seventeen? She is not a child any more.'

'Still, they are my responsibility.' He raked his hand into his hair once again, making tufts of dark hair jut out in every direction.

Georgina's fingers itched to put them back into place. Or perhaps to run through them as his had earlier.

'I understand—which is why you cannot just leave them in London. Please, do not fret about it. We have plenty of rooms and there will be many staff who can assist you and keep them company. *I* will keep them company.'

'And how are you supposed to do that when you are finding me a bride?'

She ignored the way her stomach turned to stone.

'My work shall be done before that,' she said. 'I will call on Lady Lavinia, Miss Philipps and their mothers tomorrow and extend our invitation for the party. Once they arrive in Northamptonshire, there will be every opportunity for you to get acquainted with them and woo them. I can't possibly do all the work, now, can I?'

'Hmm, I suppose…'

'I am but a shepherdess, leading the lambs to the—'

'Slaughter?' he finished.

She grinned at him. 'I was going to say fold.'

It was then that Elliot did something that took her by surprise—he smiled at her. A one hundred percent completely genuine smile that reached his eyes. Her heart fluttered madly in her chest.

'I haven't said thank you, by the way,' he said, the smile fading.

'For what?'

'For last night. And just now…with the girls. I don't think I've seen them as happy as they have been in the past half-hour in a long time.'

How she ached for those poor children.

'You may thank me by allowing the girls to come to Foxbury Hill. They will be very much welcome and very much wanted there.' She grasped his forearm. 'Please, Elliot?'

He blinked at her, his eyes darting down to where she touched him.

Realising what a presumptuous move it had been, she quickly released him. 'Apologies…' Her emotions had got the better of her and she hadn't realised she'd grabbed him. 'And for using your name—'

'No, it's all right. I did give you leave to use it if we were alone.'

And they were, as he'd pointed out, quite alone— a fact that made her heart skip a beat. 'Of course you have the courtesy to do the same.' It was only fair, after all.

He made a noncommittal sound. Then: 'Now, about your invitation…'

'Yes?'

'I accept,' he relented. 'We will travel to Northamptonshire.'

She clapped her hands together. 'Excellent. Come, let's tell them together.'

As expected, Anne-Marie and Lily shrieked in excitement when Georgina told them that they were to come to Foxbury Hill with them.

'Is this real, Elliot?' Anne-Marie asked. 'You won't change your mind?'

He huffed. 'Yes, you and Lily are coming with me to Northamptonshire.'

'Whoopee!' Lily launched herself at Georgina, wrapping her arms around her legs. 'We get two Christmases this year! Thank you, Lady Georgina.'

She patted her on the head. 'You're welcome.' Grinning, she glanced back to Elliot, who had the strangest expression on his face. 'You shan't regret this,' she assured him.

'I hope not…'

Chapter Seven

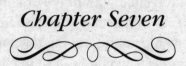

14th December

Though the process of calling on people had always been more painful than walking over hot coals for Georgina, she somehow managed to do it twice in one day. Her efforts, however, had proved fruitful, because both Lady Arundel and the Viscountess had accepted her invitation with much delight. She had known they would accept because she had mentioned the one thing that that would pique the interest of any mother with daughters of a marriageable age—the fact that there would be unmarried gentlemen present as well.

Of course that meant she also had to invite other gentlemen to Foxbury Hill, but those who would pose no threat to Elliot's prospects. Thankfully Trevor had taken care of that. He'd invited the Duke of Waldemere, as he and Lady Lavinia's sister Genevieve were practically courting, and Mr James Galwick, whom he assured her had no intention of finding a wife.

And so there would be an even number of unmarried ladies and gentlemen, if she included herself, which should satisfy the marriage-minded mamas.

Having arrived at Foxbury Hill very late in the afternoon, Georgina had refreshed herself with a short nap. She had travelled with only her lady's maid and Miss Warren, as Trevor had business to attend to in London and would not be leaving town until the next day. All their guests would be arriving today, so now she felt rested she set off to check the preparations for the festivities.

Initially, the staff at Foxbury Hill had only begun preparing for Georgina and Trevor to come, as they did every year, but thankfully Dawson had been able to send word to them about the extra guests.

Georgina went down to the kitchens and met Mrs Galloway, the housekeeper, and Mrs Laramie, the cook, to ensure everything was ready.

'The decorations are lovely, by the way, Mrs Galloway,' she said. 'They are every year, but they are particularly delightful this time around.'

Even the outside of the house was decorated, with wreaths made of fir and ribbon, and when she'd entered the hall, she'd been greeted by not one, but two Christmas trees, bedecked with all sorts of decorations.

The housekeeper chuckled, the wrinkles on her weathered face deepening. 'I would never disappoint you, Lady Georgina. Dawson sent word that Harwicke House was especially festive this year, and so of course we said we must ensure Foxbury Hill is just as splendid—if not more. After all, this is where you spend First Christmas.'

'The roast turkey will be perfect this year too,' Mrs Laramie said, rubbing her hands together. 'I've perfected a new special sauce to baste it with. And I shall be preparing all your and His Grace's favourite dishes.' Her eyes practically gleamed with anticipation. 'As well as desserts.'

'Mrs Laramie looks more excited than you were as a young child while opening your presents on Christmas Day,' Mrs Galloway commented.

'It's been so long since we've entertained,' the cook said. 'I am just happy for the opportunity to use my talents, my lady. Thank you for this.'

'You're very welcome—and I'm very eager to taste the fruits of your talents. Now, I must see to our guests.'

Georgina left the two servants and headed back upstairs. But then she remembered she'd forgotten to ask Mrs Galloway what time they would serve dinner tonight, since the guests would be arriving at different intervals.

Turning back, she retraced her steps towards the kitchens, but stopped when she overheard her name being spoken aloud.

'Lady Georgina does look different, doesn't she?' said Mrs Galloway.

'Yes, she seems happier,' the cook replied. 'Maybe it's because that pinch-faced aunt of hers is finally gone.'

Mrs Galloway laughed. 'Miss Leticia was an excellent chaperone—perhaps too excellent.' She sighed. 'It's too bad that Lady Georgina is now on her way to spinsterhood.'

Georgina winced. While her unmarried status was a fact in her in her mind, hearing about it from others still stung.

'Or is she?' Mrs Galloway said.

'Of course she is… Wait, what have you heard?'

The housekeeper chuckled. 'That the guests we are having are mostly unmarried ladies *and* gentlemen.'

The cook gasped. 'Do you think His Grace means to find a bride?'

'Perhaps. Or is Lady Georgina on the hunt herself?'

Georgina had to bite the back of her hand to stop laughing. Gossip really was quite funny in that way. When people added their own interpretations to the most innocuous news, it tended to spiral in a completely different direction from where it had begun.

'Whatever the reason, I'm glad to finally have some life and excitement here. It makes me miss the old days with the Duke and Duchess.'

Me too, Georgina thought, pressing her fist to her chest as if that would ease the sudden heartache there.

'His Grace sometimes has parties,' Mrs Galloway said.

'With his "gentleman" friends.' The cook made a disgusted sound. 'Those lot don't appreciate my cooking—not when they spend their days here carousing.

But now we will have quality people—ladies and true gentlemen.'

'It will be nice to fill the rooms of Foxbury Hill with guests once again.'

'Perhaps His Grace will find a bride and we will once again hear laughter in these corridors…'

Deciding she had eavesdropped enough, Georgina crept away from the two women and made her way back upstairs. The servants were still putting some finishing touches to the decorations, so she decided to check on their progress. Dawson told her they were in the library, and she headed there, arriving just in time to supervise the footmen and the maids.

'That's it,' she told the footman perched up on a ladder, hanging holly boughs over the windows. 'Just a little more to the right…a little more…there. Perfect. Thank you, Andrew.'

'Lady Georgina! Lady Georgina! We're here!'

She whirled around to the sound of a voice.

'Lily! Anne-Marie!' The two girls rushed towards her, stepping into her open arms. 'I'm so glad to see you.'

In truth, though they had spent only a short time together, she had grown fond of the two girls and had missed them in the last two days.

'Thank you so much for inviting us.' Anne-Marie's jade-green eyes sparkled with joy—such a contrast from the first time they had met. 'This truly is the most excitement I've had in months.'

'It was my pleasure. Are you tired? Have you eaten? Would you like some tea?'

'No, we aren't tired. We're too excited to nap,' Lily said. 'So we've decided to go exploring.'

'Foxbury Hill is perfect for that. I'll show you my favourite places.'

The little girl looked up at her expectantly. 'Now?'

'I'm afraid not, poppet. I'm a bit busy.' She nodded at the servants.

'Can we help?' Lily eyed the box of tinsel and Christmas ornaments on the table beside her.

'If you like.' She signalled to the maid waiting in the corner. 'Flora, could you show Miss Lily where those should go?'

'Yes, my lady.'

For the next half-hour or so the three of them, along with the servants, put the finishing touches to the house. Lily in particular seemed to enjoy the task given to her—spreading tinsel—while Anne-Marie assisted Georgina in directing the footmen on hanging more fir garlands.

'Lady Georgina, may I ask a question?' Anne-Marie said.

'Of course, dear girl, what is it?'

'Am I truly not allowed to join in the festivities here at Foxbury Hill?' Her lips turned out in a pout. 'I'm sixteen years old. Why can't I eat at the table instead of having my dinner upstairs with Lily?'

How Georgina wished she could trade places with

Anne-Marie. What she wouldn't do for some solitary meals for the next few days.

'I'm so sorry, but that's just how things are done here in England. Until you are out in society you must stay with the other children. Lady Arundel's youngest daughter, Lady Hannah, will be here. She's about fourteen, I believe. Perhaps the two of you can keep each other company?'

'Stupid rules,' Anne-Marie grumbled. 'I can't wait until I'm out. Then I can do what I want.'

Georgina let out a chuckle. 'You should enjoy this time, because soon you'll have even more rules and restrictions placed upon you. Unlike if you had been born a boy, like Trevor.'

'Your brother seems nice,' Anne-Marie sniffed. 'Not like mine. I bet your brother has never made you do things you didn't want—like move you away from your home twice in less than five years.'

'Twice?' Georgina asked, shocked.

'Three times,' said Lily, who had appeared between them. 'We moved three times.'

'No, ninny. The first time doesn't count. That was when Ma brought us—' She closed her mouth.

'Why did you move twice in five years?' asked Georgina. 'Where were you before you were in New York?'

'We lived in San Francisco, then New York, then here,' Anne-Marie said. 'We barely stayed long enough in one place to settle in. I was finally starting to make friends in New York and then *he* had to bring us *here*.'

Ah, so that was why Anne-Marie was so angry with Elliot. But Georgina could hardly blame the girl—change was difficult, and such big changes in so short a time would be even more so.

'I don't think I'll be out any time soon,' Anne-Marie said. 'Elliot says we must wait for the right time. When we have the right connections. So that I may have a proper society debut and no one will turn us away, like back in New York.'

Turn them away?

It was at that moment that Georgina realised her earlier suspicions had been correct.

She drew in a sharp breath.

Elliot didn't want an aristocratic wife for himself. He was doing it for his sisters. He was sacrificing his own needs—maybe even the chance of finding love—just so they could have better prospects.

A lump grew in her throat and her eyes misted.

'My lady?' Andrew said, interrupting her thoughts. 'We are finished.'

Taking a deep, cleansing breath, Georgina took a step back to examine their handiwork. 'Excellent work—thank you everyone.' As the servants began to clear up the boxes, ladders and tools, and took their leave, she turned to the two girls. 'And thank you both. I could not have done it without you.'

'Anne-Marie, Lily—there you are.'

Georgina's heart sprang up at the sound of the familiar baritone. 'Mr Smith,' she greeted him as he entered the library. 'Did you rest well?'

He bowed his head. 'I did, thank you, my lady. However, I went to the girls' room and didn't find them abed. Aren't you two tired?'

'I'm too excited to nap,' Lily declared, then gestured around them. 'Look, we helped Lady Georgina decorate.'

'I see.' He glanced around. 'Once again, you have outdone yourself, my lady.'

It did not escape her notice that Elliot did not comment on the decorations directly—declaring that he thought they were nice or he liked them. It was as if any mention of Christmas would make him spontaneously combust.

'Thank you, Mr Smith. But what do you think of the trees? And the boughs? The tinsel?'

'I helped with the tinsel!' Lily said excitedly.

'Ah, yes…' He looked around, examining the silvery bits of paper. 'Excellent choice of placement. Even distribution. And…'

'And?' Georgina asked, hopeful that he would find one actually nice thing to say.

'And…' He tapped a finger on his chin, then strode towards her, stopping when he was right beside her. 'I commend your managerial skills on picking the right person for the job.' He winked at Lily.

'I'll get you to say something nice about my decorations one day,' she said, placing her hands on her hips.

'I like *all* of the decorations,' Lily said. 'The trees, the ornaments, the—' She frowned. 'What's that?'

'What's what, poppet?'

Lily pointed above her head. 'That?'

Georgina glanced up and saw a bunch of green twigs with white berries wrapped together in a bright red ribbon. 'Why, that's—'

'Mistletoe,' Anne-Marie finished, gasping as she covered her mouth, her eyes darting from Georgina to Elliot.

'What's wrong?' Elliot asked. 'Anne-Marie, are you ill?'

She shook her head, then burst out, 'You have to kiss her!'

Georgina's cheeks burned as if someone had set them on fire. 'I… It's a silly tradition.'

Elliot cleared his throat. 'Yes, just a silly old wives' tale.'

'But you have to,' Lily squealed. 'Or you'll have bad luck!'

'There's no such thing as luck,' he retorted.

'What about all those strokes of good luck you've had, Elliot?' Anne-Marie asked. 'What if you lose your golden touch and all your money disappears?'

Lily's head bobbed up and down in agreement.

It took all Georgina's willpower to glance at Elliot without melting into a pile of shame. 'We don't have to—'

'I suppose the girls are not wrong,' he said. 'And it's just a kiss under the mistletoe.'

True. But there was one thing he didn't know.

It would be her first—and maybe only—kiss.

Elliot's mesmerising light green gaze fixed on her. 'My lady? What do you say?'

She squared her shoulders. 'Well, we can't send you to the poorhouse, now, can we?' She turned so that her cheek faced him. 'If you please, Mr Smith.'

Though she kept her gaze straight ahead, she could still see him from the corner of her eye, and her heart thumped madly in her chest as his head descended towards her. His lips were curiously soft on her cheek, though they lingered much longer than she'd thought they would. Also, his mouth was much closer to hers than she'd expected—the corner of it even touched her own. And this close she could smell the spicy scent of his cologne, which sent the most curious tingling sensation straight to her belly.

Lily clapped as soon as he pulled away. 'Hooray! No bad luck for you, Elliot.'

'Thank you.'

'Who has bad luck?'

Georgina sprang away from Elliot at the sound of a stranger's voice.

'Who—? Lady Arundel,' she greeted the older woman. 'And Lady Lavinia.' She felt that hot stab in her chest once more at the sight of Lady Lavinia. Today she looked absolutely radiant in her yellow travel gown, not a hair or thread out of place. 'Welcome to Foxbury Hill.'

'Lady Georgina!' Lady Arundel exclaimed as she strode over to her and took her hands in hers. 'Once again, thank you for your invitation. My girls and I are delighted to be here.'

'Where are Lady Genevieve and Lady Hannah?' she asked, referring to Lady Arundel's other daughters.

'Upstairs, resting in their rooms,' the Marchioness said. 'But I wanted to come and see you to thank you before going up to ours.'

'As did I,' said Lady Lavinia.

'And I see Mr Smith is already here,' Lady Arundel added.

'Good afternoon,' he greeted them with a respectful bow. 'Lady Arundel, Lady Lavinia—may I present my sisters?' He quickly made the introductions.

'How delightful they are,' Lady Arundel said. 'Are they not, Lavinia?'

'Yes,' she said. 'Anne-Marie, your dress is lovely. And Lily, you look very nice as well.'

'My...this place...' Lady Arundel's head swivelled. 'These decorations are even better than those at Harwicke House. By the way—thank you very much for giving me that catalogue of Christmas decorations, Lady Georgina. I didn't even know they were sold in such a way.'

'I only recently found out myself,' Georgina said. 'Hopefully they have not run out.'

'I helped decorate,' Lily announced. 'I did the tinsel.'

Lady Lavinia bent down to her level. 'You did a very good job. The tinsel is very beautiful.'

'Want to see?' Lily held out her hand and Lady Lavinia took it. 'Let's start over here.'

'Mr Smith would probably like to take a closer look too,' Georgina suggested.

'I would?' He frowned.

She nodded meaningfully towards Lady Lavinia. 'Yes.'

'Of course.' He took Lily's other hand into his. 'Why don't you show us, Lily?'

As Lily led Lady Lavinia and Elliot over to the fireplace, Georgina quietly moved away from the charmingly domestic scene. She turned quickly, lest the stabbing pain in her chest bury itself deeper, her steps hastening as she drew further away.

Truly, she would be happy for Elliot and the girls if he ended up marrying Lady Lavinia. She was the daughter of a marquess, her sister would soon be wed to a duke, and the Wrights were pillars of society. Elliot wouldn't be able to find a better match.

Except for you, maybe, a voice inside her said.

She clicked her tongue at that voice. In ranking and social connections perhaps she was a step above Lady Lavinia. But the truth was Georgina would make the worst chaperone and patroness for the girls. Sadly, Anne-Marie and Lily already had two marks against them—they were common-born and American. But someone like Lady Lavinia, who was experienced in manoeuvring through the waters of the Ton and avoiding the pitfalls, would help them successfully navigate the Season and increase their chances of a good match.

Unfortunately, that was not a something a reclusive spinster like Georgina could do for them.

Her hand crept up to her cheek, remembering their kiss under the mistletoe. His lips had seemingly left their brand there, the heat of them still lingering on her skin. How she wished they had been alone, with no audience. Then she could—

She stopped those thoughts before they could further grow and taunt her.

No, they would be better off with Lady Lavinia, or even Miss Philipps. And now more than ever Georgina knew she had to help Elliot make a match—not just so he wouldn't evict the girls at St Agnes's, but also to secure his sisters' futures.

She would do that, no matter how she might feel about him.

Chapter Eight

15th December

'That is the most amusing story I've ever heard,' Lady Lavinia remarked. 'Your journey on a steamship sounds exciting and not at all tedious, Mr Smith.'

'Not as amusing at the tale he told me during luncheon,' Miss Philipps said, batting her eyelashes at him.

'Won't you please tell me as well?' Lady Lavinia pleaded.

'Perhaps he can do it after dinner,' Lady Arundel said. 'So he may enjoy his pheasant. He's hardly taken a bite with all the questions we've been peppering him with.'

It was their second day at Foxbury Hill and all the guests had arrived—including Harwicke, who had been detained by some business in London. The day had been filled with amusements around the estate— a brisk walk in the gardens after breakfast, a hearty, leisurely luncheon, and then carriage rides. Before dinner, Elliot and the other male guests—Thomas Carlisle, Duke of Waldemere, the Marquess of Arundel and the Viscount—had played billiards, while the ladies had gathered in the sitting room for their own leisure activities. But now that they were complete, and their host had arrived, everyone was finally able to sit down to a formal dinner.

'It has been a delightful meal so far,' Elliot remarked.

'Yes,' Lady Lavinia agreed.

'Truly, the cook here is talented,' added Miss Philipps, flashing him a smile.

Though he didn't believe in luck, the events of the last fortnight were perhaps starting to change Elliot's mind. After all, he was in the company of not one, but two ladies of marriageable age and impeccable breeding.

Well, three, if he were to count *everyone* at dinner. But the third lady in question had already made it clear that she was not interested in marriage.

Not to him anyway.

'As I was saying, Lady Georgina, Foxbury Hill looks splendid,' said Lord Bellamy. 'Why, I don't think we have half as many decorations at my father's estate in Somerset.'

'Thank you, Lord Bellamy,' Georgina replied. 'But it was mostly the servants who did it all.'

Once again she looked incredibly lovely, in a blue satin gown trimmed with black lace, her hair pulled away from her beautiful face and allowed to cascade in waves down the back of her head.

'Ah, but surely it was your idea.' Lord Bellamy raised a glass to her and winked, which made her cheeks turn pink.

Elliot turned back to his plate and stabbed his pheasant with a knife, not caring if the poor bird was already dead and stuffed.

He's not even supposed to be here.

Bellamy had arrived earlier today with Harwicke, much to Elliot's confusion and consternation. The Duke had explained that Mr Galwick was unable to come, due to having broken his leg that morning. Not wanting to have an imbalance of gentlemen and ladies, he had invited Bellamy, who had happily accepted.

At first Elliot had been annoyed, because he did not want competition, but apparently he needn't have worried. Since he had arrived, Bellamy had not left Georgina's side. She didn't seem to discourage his attentions, either.

He sneaked another glance at them, seething as Georgina smiled at something Bellamy had said. What could she possibly see in that dandy? Sure, he was titled, but he was only the third son of an earl. Bellamy wasn't even that wealthy—at least not from what his private investigator had gathered. If she married him she would be comfortable, but extravagances like adorning an entire house with decorations every Christmas would not be feasible.

Elliot's resources, on the other hand, would allow

her to decorate an estate ten times the size of Foxbury Hill for the entire year—for the rest of her life, if that was what she wanted.

'Ah, dessert is here,' Harwicke announced.

The footmen removed the used dishes and placed a new plate in front of each guests with the evening's first dessert—a steamed pudding with raspberry cream. Everyone *oohed* and *aahed*, just as they had with every dish, and dug in heartily.

As the dinner continued, Elliot found it increasingly difficult to focus on his conversation with Lady Lavinia and Miss Philipps. He sneaked glances at Georgina and Lord Bellamy. The latter was plying her with compliments and amusing stories, and the former was seemingly open to his attentions. She did not seem to notice the others at the table and did not attempt to make conversation with anyone aside from the man beside her.

'That was a splendid meal,' Harwicke declared as he polished off his cheese, the last of the courses. 'Please convey my compliments to Mrs Laramie,' he said to the butler. 'And now we have more amusements in the parlour, as well as port for the gentlemen and sherry for the ladies.'

All the guests rose from their seats and followed the Duke to the parlour. As he'd promised, there were more refreshments for the guests, as well as sweet treats if the elaborate dinner had not satisfied them. There was also a card table, a pianoforte and even a chess set, as well as other board games for them to use.

The guests helped themselves to port and sherry and settled in. No one seemed inclined for any of the games, so they sat around the pianoforte while Miss Philipps entertained them. To Elliot's annoyance, Bellamy once again cornered Georgina at one end of the settee, so that only he would be able to converse with her.

'Do you play, Mr Smith?' Lord Arundel asked, and gestured to the chess set.

'Not very well,' he confessed.

He had no time or patience to learn more than the basics of the game.

'I love it,' he said. 'I would play for hours if I could.'

'And he does,' Lady Arundel said, bemused. 'He's very good at it.'

'Papa has a wall full of the trophies that he has won at tournaments to prove it,' Lady Lavinia added.

'Then perhaps you could teach me some strategy, my lord? I would be honoured to learn from a master.'

A little flattery wouldn't hurt. After all, Lord Arundel might very well be his future father-in-law.

Lord Arundel sat behind the white pieces. 'I would be happy to teach you.' He gestured to the seat across from him. 'Let us begin.'

At first Elliot thought he would just play along and let his opponent win and be done with it. However, the Marquess seemed to take his role as mentor seriously, explaining Elliot's every move and why it was the wrong one. But at least it was taking Elliot's mind off

Georgina and Bellamy, as they continued their conversation in their own cosy little corner of the room.

'Ah, see—I told you not to put your knight there.' Lord Arundel grabbed his queen and placed it next to the black king piece. 'Checkmate.'

'Congratulations, my lord.'

And thank goodness this game is over.

'I am only sorry that I was an unworthy opponent.'

The Marquess looked at him knowingly. 'Do not fret. You have other admirable qualities, Mr Smith.'

Elliot hoped this was some sort of stamp of approval. 'Thank you, my lord.' He stood up and glanced around the room. 'And now—'

He stopped short, and the most curious feeling washed over him. Something did not feel right.

Georgina was gone. As was Bellamy.

His stomach turned to stone. Where the devil were they? He glanced over at Harwicke, who was laughing at some story the Viscount was telling, without a care in the world, and meanwhile his sister had disappeared with a man.

Biting his lip, Elliot stifled the urge to ask if anyone had seen the couple. He didn't want to bring attention to their disappearance as it would put Georgina's reputation in peril. And people loved gossip. If anyone found out he and his sisters were here they, too, might be affected by any scandal that happened in Foxbury Hill.

'If you'll excuse me? I must refresh myself.' He nodded to the Marquess and Marchioness and discreetly left the library.

Dread and fury swirled inside him, but he could not allow his emotions to overcome him. He would find the couple and break them up before anyone discovered them. Perhaps he could persuade Bellamy to leave immediately, and he'd never have to see the smarmy fop ever again.

If I were a scoundrel, like Bellamy, where would I bring a young woman to take advantage of her?

Foxbury Hill was enormous, but surely they wouldn't be so daring as to sneak upstairs. So he began to search all the rooms downstairs, going into them one by one. When he entered what appeared to be a music room, he spied a familiar figure clad in a blue gown sitting by a harp. However, she was alone.

'Who's there?' Georgina called out. 'I heard you come in.'

Elliot stepped inside. 'It's me.'

'Oh.' Relief struck her face. 'What are you doing here?'

He paused, thinking of a good excuse. 'I got lost on my way to the necessary. This place is enormous.'

'Ah, yes, that can happen.'

'And you?'

Where was Bellamy? He glanced over to the windows. Was he hiding behind the drapes like some coward? They certainly were thick and voluminous enough that he could hide there without being detected.

'I was just feeling…overwhelmed.'

Drawing closer to her side, Elliot examined her face. Like that night at the opera, her face was once again pale, and a sheen of perspiration had collected on her brow. Her breaths came in short, shallow pants.

'What's wrong? Did he do something to you?'

'He?'

'Bellamy.'

She frowned. 'What would he do to me? He retired earlier tonight, complaining of stomach pains.'

So that's where he is.

'I didn't notice that he'd left. Are you feeling ill as well? Did you perhaps eat what has made Bellamy sick?'

'Oh, no.' She shook her head, sending waves of blonde hair shimmering under the glow of the chandelier. 'Like I said, I was feeling overwhelmed by today's activities. And sometimes, when it is too much, I get these…spells.'

Once again, guilt crept into him. This was time she usually spent alone with Trevor—for their First Christmas, she had said. It was because of him that they now had to share their home with all these near strangers.

Sighing, he retrieved an object from his pocket. 'Here,' he said, handing her the flask.

Her nose wrinkled delicately. 'I don't think liquor will help.'

'It's just water,' he clarified.

'You take water with you in a flask everywhere you go?'

'Why not? It's quite refreshing.'

Well, the truth was he'd only begun carrying it after the Rutherford ball, when he'd seen her so ill after dancing with him. He was afraid he'd over-exerted her, and he wanted to be prepared in case it happened again. That, apparently, had been good forethought on his part.

Though hesitant, she took it anyway, unscrewed the top, then took a sip. 'Thank you. That is very refreshing.'

'You're welcome.' He took the flask back and replaced the cap.

'And I'm sorry.'

'Sorry? For what?'

'Well, I promised you that I would watch over Anne-Marie and Lily, and yet I hardly saw them today.'

'Ah, I see.'

Elliot wasn't sure why, but finding them with her yesterday, decorating the house, had been disconcerting. He had meant it when he'd told her that he hadn't seen them as happy as they were when they were with her. However, seeing them laughing and joking together had sent an emotion straight to his heart that had caused a disquiet in him he'd never experienced before.

Perhaps it was best not to encourage his sisters to pursue a friendship with Georgina. Soon he would be married to Lady Lavinia, or Miss Philipps, so it would be best if the girls spent time with them instead of Georgina. Lady Lavinia seemed to be friendly with them, especially with Anne-Marie, and he'd seen them conversing during breakfast.

'I'm sure the girls are fine,' he said.

'They seem to be enjoying themselves. They are quite excited to share our First Christmas.'

His chest tightened at this reminder of why they were here. Frankly, after being exposed to Georgina's abundance of decorations, he'd grown mostly numb to the thought of Christmas.

'At least they will be able to celebrate with you, for once.' She grinned at him. 'And you'll be forced to sit down and celebrate with them on our First Christmas Day.'

Her tone was clearly meant to be light-hearted, but his mood still darkened—just as it did any time he was reminded of Christmas Day.

'Elliot, come here,' Ma had rasped. *'There is something I need you to do for me...'*

Pushing those thoughts away, he cleared his throat. 'We've been gone for far too long. We should return to the others before anyone finds—'

The sound of the doorknob turning made them both freeze.

Too late.

The hinges creaked loudly as the door began to open. Panic crossed Georgina's face, and Elliot knew he had to take action before they were discovered.

Without a single thought, he pulled her up, then

dragged her behind the first thing he saw that could conceal them—the thick brocade drapes covering one side of the room. The very same ones he had suspected Bellamy to be hiding behind. He quickly drew them aside and pressed her against the window, covering her with his body.

'Don't move…don't make a sound.'

He felt the nod of her head against his chest.

A feminine giggle came from the other side of the curtain.

'Shh…my love. Someone might hear us.'

'They are all in the parlour, Tommy. No one's going to hear.'

The female voice sounded like Lady Genevieve, and 'Tommy' could only be Thomas, the Duke of Waldemere.

'Now, kiss me,' Lady Genevieve urged.

'My pleasure…'

Elliot groaned inwardly as the unmistakable sounds of ardent kissing filtered through what he had now discovered were definitely *not* thick drapes.

'Oh, Tommy…there,' Lady Genevieve moaned. 'Touch me. There.'

Lady Georgina stiffened in his arms and their tiny hiding space suddenly shrank further. She attempted to move. But, fearing they would be discovered, he pressed against her to keep her still. Unfortunately, that meant all her luscious curves were now tucked against his body.

Damn it to hell.

'Genevieve, my love, please… I need you.' There was a rustling of skirts. 'Let me touch you…'

'Yes, it's been so long, Tommy. I— Oh, yes. That's it. Touch me. Your fingers…'

'Have you missed this?'

Lady Genevieve gasped.

'Or how about when I do this?'

'Oh! Oh! Yes, Tommy.'

Elliot quickly considered the ramifications of opening the curtains before Lady Genevieve and Waldemere progressed any further. On one hand, if they revealed themselves to the amorous couple now they wouldn't be subjected to these aural displays of affection. On the other, Georgina's reputation was still at stake, while Lady Genevieve's would be saved because Waldemere would surely marry her anyway if they were discovered.

He decided to remain, hoping 'Tommy's' fingers were skilful enough to quickly bring this torture to an end.

'Eeep…' Lady Georgina pressed her face against his chest to muffle herself.

'What was that?' Waldemere exclaimed.

'Bloody hell!' Genevieve cursed. 'Probably a mouse.'

'Or a squeaky hinge.' Waldemere sighed. 'I'm sorry, my love. Did you…?'

'No.' She sounded disappointed. 'You should return to the parlour and I'll go to my rooms. I think Mother and Father were fooled by my excuse that I was feeling ill, like Lord Bellamy, but if Hannah were to tell them I didn't go to bed right away...'

'Of course, my love. Come, let me help you right yourself.'

There was more rustling of clothing, followed by the sound of the door opening and then latching closed.

Elliot exhaled, the tension seeping out of his body. 'Are you all right?' He looked down to check on Georgina, but to his surprise she was staring right up at him, her copper-brown eyes luminous even in the scant moonlight from outside.

'Georgina, we should—'

He stopped as her hands slid up his chest, her palms resting on his shoulders. She took in a breath, making her breasts rise up and strain over her décolletage.

He couldn't.

He mustn't.

'Georgina, this isn't—'

'Elliot...' she breathed, and his name was like a reverent prayer on his lips.

She tilted her head to one side, angling it so that their lips would line up if he just lowered his mouth.

'We can't—'

'Please...'

Her unnamed request rang in his ears, and he had no choice but to grant her wish.

Just one quick kiss.

Leaning down, he let his mouth find hers as his hand cradled the back of her head. He told himself to be quick and pull away, but instead he increased the pressure of his mouth, moving it over hers until she pressed her body against his. Instantly his cock stiffened and he pinned her against the window, his hips brushing against her belly.

Her arms drew around his neck and she opened her mouth to him. His instinct was to invade her, but he held back, instead brushing his tongue inside her mouth, coaxing hers to join him in an erotic dance. Her tongue darted out hesitantly, but soon she was tasting him as eagerly as he was her.

She sighed against him, arching her body up as if they might possibly get closer. He broke the kiss so he could move down to her jaw and throat. Her pulse throbbed frantically when his mouth reached that sweet spot behind her ears, and she let out a moan when he licked at the delicate skin. His other hand, which had been resting against her waist, slid upwards to cup her breast through her clothes. He expected her to panic, or push him away, but instead she raked her fingers up the nape of his neck and gripped his hair.

He inhaled sharply, his hardened cock throbbing as she continued to undulate against him. Feeling bold, he caressed the tops of her breasts, then delved under her neckline.

She whimpered and whispered his name. He bent his head lower, raining kisses down her neck until his mouth was inches from his hand. Manoeuvring his fingers, he eased down the bodice of her gown, revealing one generous breast. He bit his lip to keep from groaning at the sight of the creamy globe topped with a delicate dusky-pink nipple which hardened at its contact with cool air.

She was so beautiful, so lushly feminine, and if he died now, having just tasted her, he would be happy. But thankfully he didn't expire on the spot, so he leaned down to take the nipple into his mouth.

'Elliot!' She clung to him, her fingers nearly ripping the hair from his nape. But he could only suckle her and lavish her nipple with his attention. She tasted so sweet…the skin of her breast so tender…

'Ah, there it is.'

They both stiffened, and Elliot pulled his mouth away from her breast.

'Thank goodness.' It was Lady Genevieve again. 'I thought I'd lost it.' She giggled. 'Next time, please be more careful, Tommy.'

'I'm sorry, my love,' the Duke said. 'I'm glad you have found your earring.'

'And I'm glad you saw that it was gone before we parted. If Papa found out…'

'Then maybe he'd let us marry before your sister does.'

'Patience, Tommy… I think the answer to our problem is already here. Lavinia may soon be wed.'

The mention of Lady Lavinia cooled Elliot's heated body, and he felt Georgina draw away from him.

'Come, let us go before anyone sees us.'

As soon as he heard the door close he let out the breath he'd been holding. 'Georgina, I'm so—'

'Do not apologise.' She turned away from him as

she adjusted her bodice. 'I... I practically begged you...' Her face turned scarlet. 'I don't... This isn't... I've never...'

'Was that your first kiss?'

'No.'

An unreasonable stab of jealousy cut into his chest. 'And who gave you the first?'

'Y-you. Under the mistletoe.'

Damn.

He was a bastard. A scoundrel. No better than Bellamy, whom he had accused of doing exactly what Elliot had now done to Georgina.

'If there's someone who should apologise, it is me.'

The air around them was much too stifling, so he drew back the curtains. The rush of cool air helped, but still his body hummed with lingering desire.

'I should not have allowed it to continue. We should forget it happened.'

'Forget?' She wrapped her arms around herself. 'Why?'

'Well, for one thing your brother would kill me.' Harwicke had warned him off that first day they'd met. 'And—'

'And you want to marry Lady Lavinia or Miss Philipps.'

And you don't want to marry me.

When he didn't answer, she continued. 'Both of them are good prospects. You have done well. I think they are keen on you. While I—' She bit her lip.

'While you what?'

'N-nothing. You should not let anything impede you in your pursuing them...seeing as they are exactly what you want. Proper English brides.'

He swallowed the growing lump in his throat. 'Yes.'

'And I, too, will get what I wish for.'

That damned building and her orphans. If he had known that number fifty-five Boyle Street would cause so much chaos in his life, he never would have bought it in the first place.

'Perhaps...perhaps you are right.' She still refused to look him in the eyes, and she stared out of the window into the cold winter night. 'We should forget this happened.'

'Agreed.' His entire chest felt as if it had been captured in a vice.

'You should leave first,' she said. 'And I will head up to my rooms. Trevor will think I'm having one of my spells, and assume I left without taking my leave.'

'A practical plan.'

He was barely two steps out of the music room when he wanted to go back to her...tell her that he did not want to forget what had just happened. And that he wanted to continue kissing her and perhaps more.

But she was right.

What he wanted was within his reach. He suspected that if he asked Lord Arundel or the Viscount for permission to court either of their daughters they would grant it to him, which would all but guarantee an engagement and then marriage. His ten-year plan would come to fruition.

Anything else—including Georgina—would simply take him off course, which he could not afford to happen.

So he would have to do whatever it took to forget that kiss, and eventually forget Georgina—hopefully before she made any further mark on his soul.

Georgina pressed her forehead against the glass of the windowpane, as if that would chill the heat that still lingered in her body. But despite the abrupt end to their passionate encounter, the fire it had ignited in her remained.

She'd been curious about kissing, of course, and perhaps a long time ago had even been interested in experiencing it for herself. She had read novels about it, and had heard other debutantes and recently married acquaintances whisper about their encounters with eager gentlemen and amorous husbands. But over the years, as she'd drawn away from society and resigned herself to spinsterhood, the interest had faded.

But now she could not stop thinking about it.

Or rather, *him*.

She blew out a breath. Elliot was right. They should forget it had ever happened. The words had hurt when he'd first uttered them—how could she forget such a wonderful thing? For once in her life she didn't feel like a stranger in her own skin. His touch had been like magic, making her soul sing and her toes curl. She wasn't Lady Georgina, spinster and on the shelf. She was just herself—Georgina.

And for once in her life she'd felt *wanted*.

Unfortunately, he had wants bigger than her—bigger than him, even. He wanted a wife who would be a patroness and advocate for his sisters, providing guidance and counsel—not someone who broke out in hives at the mere thought of going to a ball, or who would panic in the crush of a busy ballroom. Under her care, Anne-Marie and Lily would never flourish or see success during their Seasons.

She wasn't sure how long she had stood there, but knew she had to leave soon. So she quietly crept out of the music room and back to her own chambers.

Once her maid had arrived, and she'd finished undressing, she slipped under the covers and closed her eyes. Tomorrow she would have to face them all again, which would be a challenge, but she would find a way to do it. She would forget about what had happened and pretend everything was as it had been before that kiss. Thankfully tomorrow was First Christmas Eve. There would be many activities to keep her occupied, and she would be surrounded by people for the entire day, all the way until midnight.

She groaned aloud and pulled the covers over her head.

These last two days of constant activity and socialising had taken their toll on her. But perhaps she'd only have to endure it for another two days. By the time they were all headed back to London, Elliot might very well be on his way to proposing to either

Lady Lavinia or Miss Philipps, and she would save St Agnes's.

And that, she reminded herself, was what really mattered. The real reason she had concocted this mad plan to find Mr Elliot Smith a bride in the first place.

Chapter Nine

16th December,
First Christmas Eve

The following day, Georgina crept into the breakfast room early, hoping no one would be around. Usually on First Christmas Eve she would be the first to wake, as she loved walking around the house in those quiet hours by herself, admiring all the decorations. This was also the day she and Trevor, as per their household tradition, shared gifts with all the staff, the tenants and children from the village. It was the one time a year she managed to tolerate being around people and speaking with them without having one of her spells in the middle of the day.

With their guests around, though, she and Trevor had decided to let them do as they pleased during the day, while they continued with their tradition. Tonight, however, there would be more games and amusements, and the girls of course would be allowed to join them and open their presents at midnight. That meant she would at least have some peace and quiet to herself this morning.

Or at least that was what she thought until she entered the dining room.

'I can't believe you're doing this again,' Anne-Marie said, her voice shaking with anger. 'You promised we could stay until the eighteenth.'

'I *said* we could come to Northamptonshire,' Elliot retorted. 'I never gave you a date when we must return.'

'It's not fair,' Lily whinged. 'We will miss First Christmas Day if we leave in the morning.'

Georgina gasped. 'Wait…you're leaving in the morning?'

Three sets of eyes turned towards her. A small thrill raced up the back of her knees when Elliot's jade-green eyes landed on her, though he quickly averted them.

'Good morning,' Elliot murmured. 'I didn't realise you would be up so early.'

She strode into the room, hands on her hips. 'Did I hear that correctly? Do you truly mean to leave on the morrow?'

'That's what he said,' Lily cried, flinging herself at Georgina and burying her face in her skirts.

She smoothed a hand down the girl's back. 'But why?'

'I have business to attend to—an emergency that requires my presence,' he said, though he did not meet her gaze. 'Sometimes these things happen and I cannot do anything about them.'

She couldn't believe he would leave so suddenly. Was he doing this because of what had happened between them last night? Was being in her presence now so abhorrent that he could not stand being in the same house as her?

Lily moaned. 'But what about First Christmas...?'

'What about it?' Elliot shrugged. 'You still get to open your gifts tonight at midnight. And may I remind you that I bought both of you a second set of presents to open here.'

Anne-Marie let out a frustrated sound. 'Who cares about presents? I hate you so much!' With that she stomped off, Lily following her.

Elliot's jaw ticked and his hands curled into fists at his sides, but he remained silent as a rock.

'You can't mean to leave right away,' she said, once they were alone.

'We aren't. We are leaving in the morning. They can still enjoy whatever you have planned for today. Now, if you'll excuse me, my lady, I must inform my staff of our change of plans.'

Georgina's heart sank as she watched him leave without another word, without looking her in the eyes.

'My lady', he had called her.

Not Georgina, as he had done last night.

How could he be so cruel as to just leave and take the girls away? And besides, what about Lady Lavinia and Miss Philipps? How could he possibly leave now that he had spent all this time and effort in getting acquainted with them. It would all be for naught and he would end up without a wife.

Unless, of course, he already had an understanding with one of them...

She sank down on the nearest chair, her knees weakening. Her stomach was tied into knots and her chest clenched up tight. Pressing her palm against her chest, she attempted to ease the ache, but to no avail.

Perhaps he didn't need to stay any longer. Perhaps he had what he wanted and now he could go back to London and to his business, doing whatever it was he did—making money, turning everything he touched into gold, maybe finding more properties with orphans he could evict.

Glaring back at the doorway, she decided she would no longer care about what Mr Elliot Smith did. But she *did* care for those poor girls, whose lives were upturned with his every whim.

Rising to her feet, she set her shoulders with a determined shrug and marched up to their rooms.

'Anne-Marie? Lily?' she said as she knocked on their door. 'It's Lady Georgina. May I come in?'

'Yes,' came Lily's answer.

'Hello, girls.' She closed the door behind her. 'I'm so sorry you have to leave so soon.'

Anne-Marie pursed her lips and crossed her arms over her chest. 'I knew he would do something like this. I was finally enjoying myself and now he has to ruin everything.' She plopped herself on the bed. 'I hate him so much.'

'Must we go?' Lily asked. 'Can't we stay here and Elliot can leave for London by himself? We can ride back with you.'

'I wish that were possible, poppet.' She stroked her hair, tucking a stray curl behind her ear. 'But Elliot is your guardian and so you must stay with him.'

'Lady Lavinia said she would take me into the village for shopping tomorrow,' Anne-Marie said.

Georgina's ears pricked up. 'Oh? What else did Lady Lavinia say?'

'That there's a lovely little shop that sells the most precious little trinkets, like buttons and ribbons and scarves.' She pouted. 'And we were to have tea in one of the tea shops.'

'That does sound fun.'

'It does—did. Lady Lavinia is the only person who treats me like I am an adult.' Anne-Marie harrumphed. 'She came to see me yesterday, you know, while you were all in the sitting room. We had a lovely conversation in the library.'

Georgina's mouth went dry, but she managed to croak out, 'About…?'

'Oh, you know…the usual. Gossip…our favourite activities. And she asked about Elliot too.'

'I see.'

Perhaps Lady Lavinia wanted to know more about her potential suitor—which was clever, she had to admit.

'What did you tell her?'

'The truth,' Anne-Marie said. 'That Elliot is very rich and devoted to his business and nothing else. You are right, Lady Georgina. He truly is a Scrooge.'

'He hates Christmas. He's truly never celebrated it with us.'

'Never?'

'Never,' Lily said. 'I think… I think it makes him sad.'

'Sad? Why do you say that?' asked Georgina.

'I don't know. But whenever he leaves for his office on Christmas Day I see his face and he looks sad.'

Why would Elliot—or anyone—be sad on Christmas Day?

'Who cares?' Anne-Marie reclined dramatically on the bed. 'I wish we could stay here. And never leave.'

'Me too,' Lily added, lying down beside her sister.

Georgina couldn't help but feel sorry for the girls. And, while there was nothing more she could learn about Lady Lavinia and Elliot, perhaps it would be best if she used the girls' remaining time here to cheer them up.

'Girls, I'm so sorry you must leave tomorrow, but we still have today.' Placing her hands on her hips, she hovered over them. 'Come, now, get up.'

Lily raised her head. 'Why? Where are we going?'

'Well, do you know what the best part of Christmas is?'

'Christmas pudding?' the little girl answered.

Georgina chuckled. 'No, no.' Taking their hands,

she pulled them upright. 'Sharing and giving gifts, of course.'

'Giving gifts?' Lily said. 'But we're too little to give gifts. We receive them.'

'Not today—and not when you're with me,' she stated. 'Let's go.'

She led the two girls downstairs to the parlour, where Trevor and Miss Warren were already waiting for her.

'There you are, Georgie,' said her brother. 'I was beginning to think you'd forgotten.'

'Never.' She brought Anne-Marie and Lily forward. 'And I have brought some helpers.'

'Hello, girls,' Trevor greeted them. 'Are you ready to assist us?'

'With what?' Lily asked.

Trevor gestured to the pile of wrapped gifts behind him. 'With distributing gifts to our staff. It's a First Christmas Eve tradition at Foxbury Hill.'

'You give them all presents?' Anne-Marie asked.

'Of course.'

Lily cocked her head to one side. 'Why?'

'It's tradition. Our mother and father used to do this with us when we were children. And besides, everyone deserves presents,' Trevor said. 'Now, they will be here any minute, so we must be ready. Are you both willing to help?'

The two girls looked at each other and said in unison, 'Yes.'

Soon, as Trevor had said, the servants arrived in

the parlour. There were refreshments for them, like hot apple cider, tea and biscuits, that the kitchen had prepared. Since Trevor and Georgina spent the real Christmas Day in London, this had become the time to give their gifts to their staff at Foxbury Hill. As they came in, Trevor or Georgina would hand a wrapped gift to either Lily or Anne-Marie and ask them to give it to the recipient, then offer them treats. As Foxbury Hill had many servants, it took the entire morning to distribute the pile of gifts.

'That was fun,' Lily said. 'I feel like St Nicholas.'

'Who?' Miss Warren asked.

'It's from a poem,' Anne-Marie said. '*A Visit from St Nicholas*. Our butler back in New York read it to us one Christmas.'

'And who, pray tell, is this St Nicholas?' Trevor enquired.

'He's the man who gives all the boys and girls presents at Christmas,' Lily explained. 'He rides on a sleigh pulled by reindeer.'

'What?' Trevor exclaimed. 'Reindeer?'

'Uh-huh.' Lily's head bobbed up and down. 'Flying reindeer.'

'Why must they fly?'

'So they can land the sleigh on roofs and get into people's houses down their chimney,' Lily said matter-of-factly.

'It's a silly poem,' Anne-Marie said rolling her eyes. 'It's just about some guy who gives gifts to children.'

'Intriguing,' Georgina said. 'Well, my dear Saints Nicholas, I'm afraid your job isn't done yet.'

'It's not?' Lily glanced around. 'But all the presents are gone.'

'The presents for the servants *here*,' she clarified. 'But now we must go to see the tenants and take gifts to them, as well as the children in the village.'

'We are going to the village?' Anne-Marie's eyes gleamed.

'Yes,' Trevor said. 'Now, I'm afraid I don't have a sleigh, or flying reindeer, but I hope a horse and carriage will do.'

Both girls squealed in excitement.

And so they took Anne-Marie and Lily with them around the estate to deliver hampers of food and treats to the tenants. Afterwards, they went into the village to distribute the biscuits and sweetmeats Mrs Laramie had made especially for the children who lived there. As a reward for being their helpers, Trevor took the girls into the trinket shop and purchased a small gift for each of them, then they had luncheon at the tea shop before heading back to Foxbury Hill.

While Georgina was drained from all the day's interactions, as she always was, she had still enjoyed herself. How she'd loved handing out presents and seeing people's faces light up with joy. Truly, it was enough to make her forget her troubles—at least until the carriage passed through the gates of the driveway going up to the main house.

'Is that Elliot?' Trevor pointed out of the window. 'And Lady Lavinia?'

Georgina peeped out to look where his finger directed her gaze, and her heart sank. It was indeed Elliot and Lady Lavinia, out together for a walk in the front gardens, her arm tucked into his.

Trevor's gaze flickered over to the girls, who sat across from them with Miss Warren, dozing on each other's shoulders.

'It seems as if you've accomplished what you set out to do,' he told Georgina. 'Which I thought was an impossible task.'

'He's not engaged yet.'

And she wasn't quite sure how she felt about that statement.

He covered her hand with his. 'You must give yourself more credit, Georgie. And perhaps we must plan a different Christmas celebration this year...at St Agnes's?'

A small flicker of happiness lit up in her chest. 'I would like that.'

The carriage deposited them at the front door and Georgina woke the girls, instructing them to nap for the rest of the afternoon, because after all tonight they would be staying up late to join in the festivities.

The two of them of course shrieked in excitement and raced up to their rooms.

Later that evening, after she herself had taken a long, refreshing nap, Georgina prepared for the night's activities. After taking a bath, she'd had her maid assist her in styling her hair into loose waves around her head, and had changed into a new red and pink satin and velvet gown.

When the modiste had suggested it, Georgina had at first thought the colours much too bold, but now she realised they suited her quite well. The scooped neckline showed off a modest amount of skin, and the pink lace that went around the edges and tapered down to a V at the waist added a delicate touch. The underskirt was a light pink satin that draped around the front, while the overskirt was a rich red velvet.

She had, however, asked the modiste to make one design change. Instead of silk roses for the trimming on the shoulders, she had asked for holly leaves and berries, to add a more festive feel. There was also a matching holly hairpin, which her maid had tucked just behind her ear.

Satisfied with her attire, she thanked her maid and joined the others in the drawing room for drinks before dinner. Almost everyone was there, though Miss Warren had decided not to join in tonight's festivities. She was weary from their day in the village, so had stayed in her rooms.

As soon as Georgina entered, her eyes were immediately drawn to Elliot. How could they not be? His large, imposing presence overpowered everyone else in a room. Tonight, he was chatting with Lady Lavinia, Lady Arundel and Anne-Marie as they sipped on hot apple cider. Her traitorous little heart stuttered at seeing him looking so handsome in his finery.

'Lady Georgina!' Lily greeted her as she seemingly popped up from nowhere. 'You look so pretty.'

'And you look adorable, poppet.'

Lily was dressed in a green satin dress and her hair was tied with matching bows.

'I'm so glad you invited us.' She gestured around them. 'I've never had a Christmas Eve with so many people…at least people who aren't servants.'

Once again her heart went out to Lily. What a dreary existence it must be, never to have had a festive Christmas. Why would Elliot be so cruel as to leave them alone on Christmas Day? Was he truly so obsessed with making money that he could not even stop working over Christmas?

'Lady Georgina, how ravishing you look,' Lord Bellamy said as he sidled up to her.

'Thank you, Lord Bellamy. I am glad to see you up and about. How are you feeling?'

'Healthy as a horse,' he said. 'I think I overindulged myself last night, but it was nothing a good night's sleep couldn't cure.'

'I'm glad to hear that.'

'There you are,' Trevor said as he came up to them. 'Seems like everyone is here. Shall we begin?'

She nodded in agreement and took his arm. Her brother signalled to Dawson, who announced that dinner was ready, and everyone made their way to the dining room.

Though the main Christmas meal of roast turkey would be served for tomorrow's dinner, Mrs Laramie

had prepared a delicious feast of roast beef and pota-
toes, fried sole, stuffing, herbed parsnips and slices
of decadent cake.

Georgina was glad that the seating was informal,
and sat down next to Lily, who was delighted to be
at the dinner table. Anne-Marie, on the other hand,
opted to sit near the adults.

'What's this?' Lily asked, waving the brightly
wrapped package on her empty plate.

'It's a Christmas cracker,' Georgina explained.
'Here.' She picked hers up and opened it. 'See? There
are treats inside.'

Her eyes grew wide and she took her own cracker
and opened it. 'I love Christmas so much.'

Georgina chuckled. 'Me too.'

After dinner, they all went to the parlour, where
more food, drink and amusements were set up. A few
of the guests opted to play cards, including Elliot, who
partnered Lady Lavinia for a game of whist.

Georgina did her best to steer clear of them, opt-
ing to play snapdragon with Lily and Lady Hannah at
the other end of the parlour. Once in a while, though,
she would inadvertently glance towards the card table
and catch Elliot smiling at Lady Lavinia, or see her
laughing and patting his arm.

'Ow!' She withdrew her hand from the fiery bowl
of raisins. She had been so distracted by Elliot and
Lady Lavinia that she had not seen the flame flicker
towards her fingers.

'You lose!' Lily laughed. 'Lady Georgina, you must be more careful.'

She sucked her finger into her mouth, trying to soothe the pain. As she glanced back towards the card table her gaze collided with jade-green eyes. Elliot was staring at her, with the most discomfiting expression on his face. For some reason it made heat crawl up into her cheeks, and she quickly turned away.

After more games, and more food and drink, it was nearly midnight and time for presents. Georgina had prepared small gifts for all the guests, and she and Trevor distributed them.

'I'm afraid I didn't get you anything, Lady Georgina,' Bellamy confessed as she handed him the present that had been intended for Mr Galwick. 'Your brother's invitation came at short notice.'

'Do not worry, my lord, I understand. Besides, it would not be proper for you to give me a gift, even if it is Christmas.'

'I suppose not... But there is still time, as this is not really Christmas, is it?'

It was as real as actual Christmas to her, but she kept those thoughts to herself.

'Perhaps, with your permission, we could have a conversation in the sitting room tomorrow?' Bellamy went on. 'With your chaperone present.'

'Miss Warren? Why would you need her there?'

He frowned. 'Because when gentlemen call upon ladies they must have chaperones present?'

'Call—?' She clamped her mouth tightly, lest her jaw fall to the floor.

'Lady Georgina,' he began, his expression softening, 'how fortuitous that His Grace invited me here.'

The most curious desire to flee sprang into Georgina's mind. 'Er…it was because Mr Galwick broke his leg in a riding accident…'

'Oh, no! I mean, poor chap.' He clicked his tongue. 'But since we met at the opera I've been meaning to ask you if—'

'Georgina!' Lily collided into her legs, nearly knocking her aside.

'Oomph!' She managed to steady herself. 'What is it, Lily?'

'You got me a present.' She pointed to the large box by the Christmas tree.

'I did, poppet.'

'What is it?'

'Why don't we find out?' she asked, taking her hand. 'Please excuse us, Lord Bellamy.'

Relief washed over her as she allowed Lily to drag her towards the tree. Did Bellamy truly want to call on her? As if he was—she swallowed audibly—*courting* her? She could not believe it. She hardly knew him. They'd never even got the chance to dance at the ball. Why would he seek her out?

'It's a doll!' Lily exclaimed as she ripped the package open. 'Thank you, Lady Georgina.'

'You're very welcome.'

Thankfully she had enough time before they left

London to do some shopping, so she'd been able to get presents for the girls. Aside from the doll for Lily, she'd bought Anne-Marie a gold necklace. She'd also bought Elliot a jade tie pin, though she had labelled the gift as being from Trevor, as she had with all the men's gifts, while she labelled the women's with her own name. Glancing over at him, she saw him holding the small gift box in his hand, but he did not open it.

In all the excitement over the presents, Bellamy did not manage to approach her again. Just as she was sneaking off to go to her room she glanced back towards Elliot, who was walking towards Lady Lavinia with two cups of tea in his hands.

'Look, you're standing under the mistletoe!' Lady Arundel exclaimed when Elliot reached her daughter's side.

Georgina's stomach was tied into knots as that stabbing ache in her chest returned. Turning away, she quickly fled from the parlour. By the time she reached her rooms her breath was coming in short, shallow pants, and the tightening in her chest was refusing to ease.

Ringing the bell for her maid, she ripped the holly hairpin from behind her ear and threw off her gloves. She tried not to think about Elliot and Lady Lavinia kissing under the mistletoe, but it was of no use. Her mind conjured up the image, torturing her with it. What a beautiful couple they made…him so handsome and her so lovely.

'Lady Georgina, are you ready for bed?' her maid asked.

She hummed and nodded wordlessly, and the maid helped her undress and put on her nightrail. Perhaps it was a good thing he was leaving in the morning. She wouldn't have to think about him again…maybe never even see him again.

17th December

Sleep escaped Georgina. She tossed and turned for a good hour before her lids became heavy. Unfortunately, just as she was at the edge of sleep, a noise in the distance—the neighing of a horse and the rumble of carriage wheels—shook her awake. She cursed at the sound, then closed her eyes, trying to catch the drowsiness once more, and eventually she began to drift off…

'Lady Georgina?'

The small voice followed by the creaking of her bedroom door made her eyes open.

'What—?'

She blinked away the blurriness from her vision. Only a tiny stub was left of her candle, but it was enough for her to see the small head with wild overgrown curls peeping in through the door.

'Lily? Is that you?'

The head nodded.

'What's wrong, poppet?' She waved her over. 'Can't you sleep?'

The girl rushed over and stood by her bed.

'Did you have a nightmare?'

Bright red curls shook as she replied in the negative. 'No...'

'What's the matter, then?'

Her light green eyes darted left and right, as if she was afraid someone was listening to them. 'It's Anne-Marie.'

'Is she feeling sick? Did she have a bad dream?' When Lily didn't answer, Georgina sat up, and urged her to climb into bed to sit on her lap. 'Tell me, poppet. Please. You won't get into trouble, I promise.'

'I promised I wouldn't tell Elliot, but...' Lily's lower lip trembled. 'She's gone. Anne-Marie.'

'Gone?' Georgina's voice rose, but when she saw Lily's eyes widen she calmed herself before saying, 'Tell me what happened.'

'We were already in bed, and I was almost asleep. Then Anne-Marie woke me.' Her eyes filled with tears. 'She—she said she loved me, but she had to leave. She said that once she was away from Elliot she would write to me and find a way for us to be together again.'

'Where was she going?'

'Scotland, she said. She was going with a friend.'

Scotland?

And who was this friend?

Panic began to set in, but Georgina knew she could not go into hysterics now. 'What else did she say?'

'I—I...' Fat tears rolled down Lily's cheeks. 'I don't know...'

'Shh…shh, it's all right, poppet.' She hugged Lily close and smoothed a hand down her back. 'Have you told anyone else? One of your servants?'

Lily hiccupped and shook her head. 'Everyone else is still downstairs in the parlour. What are we going to do?'

Taking a deep breath, Georgina gathered her thoughts. There was only one thing to do.

'I will tell Elliot. And don't you worry. He will bring her back.'

'Really?'

'Yes.'

If there was anyone who could do it, it was him. Still, time was of the essence…

'Stay here, poppet, and try to sleep. Anne-Marie will be back before you know it.'

After tucking her under the covers, Georgina rushed to her closet and pulled out one of her looser day gowns. She quickly removed her nightrail and put it on, though she didn't bother with her corset and petticoats. The dress pinched and pulled in the most uncomfortable places without her undergarments, but it would have to do for now. She put on her slippers, then grabbed a cloak before leaving her room, wrapping it around herself as she ran down the corridor.

The party was likely to go on until morning, so she would ask one of the footmen to discreetly ask Elliot to come out. As she reached the staircase she was so busy piecing together in her mind what she would say to him that she did not notice the figure heading up the stairs—and promptly bumped into it.

'Oh!' She stumbled, but strong hands caught her by the waist and she found herself pressed up against a long, hard body.

'Georgina?'

Elliot's warm baritone caressed her skin like velvet.

'Elliot…' she said breathlessly as the scent of his cologne tickled her nose.

'What are you doing—and why in God's name are you dressed like that?'

The arm around her waist tightened, and she didn't know if that was the reason she couldn't breathe, or if it was because she was so close to him.

'Are you going on a midnight tryst?' he snarled. 'With Bellamy?'

She blinked, the spell breaking. 'I beg your pardon?' Placing her hands on his chest, she pushed as hard as she could, but his grip was like steel. 'Elliot, let go of me!'

'Not until you tell me where you're going.'

'I was coming to find *you*!'

His face slackened, as did his arm. 'What?'

'Anne-Marie's gone,' she blurted out. 'She's left.'

The dark expression returned to his face. 'Explain.'

She told him what had happened, and what Lily had said.

'Scotland? Why in God's name would she be going to Scotland? If she wanted to book a passage back to America, she should have gone back to London.'

Just as she had suspected, he had no idea what going to Scotland meant. She had to tell him, and there was no delicate and quick way to do it.

'Elliot, here in England, when someone goes to Scotland in the middle of the night, it usually means they are headed to Gretna Green.'

'And? Am I supposed to know where that is?'

'Gretna Green is a place where couples can have a blacksmith's wedding—a hasty wedding.'

'Hasty wedding?'

'Yes. To escape parents and guardians who might be against the marriage.'

The way his expression shifted from confusion to bewilderment and finally to understanding would have been comical, had it not been for the grave situation at hand.

'Goddammit.' He raked his fingers through his hair. 'I don't even know…how…? Who?'

'I don't know either, Elliot, but you must go after her.'

'Damned right I'll go after her,' he muttered. 'Where are the stables?'

She grabbed his arm. 'Come. I will—'

'I am not taking you with me,' he thundered. 'Just tell me where—'

'It's faster this way, and you won't get lost,' she said. 'Now, let's hurry. You may still be able to catch them. I don't think they left more than half an hour ago.'

If her suspicions were correct, the noise of a horse

and carriage that had jolted her awake had been Anne-Marie and her 'friend' leaving.

They made their way out of the house through the entrance to the gardens and set off for the stables. Georgina shivered and drew her cloak around her, thankful she'd thought to bring it.

When they reached the stables, Elliot hurried to the first stall and retrieved the saddle. 'Now, which way is Scotland?'

Georgina slapped her hand on her forehead. 'Of course. You don't know which way to go.'

'Do I look like I know where Scotland is? But I will figure it out. It's north, right?'

'I was merely making a statement.' She took a deep breath. 'I can show you the way. The fastest road going north leads to Derbyshire, where my grandfather's estate is located. I visit him every year.'

She didn't want Anne-Marie to feel alone once they caught up with her. While she knew Elliot would never hurt his sister, Anne-Marie was young, and likely frightened. Georgina wanted to be there to soothe her.

'No.' He whirled around. 'You cannot come with me.'

'Elliot, be reasonable. With each passing second they are getting farther and farther away. And if you get lost, you'll never find them.'

'I won't get lost because you will tell me which way to go.'

She crossed her arms over her chest. 'I won't unless I am with you. If we leave right this moment, we may be able to catch up with them and be back before sunrise.'

He muttered a curse under his breath that she heard clearly.

'Well?' she asked.

'One horse cannot take both of us—three of us when we retrieve my sister—and you are not dressed to ride side-saddle.'

'I wasn't suggesting we ride the horses. Now, take this horse's reins and come with me.' She led him to where the carriages were kept. 'We can use the phaeton.' She nodded to the small open carriage at the end of the row. 'It's smaller and lighter. We'll be able to catch up with them in this, and although it will be a tight fit, we will have room for all three of us when we return.'

He blew out a breath, but said nothing as he began to secure the horse to the phaeton. Once he'd finished, he helped her onto the carriage and sat down beside her, reins in hand. With a click of his tongue and a soft flick of the reins the horse pulled them out of the carriage house and down the path leading towards the main road.

'Which way?' he asked.

'Left,' she said. 'Then keep going until the fork.'

Elliot snapped the reins and the horse broke into a gallop. Georgina, caught unawares, let out a shout and grabbed for the nearest thing she could—his arm.

She sent him a dirty look. 'You did that on purpose.'

He didn't say anything, just snorted.

Settling back into the seat, she adjusted her cloak and pulled the hood tight around her head. The brisk pace of the phaeton blew the chilly air straight at them and she shivered again.

When they reached the fork, he asked her which way to go.

'Keep to this road for about another ten miles, and then I'll tell you,' she said, which earned her another grumble.

Oh, she wasn't about to reveal everything to him right away—lest he suddenly decide to turn around and take her back to Foxbury Hill.

Elliot slowed their pace, perhaps to conserve the horse's energy. 'How did you know Anne-Marie had run away?'

'Lily came to me, poor thing.' She told him all that had happened, including how she'd heard the horses and carriage.

His eyebrows slashed downwards. 'Why would she come to you and not me?'

'I don't know. I think perhaps Anne-Marie made her promise not to tell you, so she came to me instead. Or perhaps she was scared of you.'

'Preposterous. I would never hurt either of them.'

'I know that…but she's young.' The air was now positively freezing, despite their slower pace, and she wrapped her cloak tighter around her. 'I'm just glad I was able to find you in time. I was going to send a footman to fetch you…'

'I was the last to head upstairs. Everyone had gone to bed, thank goodness.'

'Even Lady Lavinia?'

That had come out before she'd been able to stop herself. Had he kissed her under the mistletoe? Had he liked it?

'Yes, she went to bed not much later than you, actually.' He stiffened. 'Thank you for coming to find me right away. And…apologies for what I insinuated about you and Bellamy.'

She had forgotten about that, with all the worry over Anne-Marie. 'I'm sure it was a surprise, seeing me in my cloak. But why would you even think I was going off on some tryst?'

It was bizarre and preposterous.

Elliot remained silent, his eyes gazing straight ahead at the road.

'It's not as if we are courting.'

'Not *yet*, you mean.'

Her head swivelled towards him. 'How did you…? Did he…?'

'I overheard him talking to your brother before he went upstairs.' A muscle ticked in his jaw. 'He said you have agreed to take his call in the morning.'

She didn't recall saying yes, but she hadn't said no, either.

'Would you accept his proposal?'

'He hasn't even asked to court me. It's just a call.'

'But that's where it begins, right?'

'I suppose…'

'Well? Would you marry him?'

'I don't know,' she said.

'Why not?'

'I just—' She gasped. 'Elliot!' She pointed a finger upwards. 'Look!'

'What in the world—?'

A single fat snowflake fluttered down, landing on Elliot's hand. A second one followed it, and then a third, and soon more descended from the dark sky.

'Does it usually snow at this time of the year?'

'Sometimes,' she says. 'We've had a few snowy First Christmases.'

He cursed again. 'We can't go back now.'

'I know. But this might slow them down too,' she reminded him.

With a determined grunt he said, 'Hold on tight, Georgina.'

As soon as she'd grabbed onto his arm he snapped the reins and the horse picked up its pace.

The snow continued to fall at alarming speeds, coming straight at them at an almost horizontal angle. Georgina shielded her face by burying it against Elliot's arm. Despite the protection of her cloak, she was still freezing, and she could only imagine how he was feeling.

His body shivered, giving her an answer.

Heavens, he must be miserable.

Without a second thought she slipped her arms around him, pressing her body against his to share her heat.

He stiffened. 'Georgina, this isn't—'

'Shh…it's all right. No one is around to see us, and you're shivering so hard I can hear your teeth rattle.' She moved her cloak aside, so she could wrap it around him and protect him from the snow. 'See? This is much better.'

She settled against him, the spicy scent of his cologne and the feel of his torso against her sending the most deliciously warm tingles straight down to her belly.

He answered only with a grunt.

Her thoughts went back to their encounter in the music room. She'd been trying not to remember it, as it only left her with a lingering heat in her body she could never seem to get rid of. In her decision to remain a spinster she had never considered the fact that she would never know what it was like to lie with a man. It had never seemed important. But now that she'd had a taste of it, it was difficult to ignore. It had barely been two days since that night, and she could not forget it.

What would it be like to be with a man?

No, not just any man. Elliot.

His shoulders—no, his entire body, seemed so much larger this close to hers. How she wanted to slip her hands under his coat and his shirt, to feel his naked skin. The very thought of it warmed her cheeks and sent heat pooling in her belly, enough to ward off some of the chill.

Heavens, she needed to stop her thoughts now, before she did something foolish. She moved her torso away from him, though she kept her arms wrapped around his middle.

The snow did not relent, and the air was now bitingly cold. Her cloak was soaking wet and could no longer protect them. They had been driving for about half an hour in the blizzard when Elliot slowed down.

'The horse is tiring and there is still no sign of any other carriage on the road.'

'Wait!' She squinted her eyes. 'I think I see something.'

'Is it their carriage?'

'No…' But there was a very faint light up the road. 'If I recall, that should be a coaching inn. The Steed and the Sword. Let's stop and catch our breath… maybe they'll have a fresh horse for us.'

Elliot snapped the reins once again and pushed the horse towards the inn.

'We need a new horse,' he barked at the sleepy stableboy who greeted them when they arrived.

'Sorry, sir.' The boy scratched at his head. 'We ain't got no more 'orses.'

'What do you mean? This is a coaching inn. You're supposed to have them ready.'

'Been busy, we 'ave,' the boy retorted. 'An' with this snow comin' down we probably don' expect any more until mornin'.'

'Oh, dear.' Georgina wrung her hands together. 'What are we to do, then?'

'Better go inside the tavern,' the boy suggested.

'Let yer horse 'bate for an hour or two and ye can be on yer way.'

She looked at him. 'Elliot…?'

The expression on his face was inscrutable. 'We don't have much of a choice. I'll not kill the poor creature.' He handed the reins over to the boy. 'Come, perhaps we can have something warm to drink inside.'

Chapter Ten

As soon as they'd approached the tavern Elliot placed his arm around Georgina and held her close. 'Do not leave my side and do not speak.'

She nodded.

He breathed an inner sigh of relief. Finally she had found some sense in her head to obey him. But then again, from the look of the tavern, he wasn't surprised.

The stench of ale, boiled cabbage and unwashed bodies assaulted Elliot's nose as they entered. It was nearly empty, save for a few men scattered here and there, musing over their pints of ale or conversing loudly. However, all manner of activity ceased the moment he and Georgina appeared, and all eyes went to them. The men grinned and jeered as they passed by.

Elliot would bet all the occupants here would not be able to fill a whole head of teeth between them.

Hurrying her along, he sat them down in a far corner, next to the fire. 'Do you have anything to warm us up?' he asked the barmaid who approached them.

'This ain't a tea shop, love,' she sneered, glancing over at Georgina. 'We got ale.'

'Two pints,' he said, then waved her away. 'Are you all right, Georgina?'

'J-Just cold,' she said. 'But I think I can feel my toes now.'

He smiled, then eased the cloak off her shoulders. 'It's warm in here, and the ale should help.' He shrugged off his own coat, which was now soaked through, and placed it on the empty chair next to him.

The barmaid came back with their pints, and he thanked her as he gave her a few coins. 'Have a sip,' he told Georgina.

She wrinkled her nose at the drink, but took a sip anyway. 'That is vile.' Her face scrunched up and she pushed the pint away. 'I think I'll let the fire warm me up.'

He, too, took a sip. 'I agree with your assessment.' He sighed. 'This is all my fault.'

'It's not,' she said.

'Yes, it is.' Remorse coursed through him, followed by fear. 'I just want to know that she's all right and not hurt.'

'Me too,' Georgina said. 'But this isn't your fault.'

'Anne-Marie has expressed her unhappiness in so many ways and yet I have ignored it. She hates me.'

'She does not.'

'She has said it several times now. I'm quite certain she does.'

'She does not mean it,' she assured him, taking his hand and pressing lightly.

'I just want what's best for them. So they…' He couldn't bring himself to say it aloud. 'I want them to have something better than I had.'

Could Anne-Marie not see that? He was doing all this so they would never know what it was like to live in a home with dirty floors or go to bed hungry. He'd moved them all the way here to give them the best chance in life?

Silence hung between him and Georgina, and he could not bring himself to look at her, for fear that he might drown in her copper-brown eyes. Instead, he allowed himself to revel in the warmth of her soft palm.

''Scuse me, sir.' A burly man with a scruffy beard approached them. 'My stable hand Willy says ye're sittin' down for a rest before continuin' yer journey?'

Alarm bells rang in Elliot's head. 'And who are you?'

'Beggin' yer pardon, sir, I'm the owner of this establishment. Joseph Brown, at yer service.'

'And why are you enquiring about our business, Mr Brown?'

'Well, sir.' He nodded towards the window. 'That snow's comin' down hard and not lettin' up. From my experience, I don't think it'll stop until mornin'.'

Elliot cursed silently. 'I assume you didn't come here just to tell me your assessment of the weather?'

'Well, sir. You and your…' he glanced at Georgina '…wife seem tired. Why don't ye take a room upstairs?

I run a clean establishment 'ere, and our linens 'ave just been laundered. A couple o' travellers took two rooms right before ye came in. I got one left. And if ye don't take it, I'm sure the next person who comes through that door will.'

Elliot contemplated the man's words. While he admired the man's business acumen in offering them a room, sharing a room—and a bed—with Georgina was the last thing he should be doing. Her embrace in the phaeton had nearly undone him. He would have driven off the road had he been a lesser man. Being alone in a bed with her would be pure torture.

On the other hand, the weariness on Georgina's face was evident, no matter how much she tried to hide it, and her dress was damp and no closer to drying. She might catch a cold.

'Sweetheart?' he said to his 'wife'. 'Would you like to lie down and rest for a while?'

She shook her head. 'We cannot. We need to catch up with—' Her eyes darted towards the innkeeper and she clamped them shut. 'There's no time to rest. We must hurry to our…next destination.'

'Ye won't be travellin' far in this weather,' said the innkeeper. 'Next coaching inn's about fifty miles. Besides, yer little phaeton, fast at it might be, will never hold up in those winds.'

'He's right, sweetheart.' His mind made up, Elliot said, 'Prepare the room, Mr Brown. And make sure there is a warm fire before we head upstairs.'

'Aye, sir.' He leaned forward. 'I notice ye have no

luggage… I can have me girl lend yer *wife* a nightrail. For an extra fee, of course.'

Elliot did not miss the meaning in his words. 'And I suppose this "extra fee" includes your silence?'

'Aye.' The innkeeper grinned at him, showing three missing teeth. 'I am but yer discreet servant.'

'All right. Just add it to my bill.'

'Elliot, we can't stay here,' Georgina said as soon as they were alone. 'What about Anne-Marie?'

'I know. But we can't leave either. I only hope this storm has slowed her down too.' He didn't want to think of his sister in some coaching inn like this. 'We will set off as soon as it stops.'

A few minutes later Joseph Brown came back to show them upstairs to their room. Elliot supposed it was serviceable, and not as dirty as other inns he'd stayed at, despite the musty smell. He'd noticed that everything in England tended to be old, and it had been a challenge finding his home in Mayfair because not many of those grand old mansions had modern fittings. But, despite its shabbiness, this room was warm.

'Elliot, there is only one bed,' Georgina said.

That had not escaped him. 'I won't be sleeping.' Glancing around, he found a chair in the corner and pulled it towards the fire. 'I'll sleep. You can—'

He stopped short, his mouth going dry as he watched her remove her cloak and place it by the fire.

'Elliot?' She cocked her head at him. 'What's the matter?'

He opened his mouth but, embarrassingly, nothing

came out. As he'd suspected, her dress was indeed soaked through—and quite transparent. She must not have bothered with undergarments in her haste, because he could clearly see the outline of her nipples against the wet fabric, and the darker shadow between her legs where the dress was pulled tight.

His cock immediately went hard.

'Elliot?' she repeated.

'Nothing.' He shifted around so he faced away from her, concealing his erection. 'I'm going to keep watch in case the snow slows down. You should get some rest. We will ride hard tomorrow.'

A poor choice of words, he realised, as it conjured the most erotic of images, which only tortured his poor cock further.

She didn't say anything, but his ears could hear the rustle of clothing as she began to undress. Eyes sliding heavenwards, he prayed to the Lord, promising that if he escaped this situation without embarrassing himself he would give away half his fortune tomorrow.

Elliot counted to sixty before glancing over his shoulder. Mercifully, Georgina was tucked under the bedcovers, staring up at the ceiling. He turned back and shifted in the chair, though his erection showed no signs of abating. Resigned to his fate, he leaned back and closed his eyes, trying to catch a few minutes of sleep.

'Elliot?' Georgina called.

'Yes?'

'You can't possibly be comfortable in that chair.'

No, he wasn't.

'There is enough space here in the bed.'

'No, thank you,' he bit back. 'I am perfectly fine here.'

He heard her sit up. 'No, you are not. I can see you. You won't be able to get any rest, and then you'll be too tired to drive.'

'I will be fine.'

'No, you won't. Why don't you just lie down beside me? Stay above the covers and I shall stay under.'

He sighed. 'If I do, will you go to sleep?'

'Yes.'

If she was asleep, then perhaps there would be no harm in that.

He glanced down at his lap, imploring his cock to behave. Standing up, he adjusted his trousers and headed towards the bed, where Georgina was, as promised, under the covers and facing away from him.

Heaving a sigh, he lay down beside her. His clothes were still damp. He should have asked Joseph Brown for some dry clothes as well, but he doubted he would have found anything that would fit Elliot. Besides, he would probably have charged him an exorbitant amount for a nightshirt.

He didn't dare remove any of his damp clothes, but he did untuck his shirt from his trousers and pull back the sleeves.

'Elliot?'

'What?'

'I can't sleep.' She turned to face him.

Georgina looked like an angel, lying on her side, waves of hair around her sweet face. Her coppery brown eyes were like molten pools, and as he'd suspected he was drowning in them. He could barely stop himself from touching her face. How he longed to feel her smooth skin underneath his palm…

'You must try.' He closed his eyes, which was the only thing he could do right now to block her from his sight.

'You can't sleep either.'

'Not if you keep talking to me,' he snapped.

Regret filled him as he heard her sharp intake of breath.

'Georgina…' He opened his eyes. 'What's the matter? You must be exhausted. I practically had to carry you up the stairs.'

'I know. I am tired. But my mind…it just won't rest.'

'Try not to worry about Anne-Marie.' That was his job, after all. 'There is nothing we can do at this moment.'

'It's not that.' Her teeth chewed down on her lower lip. 'You asked me a question in the carriage…'

'About what?'

'Bellamy.'

He tamped down the murderous urge that name drove in him. 'What about him?'

The smallest line appeared between her eyebrows. 'Don't you remember? You asked me if I would marry him.'

He did recall that conversation. Very much so.

'Why did you ask me that, Elliot?'

Because he very much wanted to know if she would marry Bellamy.

Would you accept his *proposal?*

Would you marry him?

And then there was the last question in his mind—one he didn't dare say aloud.

And why the hell not me?

'I don't know,' he lied.

'Do you want to know the answer?'

Not particularly.

'Will you go to sleep if I say yes?'

The corner of her mouth lifted. 'I do not think I would accept,' she said. 'I've been out in society for ten years now, and I have never received a single proposal in all this time.'

'Not one?'

Were the men of England blind?

She shook her head. 'I'm not exactly a desirable bride. In the beginning I was much too shy to attract anything more than fortune-hunters after my dowry. Trevor immediately dispatched them, before they even had a chance to court me.'

'Good.' He would do the same for his sisters.

'I went to balls, and other events, but I could hardly speak to anyone. My tongue would just tie up in knots and I would get the urge to flee. Then I would think that everyone in the room knew I was having these thoughts, which would only make me more anxious.

And then I started having these spells.' She avoided his gaze. 'You've seen them.'

'Yes.' At the ball, and just before that unforgettable encounter in the music room.

'They just got worse and worse over the years. Sometimes I wouldn't be able to leave my bed for a whole day. Socialising with a large group of people leaves me drained, and large crowds send me into a panic. My chest seizes up so tight I can hardly breathe. My stomach churns like I'm at sea, and I even broke out in hives once. So when my previous chaperone became weak, and unable to accompany me to all those events, I simply stopped going. I hadn't been to any event in three years, and I'd stopped experiencing any of those things.'

'Until I came along.'

She sneaked a glance at him. 'Yes. But see… I've grown accustomed to my solitary life. After you find your bride I will return to my reclusive ways. It's the only way I can have peace.'

Once again guilt began to eat at him. He had been causing her physical pain and discomfort. Perhaps he should release her from their bargain and allow the orphans to stay. It was only money, after all.

'I could never be the perfect society wife,' she added. 'I could never go to events with my husband or entertain guests at his estate. Trevor has pledged to care for me, no matter what happens, so I have no need of a husband ever.'

'So you plan to be unmarried for the rest of your life?'

'Yes.'

The tightening in his chest eased. It wasn't that she didn't want to marry him. She just didn't want to be married.

'Which is why I wanted to ask you something. A favour.'

'What is it?' He was already going to give her the orphanage, but he knew he wouldn't say no to anything else she might ask.

She didn't answer right away, and her eyes avoided him again. As he waited for her to speak, he searched her face for any clue as to what she might want from him. Her cheeks had grown scarlet and she was worrying at her bottom lip.

'Georgina…?'

'Will you make love to me?'

His heart—no, his entire body seized. 'I beg your pardon?'

'You heard me.' Though it should have been impossible, her face turned even redder. 'I want you to make love to me.'

His mouth went dry and he could only stare at her. 'This is ridiculous,' he finally said, when speech returned to his tongue. 'Think of what you are asking of me.'

'I have. I've thought about it for most of the ride here, and then when we sat down, right up until this moment. Elliot, I want this.'

'You don't know what you're asking.' He made a motion to turn away, but her hands quickly darted out of the covers to grab at his shirt. 'Georgina, let go.'

'No.' Her fingers tightened. 'Not until you consider my request.'

'I have. And the answer is still no.'

'Why not?'

Was she insane? 'You are a lady. I will not ruin you.'

'But you would make love to another lady?' Her voice was choked.

'That's different. She would be my wife in that case.' Gently, he took her hand and prised it from his shirt. 'I cannot do this to you.'

'But I'm asking you. Just give me this one time. I just want to know... I want to feel like I did in the music room. I want... I just want to feel wanted.'

'Oh, sweetheart...'

This was a dangerous game they were playing, and he had to stop it now before it was too late. If he ever made love to her, there was no way on God's green earth it could only be for one time.

'We cannot.'

But he wasn't sure if he was convincing her or himself.

'We should not.'

Her wrist was so delicate underneath his palms... the skin so soft.

'We can,' she whispered. 'No one will know.'

'I would know, sweetheart.' His chest tightened once again, his control barely hanging by a thread. He should leave her here now, wait out the storm downstairs.

'Then I will never make love to anyone.'

That statement stunned him, as if he'd been hit on the head with rocks.

'Georgina, don't say that.'

'It's true.'

'You will want someone else someday.' The very words left a bitter taste in his mouth.

Her chin jutted up, those coppery brown eyes spearing into him. 'It is you or no one else.'

Lord Almighty, of all the things she could have said in this moment, she just had to say that...

God, he muttered to himself, before his mouth captured hers.

Finally.

Georgina sighed as Elliot's mouth devoured her like a hungry man in search of his next meal. His fingers threaded into her hair as he pulled her closer to him.

This was it...it was truly happening.

How she'd longed for this, for him, and now he was going to make love to her.

His tongue licked at the seam of her lips and she opened eagerly for him. His hot tongue delved right into her mouth, seeking hers, while his hand threw the blankets away. It had grown hot under the covers, so the chill of the room was welcome. His hand landed on her thigh, grabbing at the fabric to raise it.

She froze.

He paused, but his lips remained barely an inch from hers. 'Do you know what's going to happen, sweetheart?'

'N-not quite,' she confessed. 'Great-Aunt Leticia promised me she would tell me before my wedding night, and since there was none…'

'She never told you?'

She shook her head and turned away from him, hiding her face against his neck.

'Do not hide, sweetheart.'

He placed his finger on her chin and tilted her head to face him. His eyes glowed bright in the light of the fire, and the most curious, delicious warmth filled her chest.

'There is nothing shameful about what happens between a man and woman. It's pleasurable for both, though you may experience some pain.'

She had overheard married women and some of the maids at home speaking of the sexual act, but she'd only been able to piece together some of the mechanics of it. 'I've heard there may be pain…down there.'

'Do you want to hear the rest of it? So you are not surprised?'

Her ears burned at the thought that he would school her on such matters. How she wished she knew more—at least enough so he did not have to teach her.

'What's wrong, sweetheart?' Concern marred his face. 'Why are you frowning?'

'It's nothing.'

'Please tell me. I do not want to do this if you are unsure.'

'I'm sure,' she said quickly, cupping his cheek, feeling the bristle underneath her fingertips. 'I'm just scared that you'll be disappointed in me. I don't know anything, and you'll have to teach me. It will be boring for you.'

He let out a soft chuckle. 'Bored is the last thing I'll feel, or disappointment.' Leaning down, he kissed her again, cradling her face with one hand. 'You please me just by being here. It will be nearly impossible for me not to feel pleasure. But I will do what it takes to make sure you feel good too.'

'I… I want to feel good. I want you to make me feel good.'

His eyes blazed. 'I will. Do you remember the music room?'

How could she ever forget? 'Yes…'

'When I touched you? And kissed you?'

'Y-yes.' Just the memory of it sent the most furious blush across her skin.

'May I do it again?'

'Please,' she said. 'I want to feel you.'

His hand cupped a breast through the nightrail. When his thumb found her nipple it hardened and poked against the rough fabric. Bending down, he placed his mouth over the nub as he continued to massage her flesh. At first, she couldn't feel his mouth, but when his tongue lapped at her, and the spot under his mouth became wet, the friction of his tongue against the fabric sent gooseflesh rising down her arms. He teased her with the flat of his tongue, further moistening the fabric. When he sucked, a jolt of pleasure made the place between her legs throb.

She gasped, and dug her hand into his hair. When she scraped her nails into his scalp, he moaned and canted his hips against her side. He removed his hand from her breast and back to her thigh. She let out the most embarrassing sigh of disappointment when his mouth released her nipple.

'What else do you remember from the music room? Did you hear Lady Genevieve? When she was crying out?'

'A little bit.' The curtains and his body had blocked out most of the sound.

'Do you know what the Duke was doing?'

'T-Touching her?'

'Do you know where?'

She had an idea, but she didn't want to say it, so she just nodded. 'Down...there?'

'Hmm-hmm. May I touch you there?'

She closed her eyes and nodded, her throat dry.

He pulled up the fabric, his fingers skimming along her thigh. It felt like for ever, and the anticipation growing within her was too much. Finally, his hand moved to the inside, all the way up. Her hips jumped the moment his fingers landed on the soft mound between her legs.

'Does this feel good?' His fingertips moved over the downy hair.

'Oh, yes. More, please.'

'Only if you open your eyes and look at me.'

Mortification flooded her. 'I cannot.'

'Yes, you can, sweetheart.' His mouth was on her temple for a gentle kiss. 'I promise this part doesn't hurt.'

Slowly, she opened her eyes. The expression on his face was a mix of wonder and contentment, yet she still felt the burning of her cheeks.

'That's it. Thank you. Just look at me. Unless you want to see what I'm doing—?'

'No.' She couldn't possibly look down there. 'Just… I will look at you.'

The corners of his mouth drew up into a sensuous smile. 'Good. Now, relax your body. Don't tense up.' He parted the mat of hair and sought out her nether lips. She gasped the moment his fingers slid against her most secret part. 'You're starting to get slick,' he said. 'The wetness will help with the pain.'

'H-How?'

'Ah, I'm getting ahead of myself.' His other hand fumbled with something at his waist and he shimmied his hips, then he took her hand and put it between them.

She gasped when the palm of her hand grasped something firm under the fabric of his shirt. 'That's your—?'

'Cock. Can you say it?'

'N-No, thank you.'

He stifled a laugh. 'Maybe later. Touch it,' he said. 'Grasp it.'

The bulge was warm under her palm, but she did not dare do as he asked. 'Will I hurt you?'

'No, just as long as you don't do it too hard—oh!' He groaned when her fingers clutched at the hardness.

She immediately let go, as if she'd touched a hot pan. 'Sorry.'

'N-No, no.' He took her hand and replaced it. 'It was good. Much better than I had imagined.'

'Oh.' She gripped the length again. It was much thicker and longer than she'd anticipated. 'Wait—you have imagined this?'

'Oh, yes, sweetheart.' He moaned when her grip tightened. 'Too many times.'

It was fascinating, feeling the hardness under the fabric. 'What do we do next?'

'Let me tell you what's going to happen…'

His fingers began to stroke her, and she found herself getting even slicker. Slowly, he pushed at her, the tip of his finger entering her. She froze once more.

'It's all right. It's going to feel good. My cock will go inside you. Right. Here.' He inched his finger into her.

Georgina couldn't find the words to describe the sensations in her body at that moment. She already felt terribly full of his finger. How was his…? How would he fit in there?

He pulled back, then pushed into her again, and

repeated the motion. 'It will feel like this, but more. Does it feel good now?'

'Y-Yes.'

'I can tell. See how you clasp at my finger, sweetheart?' He continued his gentle ministrations at her entrance. 'You'll do that for me again, around my cock. It will feel wonderful for me.'

'Oh, yes...' she moaned.

The heat was too much, and his words were blisteringly embarrassing, but she wanted him to keep going.

'That's it. Move your hips just like that.'

She hadn't even realised that she was, indeed, thrusting her hips up to meet his hand.

'How do you feel?'

'Just...so hot.'

He paused and adjusted his hand. 'There is one more place I will touch you, and you will feel even better. Do you trust me?'

'Yes, Elliot,' she panted.

His thumb brushed at the top of her mound, and her hips shot off the mattress. 'Elliot!'

His hands and fingers worked at her like magic, spreading heady pleasure all over her. She couldn't think, and her chest seemed to squeeze out every last bit of air from her. She hadn't even realised, either, that she'd grasped his length and was stroking it in the same rhythm as his fingers worked her.

The sensations made her mindless, and her body exploded in pleasure. He captured her scream with his mouth, his tongue thrusting into hers savagely.

She sank down, every bone in her body like liquid, unable to hold her up. Her eyes fluttered open as feeling finally returned to her limbs.

'How do you feel?' he murmured against her temple.

'I… Tired. But at the same time…not.'

Though her body felt sated, she knew there was more. And she wanted all of it.

'Good.' He brushed the hair from her sweat-dampened brow. 'Do you want to rest?'

'No. But, Elliot…?'

'Hmm?'

'How…how will you fit?'

It seemed impossible, with his girth, and she had already felt full with just his finger.

'That's what I meant when I said the wetness will help. And when you experience pleasure, like you did just now, your body produces even more of that slickness which will help ease me in.'

'I think I understand.'

'It hurts for many women, especially during their first time, because often the man does not prepare them in this way.'

'So it won't hurt any more? When you—?'

'It still might. You're very tight, Georgina. But that's because you have never experienced this before. I promise you, your body will accommodate me. I will do my best to ensure you are comfortable, but I cannot predict what will happen. You must promise to tell me if it's too much and we will stop.'

Lord, she didn't want him to stop.

'And you will feel pleasure too?'

'Yes. When I—' He frowned. 'There is something else. You do know this is how children are conceived?'

'Y-Yes.' She swallowed hard.

When she'd asked him to make love to her, she hadn't considered the possibility.

'There is something I must do to stop from getting you with child,' he said. 'At the last moment, I will pull out and spill my seed outside your body. That should prevent you from conceiving.'

'I... All right.' She didn't quite understand, but she trusted him.

He nuzzled at her cheek. 'You are so incredibly beautiful, Georgina.'

Normally she would not believe that, but in his arms she did feel beautiful.

'Let me look at you?' he said.

Her heart thumped in her chest. 'M-Must you?'

'I don't have to, but I want to. And this is really better without clothes.'

'Y-You as well? You'll be naked?'

'Yes, that's the general idea.'

The room felt much too bright with the fire blazing. The thought of him looking at her, and her at him, was too much for her mind to sort through. She now understood why couples did this in the dark.

'Be brave for me, sweetheart. Looking at you will give me pleasure. You don't have to look at me if you think it will frighten you.'

'N-No, I'm not frightened.' She took a deep breath and relaxed. 'All right.'

'Thank you.' He kissed her again, then proceeded to lift the nightrail over her head and toss it aside. 'So lovely you are, Georgina.' His hand slid up from her hip, over the soft mound of her belly and cupped a breast. 'So gorgeous.'

'You do not think I am…that my body is much too well-endowed?'

'Too well-endowed? Never.' His hands—rough and callused—squeezed a breast gently and thumbed a nipple into hardness. 'There's so much of you to enjoy. More for me to hold and touch and kiss.' He bent his head to lick at her nipple. 'Delectable. I could feast on you all day.'

'Oh…' That tension had begun to build in her body once more. 'Elliot…'

To her annoyance, he released her.

'One moment, sweetheart.' He moved away from her and off the bed, towering over her. Grabbing the hem of his shirt, he pulled it over his head and tossed it aside.

Georgina could not tear her eyes away from him. He was so…solid and powerful. His shoulders were wide, the muscles making him look bulky. His arms were like small tree trunks, and his large chest was covered with a mat of dark hair.

'I was always tall for my age, but then I spent ten years rowing passengers across New York's rivers, and before that I carried cargo from the ships,' he explained. 'Do you find my body displeasing?'

She shook her head. 'N-No, not at all. Just…overwhelming.'

The buttons of his trousers had already been unbuttoned and the waist shoved down to his thighs. He pushed them further down, revealing the jutting column between his legs.

Georgina swallowed hard, and quickly averted her eyes.

'I promise to be gentle.' The mattress dipped as he joined her again. 'And you must promise to let me know if it is too much. Please do not bear the pain for my sake.'

She could only nod.

He stretched his body along the length of hers. Seeking her mouth, he melded their lips together, then covered her body.

The weight of him was pleasant, though she suspected he was not putting all of it on her—after all, his great big body would crush her. He nudged her legs open and settled between them. A hand reached down to her sex, his fingers once again stroking her sensitive flesh. When she was panting, and clawing at the mattress, he spread her open and something blunt pressed at her.

She sucked in a breath as the invasion seemed to split her open. Though she winced at the pain, she felt herself open up to him as he applied pressure gently. She stretched and accommodated him, and despite the slight burning she could feel small shocks of pleasure down the base of her spine. It seemed to take for ever and he filled her until she couldn't take any more.

'I'm sorry, sweetheart, that this has to hurt. You must relax…it will ease the pain.'

That task seemed impossible, but she let out a breath and forced her muscles to obey. Just as he'd said, the pain began to ebb away and her inner muscles loosened. Reaching up, she dug her fingers into his shoulders, fascinated by the powerful contours shaped by years of rowing under the sun. When she moved her fingers, those muscles jumped under her fingers. Fascinated, she trailed them down his arms.

He moaned aloud, his body tensing. 'I must move… or else.'

'Please…'

Slowly, he began to move. There was more burning, but after a few thrusts it all but disappeared, replaced by frissons of excitement. He drew back, then pushed forward, again and again, and Georgina found herself shamelessly pushing up to meet his thrusts, as if her hips had a life of their own. With each upward movement that knot at the base of her spine tightened, waiting to snap.

He paused, then his hand slipped between them, spreading her further and caressing the bud there, making her squirm and moan louder. Then he began moving again, building the rhythm slowly, gradually, until she could feel herself completely open to him. His breath hitched, then he reached under her knees to pull them up. It changed the angle of his hips in just the right way so that her body began to shudder, the pressure building, ready to burst.

'Elliot!'

He pumped into her, riding out her pleasure until it washed over her. She heard him groan, then quickly pull out of her. A guttural moan ripped from his throat just before she felt a splash of wetness on her belly. With a rough grunt, he rolled over and collapsed beside her.

Georgina closed her eyes, her muscles refusing to move. She felt the mattress rise as his weight lifted. A few moments later, it dipped, indicating he was back. She opened one eye.

He held a washcloth in his hand. 'I need to clean you up.'

She nodded, and he used the cloth to wipe the sticky substance from her belly. He moved lower and pressed the fabric gently between her legs. She stifled the urge to wince, though he must have seen the discomfort on her face as he quickly withdrew the cloth.

'I'll place it by the basin in case you need it.'

She watched his naked back as he walked over to the washstand, admiring how the muscles moved and the light from the fire played across his golden skin.

When he came back to the bed, she turned on her side to look out of the window. 'The snow hasn't relented,' she observed.

He sidled up behind her, then nuzzled at her neck as his arms wrapped tight around her. 'Sleep. There is nothing we can do now but wait until morning. We will set off as soon as possible.'

And so she closed her eyes and let sleep take over.

Chapter Eleven

Elliot wasn't sure how long he'd slept, but it couldn't have been more than an hour or two. He did not feel as refreshed as he did after a complete night's sleep and he was more tired than usual. Of course, that probably had something to do with the woman in his arms.

He did not allow himself any regrets. What was done was done. And if Georgina was truly set against marrying, then he did not feel guilty that he was robbing her future husband of her maidenhood. No, it was a gift that she had given freely, one that he would treasure.

Still he wanted her. His cock was now rock-hard and rubbed against the smooth flesh of her buttocks.

'Are you awake?' she asked sleepily.

'Yes. But you can keep sleeping.'

She rubbed her body against him. 'Elliot... I want...'

'Sweetheart.' He gently laid a hand on her hips. 'Stop. We cannot.'

'Why not?'

'You are still sore. I do not want to hurt you again.'

'You won't.'

'Yes, I will.' He sighed. 'But we can do other things that won't hurt you.'

She flipped around to face him. 'Other things?'

'Oh, yes.' Anticipation swirled in his gut. 'Would you like me to show you?'

'Yes, please.'

He pushed her down so she lay flat on her back. 'Just lie there…' He kissed her again on her swollen lips, then trailed his mouth lower, over her neck and breasts, stopping to kiss each nipple. Then he moved lower still, until he was between her lovely thighs.

'Elliot? Are you—? Oh!'

He buried his face into her mound, spreading her thighs so he could access her sweetness. He licked at her flesh, swirling his tongue, tasting her and licking at her. He traced his tongue up and down her seam, stopping at the top to lick at her bud, to tease her until her body was shaking with need. He lost himself between her thighs, forgetting everything outside this room.

His cock rubbed painfully against the rough sheets, so he reached down and circled his palm around the shaft. He continued to pleasure her with his tongue, thrusting into her with the tip until she was panting and moaning. When her body began to shudder with her climax he increased the pressure and speed of his hand. Pumping furiously, he let himself go, the shocks of pleasure from his orgasm nearly blinding him. His body sagged into the mattress, aching deliciously from the release.

'The snow has stopped.'

'What?' The after-effects of his orgasm made it difficult to think.

'The snow.' She nodded at the window. 'It's stopped.'

'Why—?' Oh. Anne-Marie. 'We must make haste.'

His body protested as he heaved himself off her, but as the cloud of lust left him his mind began to think rationally. Anne-Marie was still out there, with God knew who, doing God knew what, and they had to catch up to her.

Elliot retrieved his clothes, which were thankfully dry, and began to put them on.

'Do you need my help?' he asked as Georgina struggled with her dress.

'No.' But when she got it over her torso, she frowned.

'What's wrong?'

'It's unfair how women's clothes are so numerous and restrictive.' She glanced over at him. 'I never realised men wore so little compared to us. All you need are your undergarments, your shirt, trousers and coats.'

'You're not wearing undergarments.' The very thought of her naked underneath her dress made his cock twitch, but he ignored it. 'And you seem to be fine.'

Her mouth puckered. 'Without the proper undergarments, this dress hardly fits at all. See how the torso and hips are too small?'

All he could see was how her luscious curves strained against the fabric. The tops of her breasts nearly spilled over the neckline of her dress and her nipples poked through the fabric. The skirt, on the other hand, hugged those full, womanly hips that had cradled him last night.

'It's awful.'

He agreed. He wanted to peel it off and—

Damn it, he had to stop lusting after her and follow after Anne-Marie.

Once they'd finished dressing, he led her towards the door. 'I shall see to the carriage. Try and see if that damned innkeeper will make us something warm to drink, and perhaps give us a loaf of bread to take with us.'

'Of course.'

'Hopefully, Anne-Marie and her "friend" were also forced to stop during the blizzard and we can catch up to them.' He opened the door and gestured for her to leave first. 'We must find—'

'Anne-Marie!' Georgina exclaimed.

'Yes, we must find her.'

'No!' She grabbed him by the lapel and pulled him out of the room. 'Anne-Marie.' She gestured to her right, down the corridor.

'Yes, of course. I—' He stopped short, finally understanding her meaning.

Anne-Marie. His sister. Standing outside one of the doors down the corridor.

Her green eyes were wide, shock on her face.

'Anne-Marie.' He didn't dare move. She looked like a frightened deer, and he was afraid she would bolt at any moment. 'Are you—? *Oomph!*'

His sister hurled herself at him, and he was caught so off guard that he could only wrap his arms around her as her body began to shake.

'There, there…' he soothed. 'I'm here.' Great heaving sobs racked her shoulders, and he held on to her tighter.

Georgina nodded back to their room. 'Elliot, should we maybe…?'

Gently, he guided Anne-Marie backwards until they crossed the threshold. As Georgina closed the door behind them, he sat Anne-Marie down on the bed. Still, she clung to him, as if her life depended on it, and her tears soaked the shoulders of his shirt.

Rage began to boil in him as all the things that blackguard might have done to her began to fill his imagination. 'I'll kill him,' he whispered. 'Then chop him into pieces so no one will ever find him.'

Anne-Marie stiffened in his arms. 'Who?'

'Whoever did this to you.'

She raised her head. 'Did what to me?'

Now he was confused. 'Whoever seduced you and convinced you to elope to Scotland.'

'How did you—? Wait…seduced me?' Anne-Marie wiped the tears from her cheeks. 'What do you mean?'

Glancing around, she cocked her head at Georgina. 'And what is Lady Georgina doing here?'

Georgina's face turned crimson, but she seemingly managed to compose herself as she sat down next to Anne-Marie.

'We came after you. Lily came to me and told me what had happened.'

'And what did she say?'

'That you'd left with a friend for Scotland.'

Anne-Marie let out what sounded like a half-hiccup, half laugh. 'I had. Lady Lavinia.'

'Lady Lavinia?' Elliot released her. 'What do you mean, Lady Lavinia?'

'It was her idea.'

Elliot raked a hand through his hair. 'I don't understand… You can't get married to her.'

Anne-Marie blew out a breath. 'I wasn't intending to. She is getting married—but to someone else.'

Georgina cleared her throat. 'Perhaps you should start from the beginning, dear girl.'

'Yes.'

Elliot crossed his arms over his chest. He definitely wanted to hear this.

'L-Lady Lavinia…she…' Anne-Marie swallowed hard. 'I thought she was my friend. She was so nice to me the entire time at Foxbury Hill. She…she let me complain about Elliot, and I told her how much I hated it here, and that you won't let me do anything fun.' Her lips pursed. 'Then she said that she was planning to run away, after the party. A friend was helping her and I could come along. We could stay with her friend and I could find a job and have Lily come join us.'

Georgina gasped. 'And then what happened?'

'I agreed, and she told me to be ready at one o'clock. Her friend came in a carriage.'

'And who is this "friend"?'

'I don't know him, but I think… I mean, at first he acted friendly to her. Then the snow storm came and we had to stop here. He rented two rooms, but instead of sharing one with Lady Lavinia, I ended up alone.'

Her lower lip trembled as hesitation crossed her face.

'It's all right, Anne-Marie.' Georgina placed a hand over hers. 'You can tell us. We won't be angry.'

'Th-this morning I caught them trying to leave without me. When I confronted her, Lady Lavinia called me a s-stupid girl. She said I was naive for believing she would take me with her to Gretna Green. And then they left.'

'They just left you here? Alone?'

'Y-Yes…' She sniffed. 'I was so scared. I just stayed in my room and…and then I heard your voice, Elliot.' She looked at him, her face so innocent and vulnerable. 'I've never been happier to see you.'

And he had never been more relieved in his entire life.

'I don't understand why she would do that,' Anne-Marie cried. 'She was so nice to me. Why would she just leave me here?'

Georgina murmured, 'Perhaps they meant to use you as a distraction.'

'How?' Anne-Marie asked.

'I think… I wonder if Lady Lavinia's lover is someone known to her family? Perhaps someone entirely unsuitable for her—which is why they had to resort to eloping. If she'd disappeared by herself, her parents would immediately have known it was this suitor and chased them all the way to Gretna Green—'

'Ah…' Elliot interrupted. 'But two missing girls would throw the household into chaos and confusion. And, knowing Anne-Marie, I would have suspected you two would attempt to return to London.'

'Or perhaps that we'd been abducted from our beds?' Anne-Marie offered.

'Either way, I would never have thought to follow you north to Scotland.'

Elliot had to admit it was a cunning plan. But he was just happy that Anne-Marie was safe. Still, even though there was no secret lover, something bad *might* have happened to his sister. His fists curled at his sides as he thought of the danger Lady Lavinia had put his sister in, leaving her here alone to fend for herself. The very thought of it enraged him.

'Elliot?' Georgina's soothing voice interrupted his thoughts. 'Why don't you get the horse ready and we can be on our way?'

'Right… Stay here.'

Rising to his feet, he marched out of the room and made his way to the stables. Knowing Anne-Marie was safe had made the tension from his body seep away. Of course now his thoughts were occupied with something else entirely.

Georgina.

They had to marry now—there was no question about it. For one thing, he no longer had any immediate prospect of his own, seeing as the one lady he had invested his time in had absconded to Gretna Green with her lover.

There was not much more time left as Christmas Day was only eight days away.

And, of course, there was the fact that he had ruined her.

Damn it all to hell.

'Morning, sir,' Willy the stable boy greeted him. 'What can I do fer ye?'

'Have our phaeton made ready at once.' He flipped a coin towards the boy and then left.

Heading back into the inn, he stopped at the bottom of the stairs to gather his thoughts. He would go up there and tell Georgina they had to get married. He should not have allowed her to come with him in the first place. Even if they hadn't slept together, someone would surely see them when they arrived back at Foxbury Hill. Harwicke would demand he marry her anyway, so he would at least gain some favour from the furious Duke by offering marriage himself first.

Yes, that was the only solution here.

Georgina would surely see reason in this matter.

Squaring his shoulders, he climbed up the rickety

stairs and entered their room. Georgina was alone, however, as she sat by the fire, staring into the flames.

'Where is Anne-Marie?'

Startled, she swung her head back towards him. 'She went back to her room to gather her things.'

'Is she…all right?' he asked.

Standing up, she faced him. 'She is.'

He swallowed. 'Did…anything happen to her?'

'No, nothing bad.' She adjusted her cloak around her shoulders. 'I believe everything happened just as she said. She spent the night alone.'

He blew out a breath. 'Thank God.' He raked his fingers through his hair. 'I never suspected Lady Lavinia…'

God, if she wasn't a woman—

'Neither did I,' Georgina answered in a quiet voice. 'She seemed so nice. And so very interested in the girls too.'

Yes, and now he knew why.

'We must go back. The phaeton should be ready soon.'

'Yes, we must. And I have an idea.'

'An idea?'

'For how we can avoid a scandal.'

Ah, yes. This was the time to talk to her about marriage.

'About that—'

'You cannot afford a scandal, after all.' She wrung her hands together. 'There is still Miss Philipps.'

'Who?'

'Miss Penelope Philipps.'

'Yes, and what about her?'

'If it came out that you and I were…and Anne-Marie had been gone the entire night…there would be a scandal. Miss Philipps would never agree to marry you. Nor would any lady from the Ton.'

He could only stare at her, dumbfounded. She was thinking of *his* marriage prospects. And probably her precious orphanage too. How could he forget that was the reason she'd even deigned to help him in the first place?

'I have a plan.' Her delicate brows drew together in thought. 'It's quite early, and we should be able to return to Foxbury Hill in less than an hour. Everyone will still be asleep, and most of the staff won't be coming in until later as they have the morning off. When we arrive, instruct your coachman to get your carriage ready and keep Anne-Marie in it. Did you bring any other staff to Foxbury with you?'

'Just my valet,' he said. 'He should be waiting for me to ring for him as soon as I wake.'

'Leave a note for him and instruct him to tell Trevor that you and the girls were called away before dawn. Tell him if anyone asks, he must say he saw you off. He can pack up all your things and then he can ride home with our servants tomorrow.'

'And Lily?'

'She should still be in my room. I shall wake her and send her to you.'

'And you? What will you do?'

'I will sneak back into my room and go back to sleep,' she said. 'See? My plan makes perfect sense.'

'Yes, it appears that it does…'

And if they were to pull it off successfully, there would be no need to marry her.

'Elliot? Georgina?' Anne-Marie whispered as she poked her head through the door.

Georgina strode over to her and placed an arm around her. 'Feeling better, dear girl?'

She nodded and embraced her. 'Thank you.'

'I will settle our bill and see you out front.' Elliot told them. Without another word, he left the room.

After paying the practically extortionate bill Joseph Brown had handed him, Elliot retrieved the phaeton and drove it around to the front of the inn, where Georgina and Anne-Marie waited. It was a tight fit, but all three of them managed to squeeze themselves into the small carriage.

As he took the reins, he could not help but glance down. Beside him, Anne-Marie sat in the middle, her head on Georgina's shoulder as she smoothed a hand over his sister's head.

His heart lurched at the sight, and for the first time in his life he felt like a failure. This was what the girls needed—a feminine hand to guide them and a shoulder to cry on. That miserable shrew who had birthed them had never shown them any care or affection, and both his sisters were crying out for some tenderness from a mother figure.

His eyes were drawn towards Georgina's lovely

face, and when those coppery brown eyes met his own, they seemed startled.

Tearing his gaze away, he snapped the reins.

Elliot drove as fast as the horse and the roads would allow them, and soon Foxbury Hill was within sight. He manoeuvred the phaeton back into the carriage house, then dropped down to untether the horse as Georgina and Anne-Marie alighted. He guided the horse back to the stables, then returned to the carriage house.

'Lady Georgina has returned to the house,' Anne-Marie informed him. 'She said I should stay here and that you would take care of everything.'

'Yes.'

So she'd left. Without even saying goodbye.

Perhaps it was better this way. All she'd wanted was one night with him. He had been a fool to think there could be anything more between them. Georgina should not have to be saddled with a husband like him, nor be responsible for the well-being of two young women—illegitimate at that.

No, she deserved someone better, who would not hurt her because of his demands that his sisters be embraced by society.

Besides, if she did marry him he would get all the benefits and she would receive nothing in return. He could not offer her the affection and love she deserved. He could not even celebrate the one time of the year that made her happy. The loss he had suffered on that day was something that had left an indelible mark on him. And he could not go through that again.

'Elliot, come here,' Ma had rasped. *'There is something I need you to do for me...'*

· *'What is it?'* Elliot would have done anything for her.

'When your pa comes home...tell him I waited as long as I could.' Her eyes had gone bright, like a candle before it burned out. *'I love you, my Harold.'*

It was on that day Elliot had sworn he would never rely on anyone, and that he would use the only assets he had: himself and time. He'd plotted out his life for the next ten years, and the ten after that, growing wealthier than he'd ever imagined. And if he just followed his current ten-year plan, he would achieve the success he'd craved his entire life.

'Elliot...' Anne-Marie's voice cut into his thought. 'I'm so very sorry for all the trouble I've caused.' Tears once again welled in her eyes. 'I was so scared when I realised I was alone, and I thought—'

He embraced her again as she began to cry. 'Don't worry. It's all right. You know I wouldn't have stopped until I'd found you.'

She nodded.

For now, he would have to forget his own desires and steer himself back onto the path he'd set out to follow. There was no other way now—only forward.

Chapter Twelve

17th December,
First Christmas Day

Georgina heaved a sigh of relief as soon as she entered her room. Her heart had beat madly the entire time as she'd sneaked into the house, fearing she would be caught by a servant or—God forbid—one of the guests. But, just as she'd predicted, everyone was still abed, exhausted from the previous night's merriment, and she'd made it to her room undetected.

'Lady Georgina?' came Lily's voice from the bed. 'Is that you?'

'Yes, poppet.' She ran over to her. 'I'm here.'

She sat up and blinked at her with sleepy eyes. 'Did you find Anne-Marie?'

'We did. And thank you for coming to me last night and telling me about her.' She kissed the top of her head. 'Now, poppet, you must do something for me.'

'What is it?'

'You must keep this a secret between us.'

'Like when you and Miss Warren came to the house?'

'Exactly.' She smiled down at her. 'Elliot will give you an extra-special gift if you do.'

It seems she, too, was not beyond bribing children.

'What's that?'

'He'll tell you when you see him. Which reminds me—you must go to him now.' She tugged the child gently from the bed. 'Go straight to his rooms and wait for him.'

She let out a yawn. 'All right...'

After she'd led Lily out of her room, Georgina changed out of her cloak and dress, hid them under her bed, then changed back into her nightrail before slipping under the covers. As the rush of excitement left her body, and left alone with only her thoughts, she could not help but think of the events of the night before.

Oh, Lord, she had taken a lover.

Not just any lover.

Elliot.

And now she understood what all the fuss was about.

Her hand went to her neck, where the bristles from Elliot's cheek had left their brand. Actually, his whiskers had left marks all over her, even between her thighs, when he—

Heat rushed over her as she recalled the delightful things he'd done with his mouth that morning. Everything about it had been wonderful, and there had been nothing shameful about it. At least, she didn't feel any shame about the things they'd done. Elliot had been considerate and kind throughout, and the pleasure had been unlike anything she'd ever felt. More than that, the fact that she had given him the same kind of ecstasy made her feel empowered. Hearing his cries of pleasure, feeling the way he'd gripped her with those rough hands, as if he couldn't get enough...

She turned to her side, hugging a cool pillow to her heated body. Now she had felt passion and pleasure, and it would have to be enough to last her for the rest of her life. It couldn't happen again, and certainly she wouldn't seek Elliot out—not if he were to marry someone else.

The very thought of him making love to another woman sent a searing pain into her chest—an emotion she recognised as jealousy.

How awful it was.

Perhaps once he'd announced his engagement and the orphanage had been saved, she would be able to think of those pleasant memories without evoking that mad, searing emotion that burrowed into her. For now, she would have to put those memories aside before they drove her mad.

Georgina could have sworn she had only momentarily closed her eyes before opening them again. However, the chill in the air indicated that the heat in her room had dissipated and no one had come in to stoke the fire.

Groggily, she got up and rang for her maid.

After performing her morning ablutions and dressing in a brand-new blue silk day gown, she headed downstairs to the dining room. Her maid had informed her that it was already noon and lunch would soon be served.

Before she entered the dining room she took a deep breath and smoothed her hand down her skirts. Would the other guests suspect anything when they saw her? Would they know she had spent the night with a lover and she was no longer a virgin?

Just go in, she told herself. *You cannot stay out here for ever.*

Scrounging up her courage, she took one step inside the dining room—the very *empty* dining room.

'Trevor?' The room wasn't completely unoccupied. Her brother was at the head of the table, enjoying his morning tea.

'There you are, Georgina.' He put his teacup down, rose from his seat and walked over to her. 'Miss Warren said you were sleeping like the dead when she peeped into your room.'

'She—she did? When?'

'Oh, I don't know…an hour ago?'

Thank heavens.

Had the companion peeped in earlier in the morning, she would have discovered Lily there and Georgina gone.

'I was much too fatigued by yesterday's activities.'

Of course she didn't mention all the activities—including those that had made her muscles sore and that place between her thighs ache.

'Um…where is everyone?'

'You missed all the excitement this morning, I'm afraid. The Marquess of Arundel and the rest of his family had some sort of family emergency. I think a cousin died.'

'You think?'

'I could not elicit the exact story as it was pure chaos and the Marchioness seemed inconsolable… poor thing wouldn't stop bawling.' He tsked. 'They were half packed by the time I came downstairs, and the daughters had already left in the first carriage.'

Georgina harrumphed to herself. It seemed she was not the only one who had thought of the plan to leave before anyone noticed the disappearance of one girl.

'Oh, that's too bad. We must send our sympathies.' *Sympathies for having a foul and malicious daughter, anyway.* 'And the others?'

'Well, you know that Elliot had already planned to return to London today, so I assume they left at first light.'

'Er…of course.'

'And, seeing as Arundel and his family had left, Waldemere declared that he wished to support them in their time of need and followed them. The Viscount and his family have decided to leave for London as well, and are packing up as we speak. I think with the lack of eligible gentlemen they decided staying wasn't worth it. Miss Philipps looked quite disappointed when Elliot remained by Lady Lavinia's side for the entirety of last night.'

Well, perhaps she will be pleased when Elliot calls upon her after she returns to London.

'Ah, I see...'

'And as for our last remaining guest—I am afraid I have bad news.'

'Last guest?'

'Bellamy.'

'Oh. Of course.' She'd forgotten all about him. 'What's the bad news?'

'He's taken ill once more, and the doctor says it's much more serious this time. He's advised Bellamy to stay abed for a few days. So he'll remain here for now, and we may not see him before we leave for London tomorrow.'

'How...terrible.'

Georgina nearly fell to her knees in thanks to the heavens.

'So it's just us for today.' A bright smile spread across her brother's face. 'Happy First Christmas, Georgie.'

She gave him her cheek as he bent down to kiss it. 'Happy First Christmas, Trev.'

They spent their First Christmas as they usually did—next to a warm fire in the library. Trevor read quietly in a corner, while Georgina was tucked under a soft blanket, embroidering a cushion and drinking tea. They had the roast turkey feast Mrs Laramie had prepared, and instructed her to serve the second bird and the extra dishes she had prepared to the servants. There was still so much leftover food, the kitchen staff had to pack everything up and send it to some of their less fortunate neighbours in the village.

The day's activities and the chance to finally be free of the presence of guests had given Georgina a chance to feel energised. However, throughout the day her mind still wandered to Elliot. Try as she might, she could not stop herself from thinking about what had happened between them—but more than that, it gnawed at her that she didn't know what he was doing and how he was feeling right now.

He'd looked incredibly relieved when they'd found Anne-Marie, but had been quiet during the entire ride back to Foxbury Hill. Did he blame himself for her running away? Would he try to mend things with his sister? Was Anne-Marie still feeling the shock of being left behind in a strange place?

Perhaps she would never know the answers. She would have to resign herself to that.

18th December

The following day they left Foxbury Hill, as planned, and set off for London.

'Welcome back, Your Grace…my lady.' Dawson greeted them as soon as they crossed the threshold of Harwicke House.

'Thank you, Dawson.' Trevor handed him his hat. 'How is everything? Nothing exciting happening, I presume?'

The normally stoic butler's face turned ashen. 'I… uh…' He cleared his throat. 'Nothing at all, my lord.'

Georgina noticed Miss Warren had sent Dawson a pointed look, but said nothing.

'I'm exhausted,' Georgina said. 'I think I shall lie down for a nap.'

Heading upstairs to her rooms, she changed out of her travel clothes, freshened up after the journey, then lay in bed. She had barely settled when Miss Warren burst into her room.

'What—? Miss Warren, are you all right?'

Her companion's face was crimson, and her nostrils flared as her breaths came in short bursts. She held a newspaper in her hand and waved it around.

'Dawson has tried to hide this from your brother.'

'Hide what?'

'This morning's *London Daily Herald.*' Miss Warren dropped the paper on the bed. 'Read it.'

Picking up the paper, which appeared to have been opened to the society gossip column, Georgina began to read:

We are delighted to reward our most loyal readers with news that is exclusive only to our paper, but we believe will be the talk of the town by tomorrow.

We have it on great authority that a certain 'Lady G', whom we have not seen in society for nearly three years now, has not mysteriously disappeared. No, it seems that the lady in question has not hidden herself away in shame after six failed Seasons, but rather has been enjoying the rewards of what she may believe is anonymity after hiding from society.

What rewards? Well, it seems the reserved, shy violet we knew has blossomed into a rose— one in full bloom and open for pollination. 'Lady G', who is said to have been carrying on a flirtation with a certain 'Lord B', was discovered by a sharp-eyed witness leaving a coaching inn in the company of another man yesterday morning. This particular inn is said to be near this vixen's family estate, well situated for a quick getaway.

Were the lovers off on an adventure or was this a one-night tryst? We do not know, readers, but we will let you decide.

Georgina's stomach dropped and she felt the blood drain from her face. 'I… There are no names…'

'Don't be daft, Lady Georgina,' Miss Warren snapped. 'Of course there are no names. Otherwise the paper would face hundreds of lawsuits a year. But they add enough detail for readers to figure out who it is. What other "Lady G" could they be referring to with six failed Seasons, who hasn't been seen in society in three years. And vixen—a female fox—is a clue to *Fox*bury Hill.'

'This Lady G could be any number of women,' she retorted. 'There's…there's… Lady Grace Ashton.'

'Lady Grace is seventy-two years old. I very much

doubt she'd be conducting a tryst at a coaching inn.' Miss Warren covered her face. 'This is my fault. I should have been there to keep an eye on you. I knew I should not have taken the night off—'

'It's not your fault,' Georgina blurted out. 'Please.' She patted her hand on top of the mattress. 'Have a seat and I will explain.'

Crossing her arms over her chest, Miss Warren sank down at the foot of the bed. 'First tell me who is the man that article is referring to? Is it Mr Smith?'

'H-How did you know?'

'I guessed as much.' Miss Warren sighed. 'I am not blind, you know. I've seen the way he looks at you.'

'L-Looks at me?'

Her companion scowled. 'Never you mind. Now, please continue.'

'All right.'

And so Georgina told her everything that had happened—at least the part about Anne-Marie running away and their finding her at the inn.

'So, you see, we weren't having a tryst of any sort at that inn. And whoever saw us leave is lying—we weren't alone. Anne-Marie was clearly with us.'

Miss Warren's lips pressed together tight. 'It doesn't matter. You were still seen away from your home at an ungodly hour in the morning with a strange man and no chaperone in sight.' She sighed. 'But at least nothing happened between you and Mr Smith, did it?'

Georgina did not want to lie, but she couldn't bring

herself to admit the truth either. However, her hesitation only confirmed her guilt.

'That vile blackguard!' Miss Warren shot to her feet, her hands curled into fists at her sides. 'How could he take advantage of an innocent girl? And one who was risking her reputation to save his sister at that!'

'Please, Miss Warren, calm down. It's not like that. And I am almost thirty years old—hardly a girl.'

'That's not the point.'

'Yes, it is. I asked him to make love to me.' Her cheeks burned, but she had to make Miss Warren understand. 'I just… I told him that I will never marry and so I wanted to…'

Her companion held up a hand. 'Please, spare me the details.'

Oh, thank heavens.

Georgina wasn't sure she'd survive the awkwardness of telling Miss Warren *everything*.

'But answer me honestly. Did he force you in any way? Coax you into doing things you did not want? Did he hurt you?'

'He didn't strike me, if that's what you're asking.' Elliot would never do that to any woman. She'd seen the care he displayed with his sisters. 'And, no, there was no force. If anything, I was the one who convinced him—'

'You may stop right there.'

'You think I am disgusting,' she accused. 'And that what I have done is shameful.'

That was what Great-Aunt Leticia would have thought if she'd been there last night. She had always called relations between a man and an unmarried woman wicked.

Miss Warren's expression fell. 'What? Oh, no.' Gently, she took Georgina's hand. 'Darling girl, I was just scared that he'd forced you into this.' She swallowed hard. 'Men are known to do that.'

He's not like other men, Georgina wanted to say.

'There was no force and it was my idea. We agreed it would only be that one time.'

'And what if you conceive?'

'I won't,' she said. 'He made sure of that.'

The relief on her companion's face was evident. 'Even so, your reputation is now in tatters. You will be a pariah by the end of the week.'

'So? It's not as if I'm searching for a husband. If anything, now I won't even have to worry about being invited to balls.'

Miss Warren clicked her tongue. 'Have you no sense? This doesn't just affect *you*. Think of your brother. The Duke will be affected by this, as will your family name. Do you think he will be able to find a wife of good quality with such a scandal staining the Abernathy name? He'll only be able to marry title-hunters. His children, too, will suffer. Many doors will be closed to them, thanks to your actions.'

Georgina wrung her hands in her lap. She hadn't thought of that. 'M-Maybe Trevor won't find out. It's just one newspaper…'

Miss Warren let out an indignant sound. 'I'm afraid once a rock starts rolling down a hill it cannot be stopped.'

19th December

And Georgina found out exactly what that meant the very next day, as her maid shook her awake. The maid told her that Trevor had ordered her to get Georgina up and dressed, and to tell her that she was to come to see him as soon as she was finished.

Sweat grew on her palms as she made her way downstairs, in her heart hoping against hope that this was not about the looming scandal.

Dread immediately filled her when she walked into his study and counted five open newspapers on his desk.

'Trev, I can explain—'

'Can you?' her brother thundered.

She flinched. In all her life, he'd never raised his voice at her.

'It was Elliot, wasn't it?'

Dropping down into the nearest chair, she nodded. 'Why?'

'I was trying to help him.'

She recounted the entire episode for him. When she'd finished, he did not seem convinced or mollified.

'Do not even try to lie to me and say that nothing happened,' Trevor said, not missing a beat.

How did he know?

As if answering her question, he said, 'I know you

very well, Georgina. Your face gives you away. You'd be a very poor poker player.'

The glib joke gave her hope that he wasn't entirely furious with her. That he didn't hate her.

'I'm sorry for the trouble I—I've c-caused you. I just wanted to help.'

'I know, Georgie.' Circling his desk, he came to her and took her hands in his. 'But what are we to do now?'

She shrugged. 'Nothing. We don't have to do anything, nor dignify those gossip rags by making it appear that we care.'

'I do not care,' he said. 'But what am I to do with you? What if you are with child?'

'There's no possibility of that.'

His mouth twitched. 'If you are saying what I think you are saying, I'm sorry to inform you that is not a guaranteed method of preventing conception.'

'But we won't know for a while, will we? And by then he may be married to someone else.'

Jealousy once again reared its ugly head as she thought of Elliot with another woman.

'True. And of course we will find a way to deal with it. But there is something I would like to know.' He placed her hands back on her lap. 'Georgie, the reason I guessed that it was Elliot, and that the story was true, is because I could see the attraction between you. I saw it in him, especially, from the beginning. But I soon started to see the signs from you as well.'

'Y-You did?'

Oh, heavens, how mortifying.

'I warned him off at first, because I know… I know you aren't keen on marriage.'

'It's not that I'm not keen, Trev. No one has ever asked me or even courted me.'

'You truly think that is the reason?'

'I…' Her brother's words made her pause. 'What do you mean?'

'Ah, I will let you think on that. But tell me, if Smith wanted you, and you wanted him, why not agree to marry? Why this farce with finding him a bride? Did you think I would disapprove because he is not a peer? Do you not trust that I would consider your happiness above all?'

The hurt on his face plucked at her chest. 'Oh, no! Dear heavens, Trevor.' She stood up to embrace him. 'Of course I trust you and love you. You've been nothing but supportive and kind since…since…'

His arms came around her. 'Since Mama and Papa died.'

She did not want to think of that right now. 'He did ask me, Trev. To marry him.'

'And you said no? After what he did?'

'What *we* did,' she corrected. 'And, no. He asked me when we first met.'

His hands dropped down to his sides. 'Explain.'

She dropped back down to the chair. 'He said he would rescind the eviction notice on the orphanage if I married him. He wants a titled wife—not for him, but for his sisters. New York society shunned them, you see, which is why he brought them here. A wife with the right name and connections could open so many doors for Anne-Marie and Lily.'

'Ah, I see. And when we couldn't find a way to save St Agnes's, you offered your services as a procurer.'

'Matchmaker,' she corrected. 'And I truly did try to find him a bride in earnest. I didn't mean for…for all this to happen.'

'I know, Georgie. You were trying to help. You've always been kind-hearted.' Her brother tsked. 'But I'm afraid no good deed goes unpunished. And now you must bear the consequences.'

'And what are those consequences?'

'For now, there are two: weather the scandal or mitigate it with a quick engagement.'

The unease swirling inside her settled deep in her belly. 'I can't… I don't want to.'

'I won't force you, Georgie,' he said. 'Legally, I cannot. And you know that no matter what I will support you.'

'Then there is no need for all this fuss,' she said. 'It's not as if I'm some debutante on the marriage mart.'

'Yes, but there are other consequences.'

Oh, yes. Those that Miss Warren had mentioned. Trevor would never show it, but he would resent her once he decided to seek a bride, or when it was his children's turn to join society. Would she really have

to choose between Anne-Marie and Lily and her future nieces and nephews?

'I must leave you for now, Georgie,' he said.

'Wh-where are you going?'

'To see Elliot. Since he has not come to see me, I
assume he hasn't seen these newspapers yet and probably has no inkling of what has happened.'

Hope sparked in her. 'If that's the case then perhaps
we do not have to tell him anything.'

'Of course we do. And also, do you not think it
strange that his name isn't mentioned in any of the
articles?'

'Is it not?'

'No. And I think he might be interested in finding
out why.'

Georgina bit her lip. 'Maybe whoever saw us didn't
know who he was.'

'Possible…but very improbable.' He kissed her temple. 'Now, stay here. Do not leave the house. I have
told Dawson to turn away anyone who comes to the
door.'

She remained in his study even after he'd left,
stunned, her limbs refusing to move. How could this
have gone so wrong? Who could possibly have seen
them at the inn? No one who might know her or Elliot,
that was for sure, based on the kind of clientele there.

Would Trevor force Elliot to marry her now?

A different sort of emotion coursed through her.
Like when she was having one of her spells, she felt

like fleeing. Her stomach churned at the thought of marriage. To be with one person for ever, until they—

She shut down her mind, unwilling to venture further. Besides, what could she do now but wait?

Chapter Thirteen

19th December

'Mr Smith, there is someone here to see you.'

Elliot did not look up from the contracts he was reading at his desk. 'Do they have an appointment, Grant?'

'N-No, sir,' his assistant stammered.

'Then send them away.'

'Yes, Mr Smith.'

With an impatient grunt, Elliot turned his attention back to the contracts. Which was, frankly, a futile effort as he'd spent the last fifteen minutes trying to decipher the same sentence. The words individually made sense, and he could read them forwards and backwards. But his mind refused to make sense of them because it was currently preoccupied with one thing.

One person.

Georgina.

He closed his eyes, allowing himself to think of her.

Just for this moment. Just for a minute. Which was a mistake, because once he began he could not stop thinking of her. Had he imagined it all? It seemed that way at times. As if she'd been a fevered dream. But the smell and taste and feel of her imprinted on his mind felt real, and no matter how much he told himself to forget her, he simply could not.

He'd questioned his every move and decision since leaving Northamptonshire. He should not have left Georgina. Should not have taken her with him to chase after Anne-Marie. Or even gone to Foxbury Hill in the first place. Perhaps he shouldn't have proposed to Georgina, or even bought that damned building.

This continued on and on, until his thoughts spiralled out of control and he had to shake himself to stop.

At the very least, his sisters were safe at home. And Anne-Marie didn't seem as angry as she usually was—at least she hadn't for the last two days. She was quiet, and there was no longer that simmering rage he'd used to feel from her.

'Mr Smith?'

'What is it now, Grant?' he asked, irritated.

'He—that is, His Lordship—insists on seeing you.'

His head snapped up. 'His Lordship?'

'Yes, sir. The Marquess of Arundel.'

Why the devil would he come here?

Elliot blew out a breath as he glanced back at the contracts. It was not as if he was getting any work done anyway. 'Send him in.'

He sympathised with the Marquess. After all, he too knew the panic and horror of having a girl under his care disappear in the middle of the night. Perhaps Arundel was here to ask for his assistance in locating Lavinia, or maybe even an insight into what she might have been thinking, running away. He wasn't sure if he had any advice for the Marquess, but he would do his best to help.

'The Marquess of Arundel,' Grant announced, and then stepped aside to let him through.

'Good morning, Mr Smith,' Arundel greeted him.

'Good morning. Please have a seat, my lord.'

Elliot observed the Marquess as he approached his desk. For a man whose daughter had eloped with a lover two days ago, he did not look distraught. In fact, if he hadn't known better, Elliot would have said he looked rather pleased with himself.

'What can I do for you, my lord?' he asked.

Arundel retrieved some newspapers he had tucked under his arm and dropped them on his desk. When the Marquess remained silent, Elliot picked them up and began to read.

At first he was confused as to why the Marquess had brought him these gossip columns. But then, as he read through the second one, it became apparent what—or who—they were about. They were dragging Georgina's name through the mud, calling her all sorts of names and making insinuations, all for the sake of selling papers.

Elliot gritted his teeth, trying to tamp down his

anger. He would not show any emotion in front of the Marquess—at least not until he'd figured out why he was here.

'I assume you did not come here so that we might discuss the latest gossip, my lord?'

'You're welcome,' the Marquess said with a smug smile.

'I beg your pardon?'

'I said, "you're welcome."'

'For what?'

'For not having your name dragged into this scandal.'

It took a moment before the words sank in and Elliot comprehended him. 'You…you have spread these vicious rumours?' His hands curled into tight fists at his sides.

'You and I both know they aren't rumours.'

'And how would you know that?'

'I have my ways.' Arundel threaded his fingers together.

'You can leave, or you can tell me.'

The Marquess paused, planting his chin on his linked hands. 'I suppose you'll find out anyway… Lavinia saw you when she returned to the inn.'

That she-devil.

'Oh? Did your dearest daughter grow a conscience and decide to return for the innocent girl she dragged into this scheme of hers?'

The Marquess's face turned scarlet. 'Your sister is

safe, as I heard it. No harm done. My daughter, on the other hand—'

'Oh, yes, please do enlighten me on the "harm" Lady Lavinia has suffered in all this.'

'Foolish girl,' he spat. 'I told her…warned her that fool was a worthless rake and fortune-hunter.'

'Who is he?'

'Some third son of a baronet—who cares who he is?' Arundel waved a hand dismissively. 'The bastard changed his mind about eloping with Lavinia once they were on the way. He turned the coach around and dropped her back at the inn—where they saw you and our dear "Lady G" as you were leaving. Thankfully, Lavinia found her way safely back to London the very same evening. I barely had time to write that anonymous letter to the *Herald* so they could print it in the following day's morning edition.'

'And now you are here to ask for my forgiveness, are you?'

He might have considered forgiving Lady Lavinia had she come back because she'd felt remorse about leaving Anne-Marie alone.

'Forgiveness?' The Marquess laughed. 'How about you show me some gratitude for excluding your name from the story?'

That fact still boggled him. 'And why would you do that?'

'Why do you think?'

'Stop wasting my time and tell me.'

The Marquess tsked. 'You know, Mr Smith, when

we played that game of chess I could read your every move even before you made it. Don't feel bad—it's an amateur mistake. Masters of the game plan everything from the beginning—which pieces to move where, and which to sacrifice in order to win. And when things do not go their way, they adapt.'

'I'm tiring of this,' Elliot said. 'Get to the point.'

'When my foolish daughter came crawling back, after she'd been spurned by her lover, she told us of an unfortunate consequence of her actions.'

'Ah, she is—?'

'Yes.'

'Congratulations on being a grandfather.'

'And that is why I left your name out of the papers.'

'What—?' Elliot snapped his mouth shut as he grasped the true reason the Marquess was here. 'So you wish me to marry your daughter and claim the child as my own.'

'You are a very rich man.' A gleam appeared in the Marquess's eyes. 'Rich enough that I can overlook your low birth. You see, as a man with only daughters I have to be smart about how to use them to my advantage. After all, you can only play the cards life has dealt you.'

Something about the comment struck Elliot straight in the gut.

'Genevieve is already going to marry a duke—Waldemere is all but in the bag. Now I need to secure my financial future and collect another powerful son-in-law.'

'Collect? Like your chess trophies?'

He laughed. 'Yes. But after Lavinia's actions… That damned fool would have cost me both you *and* Waldemere if she had gone through with it. The Duke, of course, would never marry Genevieve if Lavinia's failed elopement and her current condition became public. But, as I said, when an opponent makes a move you did not anticipate, you must adapt.'

Elliot remained silent as he gathered his thoughts and herded his emotions.

'So, Mr Smith,' the Marquess said, smiling craftily. 'Shall I accept your proposal on Lavinia's behalf? Or perhaps tomorrow's edition of the *London Daily Herald* will publish the name of "Lady G's" lover: "Mr S", the man with the famed golden touch? I daresay if they do you might very well find it difficult to procure a wife from Mayfair or Belgravia…unless perhaps you scour the kitchens for a scullery maid.'

Elliot calmly placed his palms on top of his desk and stood up. 'Allow me to clarify the situation at hand. You thought you would sacrifice a pawn—Lady Georgina—not only to shield your daughter from scandal, but also to blackmail me into marrying her?'

The Marquess did not reply, though Elliot saw the slightest tic at the corner of his mouth. Unfortunately for the Marquess, while Elliot may not be a good chess player, he knew people and could see when they were caught off guard. And from the look on the Marquess's face, he was very much caught off guard by Elliot's cool demeanour.

'Well, my lord?'

'Y-You owe m-me for not exposing your name. Think of your sisters—'

'Enough!' He slammed his fists on the table. 'You are a vile man, with an equally abhorrent daughter who put my sister in danger.' Fury rushed into his veins. 'I will never marry Lavinia, and I don't care what you say. But if I hear anyone even whisper my name or those of my sisters in connection with any scandal, I will place your head on a spike and parade it up and down Upper Brook Street.'

The Marquess spluttered. 'You dare threaten *me*? A *marquess*?'

'You doubt me? Or perhaps you would prefer ruin and shame?'

As he did with all his business prospects, he had already had his private investigator compile a file on Arundel.

'My lord, it isn't quite true that you only have daughters, is it? Hmm?' He tapped a finger on his chin. 'What about those strapping young boys hidden away in that cottage in Devonshire? They live with their mother, right? A "Mrs" Vanessa Howard.'

Arundel's face drained of colour. 'H-How did you—?'

'I, too, have my ways.' He folded his arms over his chest. 'Will you see yourself out? Or should I have you tossed out?'

The Marquess rose from the chair. 'You think you could do better than my daughter?' He harrumphed.

'I am a marquess. A common tradesman like you will never be as good as me, even if you marry the Queen!'

Elliot didn't flinch when the door slammed.

Good riddance.

Still shaking with anger, he unclenched his fists and his jaw. Though not a man of violence, Elliot had never been more tempted to hurt another person than he had this day. He imagined putting his hands around Arundel's skinny neck would feel immensely enjoyable.

But he had more important things to think about.

Such as Georgina and her ruined reputation—which was, of course, his fault.

He had to go to her…make sure she was all right. He would also go to Harwicke and explain everything, and then ask for his permission to marry Georgina. It was the only way to save her from complete ruin.

'Grant!' He shouted. 'My coat and hat—now!'

He marched towards the door and yanked it open to step outside—and promptly collided with the person who was about to step in.

'Oomph!'

Elliot stepped back, steadying himself, as the Duke of Harwicke bounced back from their crash. There was something comical about the surprised expression on the Duke's face, and Elliot nearly laughed—except the Duke's superior reflexes had him springing forward, his fist slamming straight into Elliot's cheek.

Elliot's head snapped back as pain exploded in his face. For a man who had likely never worked at any manual job, Harwicke had a mean right hook. Covering his face with his hands, he peered at Harwicke through his fingers. The Duke was hunched over, his breathing shallow, face scrunched up.

If that punch hadn't told him clearly enough, it was evident that Harwicke had already read the papers and guessed Elliot was the unknown lover.

'I had to do it.' Harwicke shook his hand and winced. It gave Elliot a modicum of comfort, knowing he had caused the Duke some pain.

'I wouldn't have expected anything less.'

He soothed his cheek with his finger. That would definitely bruise, but at least nothing was broken.

'You do not deny anything that has been said in the papers?'

Elliot stepped aside to let him in. 'Let's speak in private.'

He had hoped to see Georgina, but he supposed he should deal with the Duke first.

'Listen here, Smith—'

'I will marry her,' he interrupted.

'You damned *better* marry her. But it's not me you have to convince.'

'Convince? What are you talking about? She must marry me. She has no choice.'

'She will always have a choice as long as I am around,' Trevor said firmly. 'I won't force her, if that's what you are thinking. Besides, why do you care? Your name was never mentioned.'

'And I know exactly why. You should have seat, Harwicke. We need to talk.'

'All right.' The Duke glanced around the office. 'Damn it, don't you have anything to drink around here?'

'I have tea, coffee and water,' Elliot offered.

'No whisky or cognac?'

His eyes slid upwards. 'One moment.'

'Where are you going?'

'Someone in this damned office must have a bottle of something stronger.' Elliot poked his head out through the door. 'Grant! Find me something to drink.'

'Drink?' Grant scratched his head. 'Like…tea?'

'No, a *drink*. Pilfer it from one of those damned accountants who think they can hide their midday tipples from me.'

'Yes, sir!'

Elliot returned to his desk and sat down, indicating that Harwicke do the same. Moments later Grant reappeared, a flask in his hand.

'Give it to His Grace.'

Harwicke accepted it, opened the top and took a sip, wincing as he swallowed. 'Now, what do you know of those damned rags knowing about you and Georgina?'

'It was Arundel.'

And Elliot explained the entire situation to Harwicke, including how the Marquess had tried to blackmail him into claiming Lady Lavinia's child as his own.

'Bastard!' Harwicke spat. 'If only I'd arrived a minute sooner, I would have smashed his nose in.'

'Lucky for me, then…' Elliot groaned as the pain in his cheek throbbed.

'I still would have punched you in any case.' The Duke scowled. 'I warned you to stay away from her.'

What could he say to the man? He would not tell him that his sister had requested to be deflowered. In any case, he was the more experienced of the two of them, so he should have known better.

'I have no defence to that, but I seek to make it right and restore her honour.'

'I have told you that you will have to convince her to marry you.'

'She still does not want to marry me? After all this?'

Elliot had to admit that stung something fierce.

The Duke scowled. 'She does not want to marry at all—never had any interest in it.'

'Because of her spells?'

'You know about those?' Harwicke appeared taken aback.

'I've seen it happen and she has told me. She doesn't think she'd make a good society wife for me because she can't stand being in crowds and entertaining people.'

'Yes, but I think there may be more.'

Elliot leaned forward. 'More?'

'I suspect, anyway…' Harwicke shook his head. 'We lost our parents at a very young age, you see. She was only fourteen. They were a love match, and we had grown up with love and affection...' He cleared his throat. 'I think losing them not only destroyed her confidence, but her belief in love.'

Elliot could understand that feeling. He knew love never lasted.

'You must find a way to convince her,' said the Duke.

'I don't know how you think I can do that.'

Georgina had made herself very clear about not wanting marriage to anyone, and he would never do anything that might hurt her.

'It's not that I don't want to marry her...'

'Ah, so that's not in question, then?'

'Of course not. Who wouldn't want to marry Georgina? She's kind, thoughtful—and my sisters already love her. Lily won't stop talking about her.'

The Duke seemed pleased by what he'd said. 'I see.'

'But if she's damned set on not marrying, then I can't change her mind.' He paused. 'And I don't think I can give her what she wants.'

'Do not be too sure of that. What if she is with child?'

'I made sure—'

'You and I both know that method is not always effective.'

Damn. The Duke was right. He was a damned idiot for sleeping with her.

'What would you do if she still refused me then?' Elliot asked.

Still, the thought of her pregnant… Christ, she would look so lovely…her belly large and full.

Nine months from now he could be holding his son or his daughter.

His legacy.

'I will do whatever I need to to help her,' said Harwicke. 'Send her away to the Continent to have the child and find a couple to adopt it.'

The very thought of his own flesh and blood being raised by strangers sent Elliot into a rage.

'Are you finished with that?' He nodded at the flask.

'I was after the first sip. *Blech.*'

'Good. We're leaving for Harwicke House—now.'

Being required to stay inside and not answer any calls was usually not difficult for Georgina. In fact, if Trevor ordered her never to leave the house again, she would normally be in heaven.

But today Harwicke House, the sitting room, and the very chair she sat upon seemed like a prison.

Glancing up from her book, she saw that Trevor had now been gone for at least an hour.

'Watching the clock will not make it go faster,' Miss Warren remarked.

'I know. I just…' She'd been on tenterhooks since Trevor had left. 'I don't even know why I'm so anxious.'

Placing her book down, she stood up and began to pace across the carpet.

'It's not as if I can do anything.'

Elliot would not agree to marry her—not when he wanted a wife who could bring his sisters into society. And she certainly wouldn't marry him.

'You do realise that if certain consequences arise nine months from now, you will have to marry?'

Her hand immediately went to her belly, then quickly dropped. 'No, it won't happen.' She continued before Miss Warren could protest. 'And if it did then...then I will go to the Continent and have my child there.'

Of course with the news of her indiscretion all over London, she doubted that her sudden disappearance would go unnoticed.

'Georgina, I'm back.'

She started at the sound of Trevor's voice. 'What did you—?' She froze on the spot.

Trevor was, indeed, back—but he was not alone. Elliot stood beside him.

A jolt of shock coursed through her as his jade-green gaze collided with hers. 'Good morning, Lady Georgina,' he greeted her. 'Your Grace, may I speak to your sister alone?'

'Trev, no—'

'Of course. Miss Warren? If you please?'

'Is that wise, Your Grace?' her companion asked.

Trevor's jaw hardened. 'Miss Warren, do not make me ask you twice.'

'Yes, Your Grace.' She shot Georgina a knowing look, but turned and followed Trevor out through the door.

An awkward silence hung between them until he finally spoke. 'It was Lady Lavinia.'

'I beg your pardon?'

What was he talking about?

'She was the one who saw us at the inn. You and me.'

'She—she saw us? What was she doing there? I thought she was on her way to Scotland with her lover.'

'It's a long story.' He made his way to the settee. 'Why don't you sit down and I'll tell it to you?'

Curious—and confused at the same time—she did as he asked.

Elliot sat down beside her and began to explain what had happened from the beginning and including Arundel's visit.

'And so I told the Marquess to leave.'

Georgina could only stare at him as her mind processed the events he had recounted. 'I can't believe she did that...and he tried to blackmail you.' Lady Lavinia truly was vicious, and it seemed she had inherited it from her scheming father. 'I'm sorry.'

'It's quite all right. He'll be dealt with.'

The coldness in his eyes made her shiver.

'But you see, now we must marry.'

She shot up and away from him as if she'd sat on a pin. 'There is no need for us to marry.'

'There is every need for us to marry,' he replied. 'Your reputation is ruined.'

'But yours is not.' If there was one thing she

was grateful for in this situation it was that. 'Miss Philipps—'

'To hell with Miss Philipps!' He stood up. 'I don't want to marry her. I want to marry you.'

'Why? I would be the worst choice.'

'That's not true.'

'It is,' she insisted. 'Anyone else would be better than me, and—'

'You need a husband.'

'I beg your pardon?' She had to stop herself from chuckling. 'I do not.'

'Yes, you do. It's the only way to save your reputation. The scandal will not just affect you, but your entire family. Think of your brother.'

'He is a duke— What are you doing?' Elliot had reached out towards her. 'El—' The touch of his palm on her cheek made her gasp. 'Elliot…'

Heavens, his rough hands felt wonderful on her skin. Her knees shook and she had to brace herself on the closest thing she could reach—which was his chest.

'Weren't we good together, Georgina?'

He leaned down, bringing his mouth so close to her ear that she could feel his breath.

'It could be like that every night.'

'Huh…?'

What was he saying? She couldn't quite think…not when his lips were inches from her.

'I would make a good husband to you.'

Frustration grew in her, from wanting to feel his mouth on her bare skin, but he didn't move an inch.

'Elliot…this isn't fair.'

'What's not fair? I am merely reminding you of what was, and telling you what could be.'

She sighed.

'How about I show you how serious I am?' He drew away from her.

'How?'

Jade-green eyes stared down at her. 'I will rescind the eviction notice.'

'You mean, if I marry you?'

'Even if you do not. I had already decided to anyway…before the scandal broke.'

'Truly? When?'

'The night at the inn—before you offered yourself to me.'

She searched his face, looking for deceit or any indication that he was lying. But she found none.

'You would do that?'

'Yes. For you.'

Her heart leapt into her throat, and she could only stare at him,

'There is no downside to your marrying me,' he said. 'Only positives. Your reputation will be saved. And if we were to have a child…'

She couldn't argue with him. He was right.

'But there will be a downside for you.' Whirling away from him, she wrapped her arms around herself and began to pace. 'I know… I know why you want to marry a lady. It's not to raise your own standing, is it? It's for your sisters. You want someone who can help them gain a foothold in society once they are out. I'm sorry, Elliot, but I cannot be that wife. I cannot be the kind of wife who can guide your sisters so they will make successful matches. I am a liability, not an asset. I cannot be what you need me to be.'

'You're speaking of your spells?'

'Y-Yes.'

'They do not matter—not any more.'

'Why not?'

'Because of something Arundel told me.'

'Arundel…?'

He raked his fingers through his hair. 'They are illegitimate.'

That made her halt her pacing. 'What?'

'Anne-Marie and Lily. They are illegitimate. My father never married their mother. She was a dockside whore who dropped them off at my doorstep one night and then disappeared.'

Those poor girls.

She pressed a hand to her chest. 'Why are you telling me this?'

'Because you should know. Those girls… I just want what's best for both of them. And for them to have a fighting chance in this world.' When his voice hitched, he paused to clear his throat. 'In this world, we can only play the cards we are dealt. I want to give them the best chance, since life has not been kind to them. Arundel said something similar about his daughters, and it got me thinking... I do not want to be like him.'

'You are nothing like that scoundrel.' She clicked her tongue. 'Life may not have been kind to them, but it has dealt them *you*, Elliot.' Her soft hand covered his. 'You give yourself too little credit. Even if you weren't wealthy, they would still have a fighting chance as long as you are on their side. They do not need anyone else.'

And certainly not me.

'And I don't need a wife to open the Ton's doors for them. Anne-Marie and Lily will choose to be whatever they want to be.'

'Exactly. You don't need a wife.'

'No, but I *want* one. I want you.'

Catching her hands, he lifted them to his face and kissed her palms. The shock of the contact made her shiver.

'If you marry me, you will never have to attend any ball, tea party, opera—'

'I actually like the opera.'

He smiled against her hand. 'Noted. But if you were my wife, you would never have to take calls from anyone you don't like, or throw dinner parties. You don't even have to lift a finger. You can stay at home embroidering, drinking tea, or doing whatever the hell you want. You'll never be troubled with your spells again.'

She sighed, feeling her defences slowly breaking down. 'This truly isn't fair.'

'What's not fair? Me offering you the world and everything you want? All I ask is that you take my name and have my children.'

Her breath hitched at the idea of having children. And with Elliot.

'So, what do you say, Georgina?' He got down on one knee. 'Will you marry me?'

She was about to answer, then paused. 'Wait… Before I answer that, there is something I must know.'

'What is it, sweetheart?'

'Did you kiss Lady Lavinia under the mistletoe?'

'You want me to answer that *now*?' He gestured to himself. 'As I am on my knees, asking you to be my wife?'

'Yes.'

He blew out a breath. 'No, I did not. When Lady Arundel pointed out that we were under it, I simply pretended not to hear her and moved away. There. Does that make you happy?'

'Immensely.' She gazed into his jade-green eyes, revelling in them. 'Then, yes, I will marry you.'

Elliot got up and wrapped his arms around her, then melded his mouth to hers. Her heart nearly burst from her chest and she sighed into his mouth. She'd missed this…missed the press of his body along hers and the scent of his cologne. How different they were—small and large, soft and hard. Her hands moved up, so she could rake her fingers into the soft hair at his nape, but disappointment filled her when he pulled away, ending the kiss early.

'Elliot?'

'We cannot…not here.' Stepping back, he smoothed his hands down his front. 'Come, let's tell your brother the happy news.'

'I—yes, of course.'

Georgina knew she should be happy. St Agnes's was saved, and she would have everything she could ever want.

But a part of her still felt unsure about her decision. It felt like…falling. As if the world had been pulled out from under her, sending her stomach swooping. She couldn't understand it. She was about to get all she wanted.

But then, it could all be taken away from her.

'So she said yes?' Trevor said, as soon as Elliot opened the door.

'She did indeed.'

Her brother looked relieved. 'I'm glad.' He placed a hand on her arm and kissed her on the cheek. 'I am very happy for you, Georgie.'

'Thank you, Trev.'

'Congratulations, Lady Georgina.'

Miss Warren, who had apparently waited outside the door with her brother, smiled. Her companion seemed genuinely pleased.

'Thank you, Miss Warren.'

'We still have to deal with the ramifications of the scandal,' she replied.

'I have a solution to that,' Elliot announced.

Trevor cocked his head. 'You do?'

'Yes. Arundel gave me the idea, actually. See, I happen to know the editors of three out of the five newspapers that printed that gossip.'

'What do you mean "know" them?'

'I was looking to buy them. But I never make a purchase without doing my due diligence, so I have a private investigator who specialises in finding information for me. No one can keep anything hidden for long. Each of those owners has something to hide, and I'm sure they could be persuaded to come to our side.'

'B-But what about the freedom of the press?' Georgina said. 'You can't possibly blackmail them into printing something that isn't true.'

'I won't. I'm going to ask them to print a different piece of gossip—saying that you were with me that night. They will run the story we give them, which is that we were in love, but afraid that your brother and society wouldn't approve, so we tried to escape. Then we changed our minds and came back, and I did the right thing by seeking your brother's approval. After our version of the story has spread we will announce our engagement, and everyone will assume that was the truth all along.'

'That sounds plausible,' Miss Warren agreed.

'Quite brilliant, actually,' Trevor said. 'Not quite the truth, but not a complete lie.'

'Those three newspapers will print nothing but flattering pieces about our love story,' Elliot said. 'And the others will follow suit. The Ton will eat up the gossip and forget about our one indiscretion.'

'Because they will be too busy sneering down their noses at your supposed "love match",' Miss Warren said. 'Society will think it unfashionable. They would have respected you more if it was simply an arrangement.'

'Georgina?' Elliot asked. 'What do you think?'

All eyes turned to her as she considered the plan. 'I don't particularly care what the Ton think of us.'

Elliot beamed at her.

'So, shall we celebrate?' Trevor asked. 'Champagne, maybe? Or coffee for you, Elliot?'

'I don't mind a sip of champagne—especially on the right occasion.' Elliot smiled at her.

And although Georgina smiled back at him, that swooping feeling in her belly returned...as if she truly was falling into something unknown.

Chapter Fourteen

20th December

'Are you certain the Serpentine is not yet frozen solid enough for skating?' Lily asked.

'I'm afraid so, poppet,' Georgina said.

'How do you know?'

'Because usually, once the ice is ready, the chestnut sellers will set up over there.' She pointed to the banks of the pond.

'And how do the chestnut sellers know?'

Georgina laughed. 'How many questions do you ask a day?'

'Much more than this,' Anne-Marie interjected.

'Enough questions,' Elliot declared. When Lily made a face, he added, 'For at least the next ten minutes, so we can enjoy our walk in the park.'

Anne-Marie shivered. 'It's lovely out here, but I don't understand why we are walking in Hyde Park in the middle of a cold day. Why, there isn't anyone else here but us.'

Elliot caught Georgina's gaze. 'Exactly.'

When they'd been deciding where to go to break the news of their engagement, Georgina had suggested they take the girls shopping on Bond Street, or perhaps somewhere lively like Leicester Square. But Elliot knew those places would set off one of her spells, which was unacceptable, so they'd settled on a walk through Hyde Park.

She had seemed nervous about telling the girls, because she didn't know how they would react to her marrying Elliot. He, of course, had assured her many times that the girls would be ecstatic, but had relented and promised not to tell them until the following day. Once the girls were informed today, they would set their plan into motion. The three newspapers Elliot had 'convinced' to print their version of the rumours would publish their columns tomorrow. Then, he and Georgina would announce their engagement the day after.

Elliot hadn't expected that he would feel nervous about telling the girls. It was a strange emotion…to be so unsure of himself and a decision he'd made. While he had assured Georgina that Anne-Marie and Lily would be happy at the news, there was a small kernel of doubt in him. Despite all the years he'd spent with his sisters, it occurred to him that he didn't truly know them. What if they didn't want him to marry at all? Or—worse—what if they didn't care?

His hand came up to the breast pocket of his coat, feeling the small, rectangular object hidden away inside. Last night when he'd come home, he hadn't been able to sleep, so he'd thought a book might help him relax. Everything inside the house he'd purchased had been included with the sale, even the library books. So he had browsed the shelves, looking for something to read. As he'd approached one of the shelves, the very first book that had caught his eye had been a small, leather-bound book at the very end. The spine was thin, which meant it wouldn't be too long or boring, which would be perfect. When he had peered closer and read the title, he'd nearly laughed aloud: *A Christmas Carol* by Charles Dickens.

He had picked up the book and, sure enough, he had finished it in one sitting. And now he had some *thoughts*. Perhaps he would have time to share them later with Georgina—for he wanted to see her reaction when he told her he had read it—but for now, the tome was a comforting weight against his breast.

'What are we doing here, anyway?' Anne-Marie said, interrupting his thoughts. 'Not that I mind seeing you again, Lady Georgina.' She smiled warmly at her, then mouthed a *Thank you*.

'Yes, about that…' Elliot stopped in the middle of a path and turned to them. 'Girls, there is something I must—we must tell you.' Sidling over to Georgina, he slid his hand into hers. 'I have proposed to Lady Georgina and she has accepted.'

The two girls' eyes widened and their mouths formed into perfect Os.

'Yay!' Lily let out a scream that rang through the

empty park, then threw herself at Georgina. 'You're to be our sister!'

'Elliot… I…' Anne-Marie's gaze bounced from Georgina's to his. 'This is probably the only good decision you've ever made.' She embraced Georgina. 'I'm so happy.'

A lump formed in his throat as he saw Georgina's eyes water as she attempted to compose herself and received more hugs from the girls.

'When will you get married?' Anne-Marie grabbed at her hand excitedly. 'And will we go back to New York afterwards?'

'What colour dress will I wear?' Lily tugged at her skirt. 'Can I wear pink, please? Can I hold your flowers?'

'I—I don't know,' she stammered. 'I mean, we haven't discussed anything about the wedding or what will happen after it yet.'

'We can discuss that another time.'

It was true they hadn't ironed out the details, but he remembered that Georgina had said that their engagement period would be for at least a year.

Damned if he was going to wait that long to have her again.

Clearing his throat, he said, 'It's getting much colder than I anticipated. How about we go to the new shop that has just opened by my office? I've heard they specialise in serving hot chocolate.'

Both girls heartily agreed, though he could see

Georgina hesitate, perhaps thinking of the crowds that would surely be around the busy commercial district.

So he added, 'Maybe we don't have to go there. We can go home.'

'But I want hot chocolate,' Lily said.

Georgina tucked back a stray hair from Lily's cheek. 'Then you shall have it, poppet.'

'Are you sure, Georgina?'

'Of course. Do not worry about me, Elliot,' she assured him. 'I will be fine.'

They all returned to their respective carriages and drove towards the chocolate shop. When they reached it, it was already crowded, as Elliot had predicted. He could see the people inside standing shoulder to shoulder as they queued up to the counter, bumping into others who were already squeezed in at the tables, trying to enjoy their drinks.

'Oh, my, I don't think we will even be able to get in.' The apprehension on Georgina's face was already apparent. 'Maybe we should just…go home.'

Elliot thought for a moment. 'Actually, I think we may be able to persuade the proprietor to allow us to bring the chocolate to my office. Wouldn't that be better instead?'

'But I want to see the inside. I'm small and won't take up too much space,' Lily whined. 'They have all sorts of chocolates on display too. Can we look at the chocolates? Please, Lady Georgina?'

Georgina stammered. 'I…er…'

'Maybe Miss Warren can accompany you?' Elliot

suggested. 'I think Lady Georgina may have been chilled by our walk. Why don't I take her to my office—it's only two doors down—and the three of you can look at the chocolates? Maybe even purchase a few treats for us? Just tell the owner to send the bill to my office.'

Lily waved her hands in excitement. 'Oh, Miss Warren, could you, please?'

'I suppose that should be all right.' The companion sent Elliot a look, as if sending him a warning. 'We will not be too long.'

'Of course. You know the way to the office, correct? Then I shall see you there.'

Taking Georgina's hand, he tucked it into his arm and began to walk towards his building. He ignored the gapes and stares from his employees, concentrating only on Georgina. While she didn't seem to be having one of her spells, she certainly looked as if she was close.

'How are you feeling?' he asked when they were alone in his office.

She took a big gulp of air. 'I am fine now. Thank you.' She clicked her tongue. 'I really thought… I thought I would be all right. Lily wanted so badly to…and I couldn't…'

'Don't be upset, sweetheart. And do not worry about pleasing Lily if it is a detriment to you.'

'She's a child and I am the adult.'

'Exactly.' Drawing her into his arms, he kissed her temple. 'She's a child—you do not have to cater to her whims. I am not marrying you because I want you to spoil them. I meant it when I said that, as my wife, you will never be forced to do anything that would cause you pain.'

'Elliot…' She breathed a sigh, then lifted her face up to meet his, coppery eyes all large and luminous. 'I…'

Something shifted in the air, and her eyes darkened. Before he knew it, she'd lunged at him, pressing her mouth to his.

Though initially surprised, he quickly recovered and returned her ardent kisses. The hunger that had been stalking at the edges of his mind pounced, taking over his body and demanding to be sated. Wrapping his arms around her, he pressed her close, revelling in the delicious curves and dips of her body, which would soon be his.

She deepened the kiss, her pert little tongue demanding entrance to his. He obliged, opening his mouth so their tongues could dance together. His body was on fire and his cock twitched, hardening as her hips brushed against him.

'Georgina…' he murmured between kisses. 'I want you.'

'Me too,' she confessed. 'I haven't stopped thinking about that night.'

'I wish we had time.' His hand reached up to cup her breast through the layers of her clothing. 'I want to make slow love to you again.'

'We have some time.'

Wait… Was she suggesting…? 'Are you sure? I can't be slow. Or gentle.'

'I don't need slow or gentle,' she urged. 'Just you.'

Christ.

He backed her up until they reached his desk, which thankfully was clear of any papers or other items. Lifting her up, he placed her on top. 'You must be quiet. Can you do that?'

Coppery eyes wide, she nodded.

Spreading her legs, he lifted her skirts as high up as he could and reached between them. He found the seams of her drawers then pushed his fingers between them. She was damp, but not quite ready for him yet. Finding that nub at the crest of her womanhood, he gave it soft, gentle strokes. When she began to moan and undulate her hips, he increased the pressure and rhythm, bringing her to a quick orgasm that left her shuddering in his arms.

'Elliot,' she moaned. 'Please, I need you.'

He did not need any further instruction or invitation, and he unbuttoned his falls and grabbed his already hard cock. Manoeuvring himself between her legs, he pressed the tip at her entrance, then slowly began to push into her.

Georgina threw her head back, then moaned. 'Yes… please. It doesn't hurt at all. Oh!'

He thrust all the way inside her. 'You feel incredible, Georgina.'

Her arms tightened around him. 'Make me feel good again, Elliot.'

Gritting his teeth, he reached under her and cupped her bottom, then began to thrust into her. She let out a soft cry, then pressed her mouth to his shoulder to stop herself from making any more noise.

Elliot drove into her like a madman, as if his life depended on it. He did not want to be interrupted, so he had to quickly bring her to another orgasm. Pushing harder, he changed the angle of his hips. He must have done something right, because she was panting and biting at his shoulder. Soon she was shaking once more, and her body squeezed him, milking him, so that it took all his might not to spill into her right then and there.

He tried to withdraw. 'We must stop now... I can't...'

'No.' When he made a motion to withdraw she grabbed at his shoulders. 'Not again. Just...don't leave me.'

'Georgina, we're not married yet. I must.'

'No! Please. Stay.'

Unable to deny her anything, he continued to thrust into her, her tightness sending shocks of pleasure down his spine. He put his hand over her mouth to muffle her cries and she closed her eyes tight as her body clasped around him. In that moment his entire world was Georgina, and she was the world.

'Christ, Georgina...you're so...' He groaned as she pulsed around him.

At that second, he realised that he would do anything to keep her happy, to make sure she never suffered a day in her life. He would crawl over broken glass if that was what she wanted. Because...

'I lo—'

'Elliot!'

Georgina buried her face in his neck as her orgasm made her body shake violently, and her tightness clasping around him triggered his own. He almost went blind as pleasure burst from the knot at the base of his back, spreading over his body.

When his breathing had returned to normal and his muscles had relaxed, he withdrew from her. His heart still pounded in his chest, though, at what he'd so nearly said to her.

'Elliot?' she panted. 'What's wrong?'

He cleared his mind of all those thoughts.

'Nothing. Nothing at all.' Using the sleeve of his shirt, he wiped the sweat from his brow. 'Miss Warren and the girls could arrive at any moment.'

'Of course.'

She hopped down from the table and smoothed her skirts down, then proceeded to fix her coiffure. Elliot too, righted himself and his clothes.

'Do you think anyone will know...what we did here?'

Georgina's face was flushed, and her skin had taken on the most beautiful glow. Miss Warren would definitely figure out that something had happened.

'No, sweetheart.'

'Thank heavens.' She blew out a breath. 'I'm sorry... I don't know what got—'

'Shh…' He silenced her with a quick kiss. 'There is nothing wrong with what we did.'

'But it's broad daylight and we are in your office.'

'And? If you think our activities will be limited to the bedroom at night, then perhaps you should find a different husband.'

Her cheeks turned the most delightful shade of crimson.

'I may not be able to wait a whole year to marry you,' he said. 'I will convince Harwicke to let us marry next month.'

'Next *month*?'

'Yes. Don't you want to be married soon?'

Besides, with what happened just now, they might not have a choice.

'I do, but… I was thinking a Christmas wedding would be lovely.'

Irritation pricked him at the mention of that damned word. 'I—'

'Elliot we're here!' Lily announced as she burst through the door, waving the packages she had in her hands.

'Girls!' Georgina hurried over to them. 'What did you buy?'

'About half the shop,' Miss Warren said wryly. 'Apologies, Mr Smith. I wasn't sure if it was appropriate for me to chastise them for buying so much.'

'Not at all,' he said. 'Do not worry. I don't think they could buy enough chocolate to bankrupt me.'

'How was the shop?' Georgina asked.

'Wonderful! They had all sorts of chocolates, truffles and...'

Georgina listened patiently as Lily recounted her time at the chocolate shop, with Anne-Marie interrupting every now and then with anecdotes of her own.

For a moment, doubt entered his mind. In the throes of passion, he had nearly said the words he'd sworn he would never utter to a woman. He'd felt as if the words had been stuck in his throat, waiting for the right moment to be uttered. He had guarded himself well, though, until his own pleasure had nearly had him undone.

He could never say those words.

Love.

No, their marriage would be one of mutual respect, admiration and lust for each other. Harwicke had said that Georgina no longer believed in love. And he knew all too well the pitfalls of love, as he'd learned from watching his mother die while she called for the man she loved.

You're doing the right thing, he told himself.

The girls clearly loved Georgina already, and she them. They would grow under her care and example, and perhaps Anne-Marie's rebellious, churlish nature would be quelled. He, too, would have everything he wanted, including the fulfilment of his latest ten-year plan. And in a few short years, Georgina would bear him a passel of children, so that his legacy would live on.

That was all that mattered, and he would make damned sure nothing would stop him from marrying Georgina.

Georgina, Miss Warren and the girls stayed for another hour, but then unfortunately, they had to leave as Grant came and announced that his next appointment was in fifteen minutes. Georgina said something about taking the girls with her to visit St Agnes's the following day as they were leaving, which he agreed to.

After seeing them off, Elliot returned to his office to await his next meeting.

'Mr Charles Garret Brimsley III,' Grant announced. 'Of Brimsley & Company.'

A young fair-haired man who was perhaps a few years younger than him entered, dressed fashionably in what Elliot guessed was an ensemble from one of Savile Row's finest tailors.

'Elliot Smith,' he greeted him, and offered his hand. 'Nice to meet you, Mr Brimsley.'

The man took the hand he offered. 'Thank you for seeing me, Mr Smith.'

'Ah, you're American too,' Elliot deduced from his nasal accent.

'Chicago,' Brimsley said.

'Nice to see another American on these shores.' He gestured for Charles to sit on the chair across from him.

'Indeed… I've only been here three months, and

I'm starting to get tired of these stiff Londoners.' He laughed, his voice booming over the room.

'Yes, I know, they can be tiring. But London is a place of opportunities.'

'Indeed—which is why I'm here. I'm hoping to establish an office here. We specialise in real estate and railroad.'

'I see…'

A bit too late for that.

Unfortunately for Brimsley and his company, the English railway boom had gone bust a few years ago. The market had become much too saturated and shares in railroads had lost their value. Only the large companies were now building lines, and although Elliot predicted a small surge in interest in the railway once more in a year or two, it would likely not be as big as it had been in the beginning. If Brimsley was only entering the business now, then it was much too late.

Of course, Elliot kept that assessment to himself.

'So, what can I do for you, Mr Brimsley?'

'Well…uh…' Brimsley scratched at his collar. 'I find myself in a bit of a bind, Mr Smith.'

'What bind?'

'You see, my father and grandfather sent me to London so that I may establish an office here.'

'A clever move on their part.' Elliot knew he would have established his own office here in half the time it had taken him if he'd had someone he could trust, like a son or grandson. 'How fortunate they are to have you.'

'Indeed. They are very shrewd. My grandfather, Charles Senior, made his fortune trading fur in the Great Lakes region.'

'Congratulations to him.' Elliot tapped his foot impatiently. 'So, how can I get you out of your "bind"?'

'Yes, about that... I was supposed to acquire a building—one they had already pre-approved for me to purchase. I told them I had made an offer and they wired the money to me.'

'So, should I give you congratulations on your business deal as well?'

'No. I mean... You see...' He cleared his throat and shifted in his seat. 'Unfortunately, I found myself distracted.' He laughed. 'You understand, right? London's offerings are so much more sophisticated than those back in America. Anyway, in my distraction, someone else bought the building we intended to turn into our headquarters. That building is number fifty-five Boyle Street.'

Ah. It finally made sense why Brimsley was here.

Elliot shook his head mentally, feeling pity for Charles the II for having raised such a wastrel of a son. Of course, it did not surprise him at all. Charles the III likely had had everything handed to him on a silver platter, and prioritised his own gratification over work. He couldn't even be trusted to purchase one building—one whose owners had been eager to sell.

'I'm told you are the new owner of number fifty-five Boyle Street.'

'I am,' said Elliot. 'And what can I do for you?'

'I would like to purchase it. Please.'

Brimsley flashed him a charming smile, which Elliot guessed he used to disarm people, so he could get what he wanted. Unfortunately for him, Elliot did not care for smiles from empty-headed fools.

'It is not for sale.'

Besides, he was about to send word to the matron of St Agnes's about the cancellation of the eviction notice.

'Anything is for sale,' said Brimsley. 'Name your price.'

What a complete idiot Brimsley was. No businessman began a negotiation with 'name your price'. It was a guaranteed way to lose.

'Why did you not purchase it right away if you received the funds and arrived three months ago?'

He himself had only discovered the building was for sale at the end of November.

'I told you… I was distracted,' he replied, impatient.

'By what?'

'Does it matter?' he snarled. 'You have something I want and I have the money to purchase it. We were given a valuation of the building, and I'm willing to pay you ten percent over the asking price.' He retrieved a folder from his document case and handed it to Elliot. 'Here.'

Curious, he took the folder, opened it and began to read. It took all his might not to burst out laughing. Elliot had bought it for about half the market price because Atkinson had been so eager to be rid of this father's assets and to pay off his debts. That meant Brimsley was actually offering him *sixty* percent over what he'd paid.

'That's the starting figure for our negotiations, of course,' he said. 'How much do you want?'

Elliot closed the folder. 'You seem terribly eager. Why not purchase another building in the same area? You'll get far more value if you find a location a few streets down.'

'No, I must have this one.' Retrieving a handkerchief from his pocket, he wiped the perspiration from his brow. 'It must be number fifty-five Boyle Street.'

'But why—?' Realisation struck him. 'You've already told your father and grandfather that you have bought it, haven't you?'

His eyes bulged, then he blew out a resigned breath. 'Yes. And I have also…spent the money they sent me.'

Elliot clicked his tongue.

What a damned fool.

'Where will you get your funds to purchase the building, then?'

'I—I have my sources.'

'A bank?'

Brimsley's silence told him no. There were, of course, many enterprising businessmen everywhere, who loaned money at usurious rates.

Elliot leaned back in his chair and rested his chin on his clasped fingers. On one hand, he would love to teach this idiot a lesson and allow him to face the consequences of his actions. But on the other, making over fifty percent profit was much too tempting. Besides, Brimsley would find his comeuppance one way or another—his 'sources' were likely charging so much interest that the repayments would soar so high he would not be able to pay them. And when that happened, they would extract payment through whatever means necessary.

Of course there was the question of the orphanage—but that could easily be solved. With the money from the sale Elliot could purchase a bigger and even better home for the orphans—perhaps somewhere outside London, so Georgina would not have to deal with the crowds here.

Yes, that was what he would do. And as a wedding present to Georgina, he would not charge a single penny in rent.

'All right, Mr Brimsley, we have a deal.' He held out his hand.

'I… Of course.' He took the offered hand and shook it.

Elliot did not miss the way Brimsley's nose had turned up at the thought of shaking his hand; he was not the least bit surprised. Coming from two generations of wealth, the Brimsleys were likely the kind of family who would have shut Elliot and his sisters out of society. The very idea of taking his money was an added sweetener to this already favourable deal.

'I'll have my solicitors draw up the papers,' Elliot said. 'You can look them over and sign them, and we can finish the deal by tomorrow.'

'By the way, there is one clause I must add.'

'And what is that.'

'I must take ownership now.'

'Right now? Are you mad?'

'My father and grandfather arrive in six days. I must take ownership before then.'

'But the contracts and the funds will take a few days,' Elliot reasoned. 'And then we must wait for the deed to be transferred.'

'I don't care. I must show them a complete, functioning business office in six days.' He eyed Elliot, his nose turning up once again. 'Make it happen or the deal is off.'

Elliot considered his options. As long as there were no changes to the contracts they could be finalised in a day or two. Since they had already settled on the amount, the banks could begin to release the funds as well.

There was, of course, the question of the orphans at St Agnes's...

He snorted. How difficult could it be to move two dozen girls? He could hire people to help them, and he could afford to buy them brand-new furniture, bedding, even personal belongings. They could leave number fifty-five Boyle Street today, with only the clothes on their backs, and Elliot would ensure they would want for nothing.

'All right, Brimsley. As long as you don't cry foul on the terms we have already discussed, you can take possession in...five days.'

Yes, from his estimates, that should be enough time.

'Wonderful.' The relief on the other man's face was palpable, as if he'd just got a stay of execution. 'Just send everything to my house. I shall leave the address with your assistant.'

'A pleasure doing business with you, Mr Brimsley.'

'Likewise.'

He escorted Brimsley out of his office and as soon as he was gone turned to his assistant. 'Send word to Mr Morgan. I need him here, now.'

'Yes, sir.'

Elliot returned to his desk, then sank back into his chair, thoroughly pleased with himself.

What a glorious way to end the year.

When he'd moved to London six months ago and nothing had gone his way—the Ton refusing him entry into their hallowed halls, Anne-Marie continuously being difficult—he'd thought he would never progress on achieving the goals of his ten-year plan. Now, he had a wonderful fiancée, his sisters were happy, and he had just closed the easiest and most profitable deal of his life.

Perhaps, just this once, he would believe in luck.

Chapter Fifteen

21st December

'We cannot thank you enough, my lady,' Mrs Jameson said. 'It is because of you the girls will be able to stay in their home.'

Before they'd left his office yesterday, Georgina had asked Elliot if she could take the girls to the orphanage for a visit, and he had agreed. She'd decided that although she could not show them the more crowded and exciting sights of London, she would do her best to take them to places where she was comfortable. After all these months in England the girls had never gone farther than Hyde Park, where they would go for their daily morning walks with their governess or tutor.

So this morning she and Miss Warren had picked them up in her carriage. However, she had not arrived empty-handed. She'd had the footmen pack up one of the smaller Christmas trees at Harwicke House and brought it with her, along with several gifts for the girls and Elliot. The girls had shrieked in excitement as soon as they'd seen it. Georgina instructed their butler and housekeeper on how to put it up, and then she and the girls had driven to Boyle Street together.

'There is no need to thank me, Mrs Jameson.' Georgina patted her hand. 'First of all, it was a misunderstanding. Mr Smith had no idea he had bought an orphanage! Can you imagine his shock upon his discovery?'

That wasn't a complete lie, of course, as Elliot had said he wasn't aware there were people living in the building he had bought. However, she didn't want anyone to think he was the kind of man who would deliberately toss orphans out on the street during Christmas.

'He must have been beside himself...' Mrs Jameson tutted.

Thinking of his initial reaction—which had been to try to bribe her into marriage—Georgina nearly choked, trying not to laugh. 'That's one way to put it... But all is right in the world again. We needn't worry—at least not for the foreseeable future.'

'Still, I am glad you could make Mr Smith see the error of his ways. Why, it must be the spirit of Christmas working its magic.'

'Er...indeed.'

'Lady Georgina!' Lily waved at her from the top of the stairs, where she stood with five or six girls around her age, including Charlotte and Eliza.

'Look at me!'

'Look at what—? Lily, no!'

The little girl had climbed on the banister and was sliding all the way down, much to the delight of the other girls.

'Hooray, Lily!' Charlotte cried.

'So brave!' Eliza screamed.

Georgina's heart leapt into her throat as she sprang towards the stairs, catching Lily just in time before she reached the bottom. Setting her down, she said, 'Lilian Smith, don't you ever scare me like that again.'

'But it was fun!' Her jade-green eyes sparkled. 'None of my governesses ever allowed me to do this.'

'Oh, dear…is she all right?' Mrs Jameson asked. 'And did you say her name was Smith?'

'Er…yes.' She had introduced Lily and Anne-Marie to Mrs Jameson earlier, but had not mentioned the connection to St Agnes's new landlord.

'As in Mr Elliot Smith?' Mrs Jameson said.

'Elliot is my brother,' Lily stated. 'And he's marrying Lady Georgina. She's going to be my sister.'

That was another thing she hadn't mentioned to Mrs Jameson, as she'd been afraid the matron would make the connection between the cancellation of the eviction notice and her engagement.

'I see.' A knowing smile spread across the matron's face. 'Perhaps it's not the Christmas spirit that has inspired Mr Smith's generosity. But rather *love*?'

Georgina's heart seized at the word. 'Er…um…' It was difficult to breathe, as if her corset was laced too tight. 'Excuse me. I must…head to the necessary.'

She turned on her heel and hurried away from them,

down the long narrow corridor that led to a sitting room at the end. Once she was inside, she closed the door and leaned against it, closing her eyes as she took deep, calming breaths.

Perhaps she was having one of her spells. But no, it couldn't be. She never had them here at St Agnes's. The anxiousness felt similar, but worse in some ways, as if she wanted to burst out of her own skin.

Could it be what Mrs Jameson had said?

It was a preposterous notion. The love match was a story they'd concocted to save her reputation. It was no more real than…than the St Nicholas that Lily had spoken of, who gave away toys to children.

No, Elliot couldn't possibly love her.

Her breathing returned to normal, and with a determined shrug of her shoulders she marched out. When she reached the main hall, Mrs Jameson was nowhere to be found.

'Girls, where did Mrs Jameson go?'

'Someone knocked on the door,' Eliza said. 'And she went to answer it.'

'I see.' Georgina headed towards the front door, arriving just in time to see the matron close it. 'Apologies for running off. I was— Mrs Jameson? Is something the matter?'

Mrs Jameson was shaking her head, her face utterly distraught.

Concerned, she hurried over to the matron's side. 'Who was at the door? Did they upset you?'

'Mr Morgan.' The matron lifted her head to meet Georgina's eyes. 'Mr Smith's man of business.'

'What did he want?'

'H-He…' She swallowed. 'He came to reiterate the terms of the eviction.'

'What?' Georgina asked, incredulous. 'There must be some mistake.'

'I—I'm afraid not, my lady.' She handed her a piece of paper. 'We must vacate in four days' time.'

'Four days—on Christmas Day?'

Snatching the paper from her, she read it, her heart sinking with every word.

No, it couldn't be true. There had to be some mistake.

Perhaps Elliot had forgotten to tell his man of business that he was rescinding the eviction. Whatever the reason, she would get to the bottom of this.

'I shall speak to Mr Smith and clear up this misunderstanding.' Hopefully she sounded cheerful enough that the matron would not worry. 'Could you let Miss Warren know I have had to leave for a short while?' Last time she'd seen her companion, she and Anne-Marie had been on a tour upstairs. 'I will be back soon.'

'Certainly, my lady.'

Georgina's stomach was tied up in knots for the entire carriage ride to Elliot's office. She could not believe he would go back on his word, despite the evidence written in his own hand. The letter was dated today, which meant he had given the order to send it sometime between yesterday and this morning.

Her worry shifted into anger when she realised the suspicious timing of the eviction. The gossip columns were set to print the story of their supposed love match today, which would pave the way for the engagement announcement tomorrow.

Indignation rose in her. Did he think he could betray her now that it was impossible to break their engagement without ruining her reputation?

By the time she had alighted from her carriage in front of his office building she was brimming with rage. She ignored Mr Grant's greeting and burst into Elliot's office.

'Georgina?' He looked up from the papers he was signing. 'Sweetheart, what are you—?'

'Do not "sweetheart" me.' Marching over to the side of his desk, she tossed the eviction notice in front of him and crossed her arms over her chest. 'Tell me this is a mistake.'

A twinge plucked at her chest. *Lord, please let it be a mistake.*

He picked up the eviction notice and scanned through it. 'Where did you get this?'

'I was at the orphanage, with the girls, when Mr Morgan came to deliver it.'

'You weren't supposed to see this,' he said, his voice calm.

'Ah, so it is true?' Fury swirled inside her. 'You're breaking your promise to me now because it's much too late to stop the newspapers and I have no choice but to marry you.'

He sprang to his feet. 'Too late? What in God's name are you talking about?'

'Oh, you very well know what I'm talking about,' she shot back. 'The gossip columns about our lo—our postponed elopement will come out today and we are announcing the engagement tomorrow. Now that it's all done, you have decided to proceed with the eviction because you have already got what you wanted!'

His expression fell. 'No, that's not it. That's not it at all.'

'Is that so? This eviction is a joke, then? A mistake? You're not really tossing over two dozen orphaned girls into the street?'

'I—' He snapped his mouth shut. 'It is not a mistake.'

The confirmation of his actions made her heart sink and turned her stomach to ice. 'H-How could you?' Her throat felt raw…as if she'd swallowed nails.

'Morgan should not have come… He must not have known you were going to be there. I wanted to tell you…' He raked his fingers through his hair. 'Someone has made me an offer on the building—a very good one—but they asked that the premises be vacated quickly.'

'By Christmas.'

'What?'

'Christmas Day,' she reiterated. 'That's when the girls have to leave.'

Frowning, he glanced at the calendar. 'I had no idea…'

'Of course you didn't,' she spat. 'Why would you?'

He harrumphed. 'If you'd just let me finish—'

'Go ahead. I'm not stopping you.'

'As I said, I'm selling the building for an enormous profit. With the money I'm making on the sale I've arranged to purchase a house in Camden. Twenty-two rooms, two gardens, and a stable with two carriages and horses. The owners have accepted my offer and the girls can move in on the twenty-fifth.' His shoulders sank. 'Did you really think I was so heartless as to leave them homeless, knowing how much they mean to you?'

'I—' Her throat tightened and she stiffened under his scrutinising gaze. 'Y-You still cannot ask them to leave on Christmas Day. Go away from the only home they've known. It's cruel.'

He huffed. 'What does it matter what day they move? They're children—it's not as if they'll know the difference. It's just another day.'

'Just another—' she spluttered, brimming with indignation. 'You really are a Scrooge. You planned this eviction and this move so you don't have to celebrate Christmas, I bet.'

Anger rippled along her spine, and the dam that had held her emotions broke.

'Is this what it's going to be like, Elliot? For the rest of our lives will you find ways to completely avoid Christmas? Will you hide away in your office every

December the twenty-fifth, while the girls and I—and our children—celebrate Christmas on our own?'

'Now, wait a damned minute here.' He took a step towards her, towering over her. 'How in God's name did we even arrive at this conversation? What does Christmas have to do with anything?'

'I just don't understand, Elliot. Why don't you celebrate Christmas? You act as if it were the worst thing in the world.'

Her questions were met with stone-cold silence, but she continued.

'Anne-Marie and Lily have noticed. You provide the girls with every material thing they want, but not what they need—you to understand them and listen to them. To treat them as something more than an extension of yourself or a way to right the wrongs that fate has set upon you. Why won't you open yourself up?'

'That's rich, coming from you,' he sneered.

'I beg your pardon?' she asked, taken aback.

'You come in here, accusing me of these terrible things without even asking me for an explanation.' Bitterness sharpened his voice as he continued. 'Why do you assume the worst after everything that's happened between us? Have I not proved myself worthy of you?'

A slash of guilt struck her in the chest. 'Elliot—'

'And now what? You want to end the engagement? You're walking away from me because you cannot get your way? Can there be no discussion, no compromise?'

'I didn't—'

'Or did you just want a reason not to marry me? What are you truly scared of, Georgina?'

'Wh-what do you mean?'

Her back hit something solid—the wall behind her. When had he backed her into a corner? She'd been so blind with rage she hadn't even noticed.

'Why have you been hiding yourself away all these years? Why haven't *you* opened yourself up to the possibility that you could find someone to share your life with?'

Anxiety built in her chest, making it difficult to breathe. 'I... I told you...my spells... I'm not making them up.'

'I know that. But at some point perhaps you've begun to use them to hide behind the fact that you're afraid.'

'Afraid of what?'

His eyes burned with an emotion that stole her breath.

'Of meeting someone who loves you deeply and passionately with all his heart. Someone who would do anything for you and give you the world.'

'I... I...'

The anxiety erupted into full-blown panic and Georgina felt the walls and Elliot closing in on her. So she did the only thing she could—she fled.

Ducking away from Elliot, she raced out of his office, nearly tripping as she took the stairs all the way to the ground floor. Her carriage was waiting outside, and she didn't even bother to wait for the footman to open the door as she grabbed the handle herself and hurried inside.

Tears burned at her throat and she clawed at her chest, wanting to rip off her clothes so she could breathe.

'Lady Georgina?' came the voice of the footman. 'Where would you like to go?'

'Home,' she called out. 'Take me home.'

The moment the carriage lurched forward Georgina burst into tears.

Heavens, this was a mess.

She buried her face in her hands. Was he right? Had she come here accusing him and thinking badly of him because she wanted a reason not to marry him? Her spells felt so real to her, and there were truly times when she physically could not breathe. But perhaps... perhaps they were rooted in something else. A fear of some kind.

'We've arrived, my lady.'

Using the sleeves of her dress, she wiped her face, and then she composed herself, took a deep breath and stepped out of the carriage. 'Could you please go back to St Agnes's and fetch Miss Warren a-and the girls?'

'Of course, my lady.'

Nodding her thanks, she dashed into the house, hoping to reach her room before anyone saw her.

Unfortunately for her, she ran smack into the one person she didn't want to see right now.

'Georgie?' Trevor exclaimed, grabbing her arms to steady her. 'Have you been crying? What's wrong?'

'I—n-nothing,' she stammered.

'It's not nothing.' His voice was soothing. 'Tell me. I'm your brother.'

She promptly burst into tears. 'Oh, Trev…'

Georgina wasn't quite sure what happened, but somehow she started babbling about the eviction and Elliot and their broken engagement. At some point Trevor gently guided her into the parlour, closed the door and led her to the settee.

'I've made a mess of things,' she said, blowing into the handkerchief he offered. 'I was wrong, wasn't I? Not to trust him?' She sighed. 'I don't even know why.'

Trevor's gaze pinned her to the spot. 'Are you sure you don't know why?'

'I swear, I don't.'

He placed an arm around her and she laid her head on his chest. 'Georgie…you were so young when we lost them.'

'Who?'

'Mama and Papa.'

The heart stopped. 'Trev, I don't want to talk—'

'But perhaps we should. The days and months after they died I was too busy with the estate and all the arrangements. I never had the time to talk with you and ensure you were all right.'

'You were busy with far more important things. I was—I *am* fine. But why are you bringing this up now?'

'Why do you think? Georgie, have you ever thought that perhaps…perhaps you shy away from others?

From forming attachments because you are afraid? Afraid of the pain of losing someone you love?'

She shook her head. 'N-No, that's not true. My spells—'

'Is it not true?' He kissed the top of her head. 'Have a think. And do not despair. I do not think Elliot will allow you to break the engagement that easily.'

Oh, heavens, she had just run out on him. 'I'm not so sure...'

'Do not discount yourself. I believe he will come to you.'

She sat there, staring at the wall, for what seemed like a lifetime after Trevor left. When she finally shook herself out of her trance, her mind began to whirl with possibilities? Was Trevor correct? Was she hiding herself because she didn't want to be hurt by love?

And what was she to do now?

Chapter Sixteen

24th December

Whenever Elliot faced a problem he could not overcome, he did the one thing that he did know how to do—he worked. He worked on the issue until it was solved, never relenting or giving up. Of course, the current problem he faced could not be solved, even with all the skills he'd learned over the years. So, without any obvious solution, he decided just to *work*.

And that was what he'd been doing for the past two days. He was at the office from sunrise all the way to midnight, going home only to refresh himself and change his clothes. The exhaustion allowed him to sleep peacefully for a few hours, then he awoke and returned to the office once more. Keeping himself busy was the only way he could stop himself from going mad.

I shouldn't have told her those things.

He should never have accused her of not trusting

him or claimed her spells were a manifestation of her fears.

And he certainly should never have confessed his love for her.

While he hadn't actually said the words, he'd all but admitted it, and it had sent her running from him.

'Mr Smith, will that be all?'

'What?' Bleary-eyed, he looked up at Grant, who stood in front of his desk. 'Will what be all?'

'Uh…for today, sir? It's five o'clock.'

'Is it?'

Grant hesitated, as if Elliot would deny his claim. 'Y-Yes…'

'I see. Go home, then, and have a good evening.'

'Thank you, sir. And…uh… Happy Christmas Eve…'

What?

Before he could say another word, Grant hurried out.

Blinking away the blurriness from his vision, Elliot looked at the calendar. It was, indeed, the twenty-fourth of December.

Grunting, he turned back to his papers and continued to work.

25th December

There was an unfamiliar ache in Elliot's neck when he woke. When he opened his eyes it was light outside, and he was sitting in his chair, face resting on his desk.

He had fallen asleep at the office.

Rising to his feet, Elliot stretched his arms over his head. Perhaps it was time to go home. The banks and other businesses were closed anyway, and his deal with Brimsley had been signed and stamped, with the money now sitting in the ES Smith Consolidated Trust's bank accounts. And as far as he knew the Camden house was now in his name, and Morgan had hired people to help the occupants of number fifty-five Boyle Street pack up their things so they could move.

His stomach growled unhappily. Usually when he was in the middle of business negotiations the drive to succeed made him forget all his needs, including sustenance. But now his body clamoured for food…perhaps some coddled eggs, toast and a big pile of bacon.

His stomach clenched and his mouth watered at the thought.

Mind made up, he retrieved his coat and hat and sent for his carriage.

As soon as he arrived at the house, he asked Fletcher, 'Is breakfast ready?'

'Sir?' The surprise on the butler's face was apparent. 'You're having breakfast now?'

'Yes,' he snapped. 'Now, call the girls so that we may eat. I'm famished.'

It had been two—no, three days now since he had seen Anne-Marie and Lily, so surely they would be glad he was home, and maybe even overjoyed that he was actually here for Christmas.

'I shall wait for them in the parlour.'

After leaving his hat and coat with Fletcher, Elliot

headed to the room on his right. To his surprise, there was a Christmas tree there, with presents underneath. Upon closer inspection he saw the loopy, feminine handwriting on the tags, indicating who they were from. He picked up one gift with his name on it—a small, rectangular object wrapped in pretty green paper. He turned over the tag to read it.

To Elliot,
May you honour Christmas in your heart and keep it all year. Live in the past, present and future.
Yours always,
Georgina

A dull ache formed in his chest. How he missed her so. Perhaps it was time he went to her, so they could make things right between them. Surely whatever had broken between them could be mended?

'Sir!' came Fletcher's urgent call.

He whirled around to face the butler. 'What is it?'

'S-Sir.' Fletcher's face paled. 'Miss Anne-Marie and Miss Lily...they are gone.'

'What?' He had to stop himself from leaping at the butler and grabbing him by the lapels. 'What do you mean, gone?'

'They are not in their rooms.'

Alarm bells rang in his head, but he remained cool. 'Then check the other rooms,' he said, irritated. 'Check all the rooms.'

'Yes, sir.'

Minutes ticked by as he waited for Fletcher to return. Perhaps the girls were playing a joke on them. Or they were hiding in a closet or in the attic. Hell, there were rooms inside this house he'd never been in—perhaps they'd found some hidden chamber and were accidentally locked inside.

'Where are they?' he barked at Fletcher as soon as he returned.

'They are not in any of the rooms in the house, sir.'

'Are you certain?'

'Yes, sir. The maids are checking every room and closet once more, but they said they hadn't seen the young misses since last night.'

'How could this have happened?' Worry, fear and dread swirled in his chest. 'Where could they have gone?'

'I don't know, sir. According to Mrs Murphy, after the girls opened presents at midnight, they went up to Miss Anne-Marie's rooms and haven't come out since.'

They must have sneaked out.

'Have my carriage ready at once,' he ordered.

As the butler scurried away he calmed himself, tamping down the panic rising in him. Where would Anne-Marie and Lily go? And why would they have left? Were they angry that he hadn't seen them in three days? He often didn't see them for longer than that, especially when he was closing a deal.

He wondered if the girls had got wind of his quarrel with Georgina.

Yes, that had to be it. And they had to have gone to her.

'Sir, the carriage is outside,' Fletcher said, Elliot's hat and coat in his hand.

'Thank you, Fletcher.'

Rushing outside, he barked at his driver to take him to Harwicke House. 'And be quick about it!'

He could barely stay still as the carriage began to move. The ride seemed to take for ever, and when they stopped he nearly leapt out.

Just as his feet landed on the ground, he heard someone call his name.

'Elliot?'

Slowly, he raised his head. Georgina stood just outside her door, staring at him, mouth agape. She looked so lovely, standing there in the morning sun, it made his heart clench.

'What are you doing here?' she asked as he approached.

'I...' He'd forgotten, just for a moment. 'The girls. Are they here? With you?'

'Anne-Marie and Lily? No, of course not.' She frowned. 'Why would they be?'

'I— Never mind.' When he made a move to turn away, she reached out to grab at his arm.

'Elliot, what's the matter? Where are the girls?' Her tone was firm as her grip tightened. 'Tell me, please.'

'They are gone. I think they ran away.'

'They ran away?' she echoed. 'How? Why?'

'I'm not sure.' He released the breath he was holding. 'I think they're angry with me. I haven't seen them in three days.' He thrust his fingers into his hair.

'Why not?' she asked in a quiet voice.

Why do you think?

'I've been busy. In any case, I shall go and look for them—'

'Where? I mean, where would you start? London is a colossal city. They could be anywhere.'

'Don't you think I know that?' he barked, then instantly regretted it. 'My apologies. I'm—'

'I know, you're frightened for them.' She smoothed her hand over his arm. 'But you cannot just run around London hoping to find them. You must think clearly. Where could they have gone?'

'I don't know.' He thought for a moment. 'If I had to guess…perhaps they might try to book a passage to America?'

'Hmmm… How? Do they have funds? Do you give them pin money?'

'No, all the bills for everything they may need or want get sent directly to me.'

Anne-Marie was still far too young to have an allowance of any sort.

'All right.' She chewed at her lip. 'Without any money, they wouldn't be able to hire a hansom cab. Which means they are on foot. How long have they been missing?'

'Since midnight, maybe. Fletcher said they opened

their presents, then went to bed. When I came back from the office this morning they were already gone.'

'They don't really have anywhere to go. They haven't been to many places except Hyde Park.'

'And here,' Elliot supplied.

'Which is why you thought to come here.'

'Yes. Christ.' He raked his fingers through his hair. 'I just want them to be safe.'

'I do, too.'

To his shock and surprise, Georgina reached up to smooth the sides of his hair, her soft fingers brushing the outside of his ear. He suddenly became aware of how close she was, and his stomach knotted itself with the yearning he felt for her.

'There is one other place they know in London.'

'And where is that?'

'St Agnes's. I took them there.'

Realisation struck him. So they'd likely know about the eviction, perhaps overhearing talk of it while they were there. And since Elliot hadn't explained to them what had happened…

'I must go there now.'

She did not release him. 'I am coming with you.'

'No, you are not.' He attempted to shake off her grip, but she clung to him like a python. 'Release me, Georgina.'

'I am coming with you, one way or another.' A determined look set on her face. 'I need to know if those girls are safe. Please, Elliot, take me with you.'

'Where is your carriage?'

'It will take for ever to get it ready.' She nodded at his carriage. 'We can take yours. It makes more sense.'

'You can't ride with me in a closed carriage. Where is Miss Warren?'

'She has the next few days off,' she said. 'Please, we are wasting time.'

'Georgina…' he warned. However, she still refused to release him, so he let out a resigned breath. 'All right, let's go.'

He led her to his carriage and settled in across from her. The entire ride to Boyle Street was silent, and Georgina stared out of the window, wringing her hands on her lap. Had it been four days since he'd last seen her? She had run so fast from him he hadn't even had time to think.

It had occurred to him that that might have been the last time he would see her. He should not have pushed her so hard. Would it really have been so terrible to cancel his agreement with Brimsley? Or perhaps he should not have even entertained his offer at all. What had he been thinking? It was only money, after all, and he already had lots of it.

'We're here,' Georgina announced.

Alighting from the carriage, he helped her down and they bolted towards the front door of St Agnes's. He knocked furiously, not stopping until it was opened.

'Can I help you sir?' The woman's tone conveyed her annoyance. 'And what—? Lady Georgina?'

'Mrs Jameson,' Georgina began, 'are Lily and Anne-Marie here?'

'Why, yes— What do you think you're doing?' she cried when Elliot pushed himself inside.

He ignored the woman's shouts of indignation and began to call for his sisters. 'Anne-Marie! Lily!' he called. 'I know you are here! Come down right this minute.'

'I'm sorry, Mrs Jameson,' Georgina said. 'He thought they'd run away and he has been worried sick.'

'Girls!' he bellowed. 'Come here—Anne-Marie! Lily!'

The heaviness in his chest disappeared at the sight of his sisters as they stood at the top of the stairs.

'I'm so glad to see you both.'

He broke into a run towards the stairs and began to climb them, but just before he reached the top, he found himself blocked as an army of little girls began to pour down the steps. They surrounded him, their faces drawn into scowls as they stared up at him in challenge.

'What is going on?'

'We're not coming home with you,' Anne-Marie declared.

'We're staying here,' Lily said, nodding in agreement.

'Girls, you cannot stay here,' he said. 'You belong with me, at home. And these very lovely little ladies will soon be at their wonderful new home. I am sure they will enjoy themselves there. Why, there are even ponies for them to play with.' He glanced down at the child by his left leg, the smallest of the bunch. 'Wouldn't you like that?' he asked.

The girl only bared her teeth and growled.

Elliot blew out a breath. 'All right, what do you want?'

'We want you to make up with Lady Georgina,' Anne-Marie said.

'I want her to be my sister,' Lily wailed.

Elliot too, wished for that, with all his heart. 'I'm sorry, girls, but that's not up to me.'

'Can't you do something—? Lady Georgina?' Anne-Marie exclaimed.

Lily gasped. 'You're here.'

'Yes, I was very worried about you.' Georgina stood at the bottom of the stairs. 'Girls,' she said to the swarm surrounding Elliot, 'would you please let Mr Smith through? I think he and I need to speak alone.'

Smiling, she held out her hand towards him.

The children parted like the Red Sea, and so Elliot, like Moses, followed the trail downwards. He reached out and took Georgina's hand and allowed her to lead him away into the nearest room.

Closing the door behind her, she motioned for him to sit on the large settee by the fireplace. He did, and she joined him.

'I'm sorry—'

'Forgive me—'

They both stopped, and Elliot was sure the shock on his face mirrored hers.

'Georgina,' he began again. 'Forgive me. I should

not have entertained that offer. I... I justified it because of the money, and because I wanted to teach someone a lesson. I made you a promise, and I broke it. Please forgive me.'

She blew out a breath. 'Elliot, I said some things to you that day that I regret so much. You're right, there should have been a discussion, a compromise of some sort, before I decided to run out on you. I was just scared—'

'Because I love you.' A lightness filled his chest as he said it aloud. He didn't care if she heard it or if it scared her. She *had* to know.

Her breath hitched audibly and tears welled up in her eyes. 'You were right. I was afraid. Afraid of the pain I felt when I lost Mama and Papa. They loved each other so much. I don't... I never thought I would ever have something like that. And even if I did, I knew it wouldn't last. I told myself I didn't want to feel it and have it taken away. I never wanted to feel...' She swallowed, and then she spoke in barely a whisper. 'I don't know what I would do if I lost you too.'

'Georgina.' Unable to help himself, he gathered her into his arms. 'Don't cry.'

'B-But I lost you anyway,' she sobbed. 'I ran away from you. And now you—'

'I am here,' he soothed. 'And I love you.'

'I...' Pulling away from him, she lifted her face to his. 'I love you too.'

Cradling her face in his hand, he leaned down to kiss her. A warm glow wrapped around him and his heart seemed to expand to twice its size and burst out of his chest. Her mouth was soft, and as sweet as he'd remembered, maybe even more. He couldn't get enough of her—but he would have to stop now before he went too far.

'Sweetheart…' he breathed. 'Will you marry me?'

'I haven't said I wouldn't,' she replied, smiling against his mouth. 'Will *you* marry me?'

'A thousand—no, a million—times over.'

'I just need the one.' She pulled away from him. 'I… I love you just the way you are. You are set in your ways, and I understand, as I am in mine. And if you can learn to accept me as I am, then I can accept you too.'

'What do you mean?'

'I know you don't seem to like Christmas, so if you'd prefer not to celebrate—'

He pressed a finger to her lips to stop her. 'Oh, no, sweetheart. Please don't… I don't.' He sucked in a breath. 'It's not that I hate Christmas, it's just…'

He closed his eyes, trying to forget the memory. But perhaps it was time for him to let go.

'My ma died on Christmas Day.'

She gasped. 'Elliot, I'm sorry.'

'It's all right.' He gathered his hands into his. 'The day never held any pleasant memories for me, even before that. We were too poor to celebrate. But that Christmas Day she died, crying out for my good-for-nothing father, was the day I decided I was going to make something of myself. I worked myself to the bone, accumulating wealth and power, trying to fill that hole she had left inside me. I came up with my ten-year plans so I wouldn't notice how real life was passing me by as I pursued my goals. I didn't stop— I couldn't stop. Because I was afraid when I did I would realise that having all the money in the world didn't matter. That *I* didn't matter.'

'But you do, Elliot.' Smiling up at him, she smoothed his hair back. 'You matter to Anne-Marie and Lily. You matter to me.'

'And you matter to me. All of you. I don't care about my ten-year plan any more. I want to slow down, enjoy my life with you and the girls…and our children.'

With an excited cry, she sprang at him, wrapping her arms around his neck as she crushed her lips to his. He toppled back and she landed on top of him, her curvy, soft body pressed against his. He groaned as her hips made contact with his lap and—

'Are you done kissing?' came Lily's faint voice from behind the door.

'And are you engaged again?' Anne-Marie added.

'We never stopped being engaged,' Elliot called out.

'May we come in now?' Lily asked.

They looked at each other and Georgina giggled. 'One moment!' She moved off him and then sat down on one side of the settee, arranging her skirts. 'All right, come in!'

Anne-Marie and Lily bounded inside, their faces bright with excitement.

'Have you truly made up?' Anne-Marie asked.

'Yes,' Elliot confirmed. 'We have. Can we go home now?'

'But we want to spend Christmas here,' Lily whined. 'And help the girls with packing for their move to Camden.'

'What if I told you they don't have to move to Camden?' Elliot said. 'And they can stay here.'

'Elliot?' Georgina stared at him, slack-jawed. 'Are you sure?'

'Yes. I will cancel the sale to Brimsley.'

Young Charles the III would have to face the consequences of his actions when the senior Brimsleys arrived—which, he supposed, was still a way for the fool to learn his lesson, even if Elliot did not profit from it.

'And the girls do not have to move out.'

'Hooray!' Lily raised a fist in the air.

'But what about the house in Camden?' Georgina asked. 'Won't it be a waste to have all that space?'

'I suppose... But it's still the perfect place for a new orphanage. Perhaps that could be a project for you?'

'Me?'

'Yes. I was planning not to charge St Agnes's rent on the place anyway, as my wedding gift to you. But now I'm thinking I should give you the deed instead and you can establish a second orphanage.' He'd noticed she had no trouble being around crowds of children, so it would be perfect for her. 'Would you like that?'

The smile on her face practically lit up the room. 'Yes, I would.'

'Can we still stay here?' Lily asked. 'And have our Christmas dinner here tonight with all the girls?'

'I think that would be lovely,' Georgina said. 'What do you say, Elliot?'

'I think I am outvoted,' he said with a resigned sigh. 'All right.'

And so the four of them stayed for the entire day, playing games, singing carols and eating Christmas pudding. Georgina and Trevor had already planned to spend Christmas at the orphanage anyway, so the Duke arrived later that day. He looked overjoyed to see that Georgina and Elliot had made up.

Trevor did not come empty-handed. He had brought two roast turkeys for dinner. And Elliot had sent word to his own staff, who'd brought over the feast they had prepared.

They all sat in the orphanage's massive dining room as Elliot and Trevor carved the turkeys, and after dinner all the girls went upstairs to their rooms to continue with their merrymaking. Now Trevor had gone home, but Georgina had decided to stay for another hour or two.

She and Elliot sneaked back into the parlour so they could be alone.

'Happy Christmas,' Georgina said to Elliot as she laid her head on his shoulder and he put his arm around her. 'Your first. First time celebrating it, anyway.'

'And not the last.'

Georgina snapped her fingers. 'Oh, that reminds me—I have a gift for you. It's under the tree I had brought to your house.'

'I know. I saw it.'

She grinned slyly at him. 'I think you'll like it.'

'I think I will.' He already had a suspicion about what it was. 'But I'm afraid I've already read *A Christmas Carol*.'

'You have?'

Reaching into his coat, he retrieved the book from his pocket. He wasn't sure why he'd carried it around all this time, but now he realised it was the only way he could keep her close to his heart.

'Well, I had to—especially since all three of you had accused me of being a Scrooge.' He tickled Georgina's nose, sending her into a fit of giggles. 'Did you hope it would cure me of my Scrooge-like ways?'

'Possibly,' Georgina said.

'Perhaps I am cured. But I wouldn't give credit to Dickens for the change.'

'Oh?'

'No, sweetheart.' He stared deep into her coppery brown eyes, finding the love shining in them. 'If anyone has brought Christmas into my heart, it's you.'

* * * * *

MILLS & BOON®

Coming next month

ONE WALTZ WITH THE VISCOUNT
Laura Martin

Sarah made the mistake of looking up and for a long moment she was lost in Lord Routledge's eyes. Of course she'd noticed them before—even in the semi-darkness it was impossible to ignore the man's good looks. His eyes were a wonderful deep brown, full of sadness and intrigue.

She swallowed, her pulse racing and heat rising through her body.

She knew she was passably attractive, and there had been offers from a couple of young men of her acquaintance to step out over the last couple of years. Never had she been tempted. But, right now, if Lord Routledge asked her to run away into the night with him, she would find it hard to refuse.

Silently she scoffed at the idea. As if the poised and eligible Lord Routledge would ask her that. No matter what he said, he probably had five or six elegant and well-bred young women waiting for him downstairs.

'You look sad,' he said, an expression of genuine curiosity on his face. 'The waltz isn't meant to be a melancholy experience. At least not if I'm doing it right.'

With a press of his fingers he spun her quickly, and somehow they ended up closer than they had begun, her body brushing against his. She inhaled sharply, and for a moment it felt as though time had stopped. Their eyes met. Ever so slowly, he raised a hand to her face, tucking a stray strand of hair behind her ear.

In that instant Sarah wanted to be kissed. She felt her lips part slightly, her breathing become shallow. She'd never been kissed before, but instinctively her body swayed towards Lord Routledge. Her heart thumped within her chest as he moved a fraction of an inch towards her, and then stopped.

Continue reading

ONE WALTZ WITH THE VISCOUNT
Laura Martin

Available next month
millsandboon.co.uk

COMING SOON!

We really hope you enjoyed reading this book.
If you're looking for more romance
be sure to head to the shops when
new books are available on

Thursday 19th December

To see which titles are coming soon, please visit

millsandboon.co.uk/nextmonth

MILLS & BOON

afterglow BOOKS

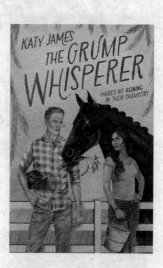

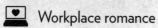 Workplace romance

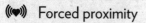 Forced proximity

 Spicy

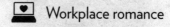 Workplace romance

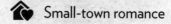 Small-town romance

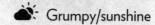 Grumpy/sunshine

OUT NOW

Two stories published every month. Discover more at:
Afterglowbooks.co.uk

LET'S TALK

Romance

For exclusive extracts, competitions and special offers, find us online:

 MillsandBoon

 @MillsandBoon

 @MillsandBoonUK

 @MillsandBoonUK

Get in touch on 01413 063 232